"A CHEER FOR THE GODDESS OF LIBERTY" (page 47)

ROBERT TOURNAY

A Romance of the French Revolution

BY

WILLIAM SAGE

WITH ILLUSTRATIONS BY ERIC PAPE
AND MARY AYER

BOSTON AND NEW YORK
HOUGHTON, MIFFLIN AND COMPANY
The Riverside Press, Cambridge
1900

TO MY MOTHER

TO WHOM I OWE EVERYTHING
I LOVINGLY DEDICATE
THIS STORY.

CONTENTS

LIST OF ILLUSTRATIONS

ROBERT TOURNAY

CHAPTER I

HOW TOURNAY CAME TO PARIS

THE Marquis de Lacheville sat in the dining-
hall of the château de Rochefort. In his hand he
held a letter. Although it was from a woman,
the writing was not in those delicately traced char-
acters which suggest the soft hand of some lady
of fashion. The note-paper was scented, but the
perfume, like the color, was too pronounced; and
the spelling, possibly like the lady's character,
was not absolutely flawless.

A smile played about the cold thin lips of the
marquis; he carelessly thrust the missive into his
pocket, as one disposes of a bill he does not intend
to pay, and lifting his eyes, allowed his gaze to
wander through the open window toward the figure of a young girl who stood outside upon the
terrace.

She was watching a game of tennis in the court
below, now and then conversing with the players,
whose voices in return reached de Lacheville's
ears on the quiet summer air.

A few minutes before in that dining-hall the

Baron de Rochefort had betrothed his daughter Edmé to his friend and distant kinsman, Maurice de Lacheville. In the eyes of the world it was a suitable match. The marquis was twenty-five, the girl eighteen. She was an only child; and their rank and fortunes were equal.

They did not love each other. The marquis loved no one but himself. Mademoiselle had been brought up to consider all men very much alike. She might possibly have had some slight preference for the Marquis de St. Hilaire, who was now playing tennis in the court beneath; but it was well known that he was dissipating his fortune at the gaming-table. Mademoiselle did not lack strength of will; but, her heart not being involved, she allowed her father to make the choice for her, as was the custom of the time.

De Lacheville continued sitting at the table, now looking dispassionately at the woman who was to become his wife, now looking beyond toward the wide sweep of park and meadow land, while he calculated how much longer his cousin, the baron, would live to enjoy possession of his great wealth.

What the young girl thought is merely a matter of conjecture. She was as fresh and sweet as the pink rose which she plucked from the trellis and gayly tossed to the marquis below. He caught it gracefully and put it to his lips — while she laughed merrily with never a thought for the marquis within.

Near the tennis court stood another man. He

was tall and well-made, with dark eyes and a sun-browned face. Beyond furnishing new balls and rackets when required, he took no part in the game, for he was the son of the intendant of the château and therefore a servant.

He watched the rose which the lady so carelessly tossed, with hungry eyes, as a dog watches a bone given to some well-fed and happier rival. At the call from one of the players he replaced a broken racket, then took up his former post, apparently intent upon the game, but in reality his mind was far afield.

It was in the early summer days of the year 1789. Looking out over the baron's noble estates through the eyes of a girl like mademoiselle, the world was very beautiful. Glancing at it through the careless eyes of the prodigal St. Hilaire, it seemed very pleasing; but in spite of these waving crops, and wealthy vineyards, in spite of the plenty in the baron's household and the rich wines in his cellar, throughout France there were many who had not enough to eat. Men, and women too, were crying out for their share of the world's riches.

A new wave of thought was sweeping over France. A thought as old as the hills, yet startlingly new to each man as he discovered it. Books were being written and words spoken which were soon to cause great political changes in a land already seething with discontent. Change and Progress at last were in the saddle, and they were riding fast. As the careless noblemen batted their tennis balls back and forth, thinking only of their

game; as the young girl leaned over the rose-cov-
ered terrace, thinking of the sunlight, the flowers,
and the beauty of life, Robert Tournay, the intendant's son, pondered deeply on the " rights of man "
while he ran after the tennis balls for those who
played the game.

As if wearied by the contemplation of his pro-
spective married bliss, Monsieur de Lacheville
yawned, arose from his seat and strolled leisurely
from the room, descended the staircase and came
out into the park in the rear of the château, unobserved by the tennis players. The note in his
pocket called him to a rendezvous; and the marquis, after some deliberation, had decided to keep
it. Once in the wooded park and out of sight of
the house, he quickened his pace to a brisk walk;
proceeding thus for half a mile he suddenly left
the driveway and plunging through the thick foli-
age by a path which to the casual eye was barely
visible, came out into a shady and unfrequented
alley.

A few minutes after de Lacheville's disappearance into the woods, the other noblemen, wearied
of their sport, retired into the house for refreshment.

This left young Tournay free for the time being,
and he availed himself of the opportunity to go
down toward a pasture beyond the park where
some young horses were running wild, innocent of
bit or bridle. It was Tournay's intention to break
one of these colts for Mademoiselle de Rochefort.
She was a fearless rider, and it gave the young

man pleasure to be commissioned to pick out an animal at once gentle and mettlesome for the use of his young mistress.

The Tournays, from father to son, had been for generations the intendants of the de Rochefort estate. With the baron's permission Matthieu Tournay had sent his son away to school, and he had thus received a better education than most young men of his class. He was of an ambitious temper, and this very education, instead of making him more contented with his lot in life, increased his restlessness. It only served to show him more clearly the line that separated him from those he served. In his own mind he had never defined his feeling for Mademoiselle de Rochefort. He only knew that it gave him great pleasure to serve her; and yet, as he did her bidding, he felt a pang that between them was the gulf of caste; that even when she smiled upon him it was merely the favored servant whom she greeted; that although he might be as well educated as the Count de Blois, a better horseman than St. Hilaire, and a better man than de Lacheville, *they* could enter as equals into the presence of this divine being, while such as he must always take his place below the salt.

It was with such thoughts as these revolving in his brain that the intendant's son walked through the woods of the park. He followed no path, for he knew each tree and twig from childhood. Suddenly he was interrupted in his reverie by the sound of voices, and stopping short, recognized

the voice of the Marquis de Lacheville in conversation with a woman.   Tournay hesitated, then
went forward cautiously in the direction whence
the sound came.   Had he been born a gentleman
he would have chosen another way; or at least
would have advanced noisily.   Indeed, such had
been his first impulse, — but a much stronger interest than curiosity impelled him forward; and
drawing near, he looked through a gap in the
hedge.

On the other side stood de Lacheville facing a
young woman.   Her cheeks were flushed, and the
manner in which she toyed with a riding-whip
showed that the discussion had been heated.   Although she was handsomely dressed in a riding-
habit and assumed some of the airs of a lady,
Tournay recognized her at once as a young girl
who had disappeared some months before from
the village of La Thierry, and whose handsome
face and vivacious manner had caused her to be
much admired.   Near her stood the nobleman,
calm and self-composed.   Before men, de Lacheville had been known to flinch; but with a woman
of the humbler class the marquis could always play
the master.

"And now, Marianne," said the nobleman
slowly, "you had better go, — and do not make
the mistake of coming here again."

Although she had evidently been worsted in the
argument, a defiant look flashed in her dark eyes
as she answered him: "If I believe you speak the
truth I shall not come here again."

DE LACHEVILLE FACING A YOUNG WOMAN

"Of course I speak the truth," replied de
Lacheville lightly. "I shall marry Mademoiselle
de Rochefort " —

The young woman winced, but she did not
speak.

De Lacheville went on slowly as if he enjoyed
the situation — "In a year or two — I am in no
hurry. She is very beautiful " — here he paused
again — "but I prefer your style of beauty, Marianne ; I prefer your vivacity, your life, your fire ;
I like to see you angry. My engagement to
Mademoiselle de Rochefort need make no difference in my regard for you. That depends upon
yourself." Here the marquis stepped forward
and kissed her on the lips.

Tournay controlled himself by a great effort,
his heart swelling with the resentment of a man
who hears that which he holds sacred insulted by
another. And this man who held Mademoiselle
de Rochefort in such slight esteem was to be her
husband.

"And now, Marianne," said the nobleman, "you
must ride away as you came," and suiting the action to the words he swung her into the saddle.
She was docile now and gathered up the reins
obediently. "And, Marianne," continued the nobleman, "never write letters to me. I am rather
fastidious and do not want my illusions dispelled
too soon. Good-by, my child."

She flushed as he spoke, and a retort seemed
about to spring to her lips ; but instead of replying she shrugged her shoulders, gave a sharp cut

of the whip to the horse, and rode off down the
pathway.

De Lacheville laughed. "She has spirit to the
last. She pleases me;" and turning, beheld Robert Tournay in the path before him.

For a moment neither spoke; then the nobleman asked sternly, "Have you been spying upon
me?"

"I have heard what has passed between you and
that woman," replied Tournay with a significance
that made the marquis start.

"You villain," replied the nobleman hotly, "if
you breathe a word about what you have seen I
will have you whipped by my lackeys."

Tournay's lips curled defiantly.

"Or," continued the marquis, "if one word of
scandal reaches the ears of Mademoiselle de Rochefort" —

Before the words had left his lips, Tournay
sprang forward and had him by the arm.

"Do not stain her name by speaking it," he
cried fiercely. "I have heard you insult her; I
have seen how you would dishonor her; you, who
are not worthy to touch the hem of her garment.
What right have you to become her husband?
Your very presence would degrade her. You
shall not wed her."

White with rage, if not from fear, the marquis
struggled to free himself from Tournay's grasp,
but he could neither throw off his antagonist nor
move his arm enough to draw his sword. Finding himself powerless in the hands of the stronger

man, he remained passive, only the twitching of his mouth betraying his passion.

"And you would prevent my marriage," he said coldly. "So be it. Go to the baron; tell your story. Go also to mademoiselle, his daughter; repeat the scandal to her ears; say, 'I am your champion;' and how will they receive you? The baron will have you kicked from the room and mademoiselle will scorn you. Championed by a servant! What an honor for a lady!"

The truth of what he said struck Tournay harder than any blow; his arms dropped to his side, and he stepped back, as if powerless.

The marquis arranged the lace ruffle about his neck. Placing his hand upon his sword he eyed Tournay as if debating what course to pursue. He smarted under the treatment he had received, and his eyes glittered viciously as if he meditated some prompt reprisal. But above all the marquis was politic, and he also knew that in his biting tongue he possessed a weapon keener than a sword.

He stooped and plucked a flower from the border of the path, and as he spoke a sarcastic smile played mockingly about his lips.

"I shall marry mademoiselle," he began, slowly dwelling on each word, while he plucked the petals from the flower, and tossed them, one by one, into the air. The gesture was a careless one, but there was a vicious cruelty about his fingers as he tore the flower. "And you," continued the marquis, — "you, who one might think had dared to raise your eyes toward the lady's face" —

Tournay stood dumb before his inquisitor. His heart raged and he writhed as if under the lash, but still he stood passive and suffering.

"And you shall be our servant," ended the nobleman, with a laugh, turning and walking haughtily up the path, but with his hand still on his sword-hilt lest he should be again taken by surprise.

As the heels of the marquis crunched the gravel-walk Tournay felt the truth of each word that he had spoken borne in upon his mind with overwhelming force. It was not fear of the marquis's sword that had kept him silent. It was the hopelessness of his own position. What right had he to speak? And who would listen to him?

Silently the young man slipped into the forest as if to seek consolation from the great murmuring trees. As he walked slowly beneath their green arches as under some cathedral roof, a quiet strength came to his soul. He seemed to feel that the day would come when his voice would be heard and listened to. Until then he must bide his time; and in this frame of mind he went back to the château.

When Tournay reached the house he was greeted by an order from the baron. The tracks of a boar had been recently discovered in the forest by one of the gamekeepers, and the intendant's son, who was himself a keen huntsman, was directed to escort the party of gentlemen through the woods to a glade where the animal was supposed to have his lair.

After he had collected the guns and ammunition, called up the dogs and ordered the grooms to bring round the horses, Tournay went to the front of the château to await the pleasure of the young gentlemen who intended participating in the hunt.

There were half a dozen of them standing under the porte-cochère, and Tournay disliked them all in greater or less degree; excepting perhaps the Marquis de St. Hilaire. St. Hilaire was the eldest of the group, the tallest and the handsomest. He rarely addressed any remark to Tournay, but when he did, it was with perfect politeness. When the Marquis de St. Hilaire rode his horse he did it with a grace none could surpass; when he shot, he hit the mark. He had the reputation of being one of the most dissipated young noblemen in the kingdom. He certainly spent money more lavishly than the most prodigal. This reputation was at once the envy and admiration of a host of young followers; and yet if asked, no one could mention any particular debauchery of which he had been guilty. When his companions, under the excitement of wine, committed extravagant follies and excesses, St. Hilaire, although by no means sparing of the winecup, maintained a certain dignity essentially his own. At the gaming-table it was always the Marquis de St. Hilaire who played the highest. He won a fortune or lost an estate with the same calm and outward indifference. On every occasion he was the cool, polished gentleman.

As Tournay approached the group of noblemen, the Marquis de Lacheville, determined to keep him in a state of submission, greeted him with an arrogant rebuke.

"You have kept us waiting a pretty length of time."

"I only received notice of your intended hunt a short time ago, and various preparations had to be made," was the rejoinder.

"Make no excuses," continued the marquis, — "you always have plenty of those upon the end of your tongue."

Tournay bit his lip to keep from replying.

"Whose horse is that?" called out the marquis a moment later, pointing out one of the animals among the number which were being led up by the grooms.

"My own, monsieur le marquis — a present from the baron."

"Well, it is by all odds the best one among them; I will ride it." And the marquis swung himself into the saddle without waiting for a reply.

Tournay made no audible reply, but the color deepened on his cheek, as he quietly took another horse.

"We shall never see that boar if we delay much longer," called out St. Hilaire, who was long since in the saddle. "Are you ready, gentlemen?"

With one accord they all started down the avenue at a swift gallop; Tournay following a short distance behind them.

For a mile or so they swept along the parkway

until they arrived at the gate which led into the
wood.   De Lacheville had been correct in his
judgment of the horse, and was the first to reach
the gate.   This seemed to make him good-natured
for the time being ; and as they cantered through
the forest he allowed Tournay, who was best ac-
quainted with the ground, to ride in advance.

On approaching the entrance to the glade, the
party dismounted and the horses were fastened to
the trees.   The Counts d'Arlincourt and de Blois
went to the right ; the Marquis de St. Hilaire to
the left ; Tournay took two dogs and went toward
the northern end ; while de Lacheville remained
near the entrance.

It was arranged that Tournay with the dogs
should rout the animal from its lair in the upper
end of the dale, and, the thicket being surrounded,
one of the gentlemen would be sure to bring it
down with a shot as it ran out.

Tournay had not gone half the distance when he
heard a noise in the underbrush, and looking in
the direction whence it came, saw the boar making its way leisurely down the glade, snuffing from
time to time at the roots of trees for acorns.

Tournay tried to work down ahead of the animal and drive him off to his right in the direction
of the Marquis St. Hilaire, as he was the best shot
in the company, and with a sportsman's instinct
Tournay wanted to give him the opportunity to
win the tusks.   One of the dogs, however, upset
this plan by slipping the leash and bounding off
in the direction of the boar ; that animal took the

alarm at once and started on a run down the glade with Tournay and the two dogs after him in full pursuit.

"The Marquis de Lacheville will be the one to shoot him," thought Tournay bitterly.

The boar, plunging through a thicket, made straight for the spot where the horses had been tied, and where the Marquis de Lacheville had taken up his position.

"Why does he not fire?" was Tournay's mental inquiry as he followed the trail at full speed, with ear alert in the momentary expectation of hearing the sound of a gun. "Can it be that the marquis is going to risk attacking him with the knife?" And he dashed into the thicket, regardless of the brushwood and briars that impeded his progress, to come out on the other side, leaving a portion of his hunting blouse in the grasp of a too-persistent bramble.

Here he beheld so ludicrous a sight that it would have moved him to merriment, had it not overcome him with wonder. The marquis lay sprawling on the grass, his eyes rolling with terror and his loaded gun lying harmlessly by his side. The horses were straining at the tethers and neighing with fright, while in the wood beyond, the boar was disappearing from sight with the dogs upon his haunches.

As Tournay approached, the marquis struggled to his feet. For a moment he stood silent and then said gruffly : —

"The brute sprang through the bushes before I

expected him; my foot slipped and I fell, so he got by me."

In the instant it flashed through Tournay's mind that the marquis had fallen in trying to avoid the boar. He received the explanation in silence, his face clearly betraying his suspicion.

The marquis eyed him savagely. "Where are the others?" he demanded.

"They have evidently missed all the sport," was the curt rejoinder.

The marquis scowled, but his anxiety to conceal the mishap from his companions led him to overlook the ring of sarcasm in Tournay's voice.

"Did they hear or see the boar?" he inquired.

"I fear not. The animal started too near the centre of the glade, and luckily for him made straight for you."

"We have not seen him, either," was the cool rejoinder.

"But I saw him," exclaimed Tournay with open-eyed astonishment.

"Up in the thicket beyond? Possibly," admitted the marquis, who had now regained his self-possession and had resolved to put the best possible face on the matter.

"No! Right here in the open, as he ran into that clump of beeches."

"You are mistaken. I did not see him," the marquis insisted, approaching his horse and untethering him.

"Monsieur le marquis was possibly not looking in the right direction."

De Lacheville mounted his horse. He bent down from the saddle, saying fiercely, "Twice this day you have ventured to oppose me. Have a care! You will rue the hour when you dispute any statement of mine."

Tournay looked up at him defiantly, and with a significance too deep to be misconstrued, said: "I will not lie at your bidding, Monsieur de Lacheville."

"You insolent villain!" and the marquis' whip fell viciously across the defiant brow. The next instant the nobleman was dragged from the saddle and his riderless horse galloped off through the woods.

For a moment the two men stood looking at each other.

Tournay was the first to speak: "You will fight me for that blow, Monsieur de Lacheville."

The marquis gave a harsh laugh: "We do not fight lackeys — we whip them."

"We are alone, and man to man you shall fight me with my weapons, monsieur le Marquis." Tournay spoke with a certain air of dignity and with a suppressed fierceness that made the marquis draw back; yet such was the nobleman's contempt for the man of humble birth that he made no response beyond flicking the whip which he still retained in his hand, and looking at him disdainfully.

"You have a hunting-knife at your side; arm yourself," commanded Tournay sternly, at the same time drawing from beneath his hunting-blouse a long, keen blade.

The marquis turned pale. " I do not fight with such a weapon," he faltered, looking about him as if in hopes of succor from his friends.

" Then for once the low-born has the advantage," replied Tournay pitilessly, " and unless Heaven intervenes, I shall kill you for that blow."

The blow itself was forgotten even as he spoke, and he felt a fierce joy as he whispered to himself, " If heaven so wills it, you shall never marry her, Marquis de Lacheville."

There was no fire of revenge in his eyes as he advanced, but the marquis saw the light that burned there and, realizing his pressing danger, drew his own hunting-knife.

There was a thrust and parry. Tournay closed in upon him, and the nobleman fell backward with a groan.

The next instant Tournay threw aside the knife and stood looking with awe upon the prostrate body. The bushes behind him parted with a rustle and he looked over his shoulder to see the Marquis de St. Hilaire standing by him.

" What's the matter? " inquired the latter sternly. " Has the marquis injured himself ? "

" He struck me," exclaimed Tournay, his face, except for a bright red line across the brow, deadly pale. " And I — I have killed him."

St. Hilaire stooped down and undid the marquis's waistcoat, Tournay giving way to him. " He's not dead," said St. Hilaire, after a short examination. " Your blade struck the rib. He is not even fatally hurt, but has fainted."

Tournay stood passive and silent.

St. Hilaire rose to his feet and proceeded to cut some strips from his own shirt to make a bandage for de Lacheville's wound.

"As far as you are concerned, you might as well have killed him," he said as he bound up the wound. "The penalty is the same."

"I'm not afraid of the penalty."

"Young man," said St. Hilaire, busying himself over the wound, "mount that horse of yours and ride away from this part of the country as fast as you can. I shall not see you."

"I'm not a coward to run away."

"Don't be a fool and stay," replied St. Hilaire sharply, without looking up from his occupation. "You have acted as I would have done had I been in your place, but I should not stay afterward with all the odds against me. Come, you have only a minute to decide. I'll see the marquis has the proper care."

In another minute Robert Tournay was on his horse's back riding swiftly away from the scene. He only thought of one point of refuge and that was the city of his dreams, the great city of Paris. Toward it he turned his horse's head. When he had gone far enough to no longer fear pursuit he dismounted and turned the horse loose, knowing that a man riding a fine animal could be more easily traced; so the rest of his journey of a hundred miles was made on foot.

It was about the noon hour, July 12, 1789, when he entered the southern gates of the city. He

had been walking since early morning, yet when
once in the town he was not conscious of any
fatigue.

It seemed to him that there was an unwonted
excitement in the air, and the faces of many people
in the crowded streets wore an anxious or an ex-
pectant look. Several times he was on the point
of stopping some passer-by to ask if there was any
event of unusual importance taking place, but the
fear of being thought ignorant of city ways deterred
him. So he wandered about the streets in search
of some cheap and clean lodging suitable to the
size of his purse, where he could be comfortably
housed until his plans for the future matured.
He went through narrow, ill-smelling streets, where
strange-looking faces peered at him curiously from
low wine-shops. Thence he wandered into the
neighborhood of beautiful gardens, where he mar-
veled at the splendid buildings, any one of which
he fancied might be the home of the Marquis de
St. Hilaire. Finally, he came upon a number of
people streaming through an arcade under some
handsome buildings. Judging that something of
unusual interest was going on there, and being
moved by curiosity, he pushed his way in with the
rest, and found himself in a quadrangle of buildings enclosing a garden. This garden was filled
with a dense crowd. Turning to a man at his
elbow, he asked the reason of such an assemblage.

" The king has dismissed Necker," was the
reply, " and the people are angry."

" I should think they might well be angry,"

replied Tournay, who admired the popular minister of finance. "Did the king send away such a
great man without cause?"

"I know not what cause was assigned, I do not
concern myself much with such affairs, but I know
the people are very wroth and there has been much
talk of violence. Some blood has been shed. The
German regiments fired once or twice upon a mob
that would not disperse."

"The villainous foreign regiments!" said Tournay. "Why must we have these mercenary troops
quartered in our city?" He had been in the city
but a few hours, but in his indignation he already
referred to Paris as "our city."

"The native troops would not fire when ordered,
and were hurried back to the barracks by their
officers. Worse may come of it. There is much
speech-making and turmoil; I am going home to
keep out of the trouble;" and the stranger hurried
away.

Tournay elbowed through the crowd. Standing
upon a table under one of the spreading trees, a
young man was speaking earnestly to an excited
group of listeners that grew larger every moment.
Tournay pressed near enough to hear what he was
saying.

He was tall and slender, with dark waving hair
and the face of a poet. He spoke with an impas-
sioned eloquence that moved his hearers mightily,
bringing forth acclamation after acclamation from
the crowd. He denounced tyranny and exalted
liberty till young Tournay's blood surged through

his veins like fire. He had thought all this himself, unable to give it expression; but here was a man who touched the very note that he himself would have sounded, touched the same chord in the heart of every man who heard his voice, and by some subtle power communicated the thrill to those outside the circle till the crowd in the garden was drunk with excitement.

"Citizens," cried the young man, "the exile of Necker is the signal for a St. Bartholomew of patriots. The foreign regiments are about to march upon us to cut our throats. To arms! Behold the rallying sign." And stretching up his arm he plucked a green leaf from the branch above his head and put it in his hat.

The next instant the trees were almost denuded of their leaves. Tournay, with a green sprig in his hat, swung his hat in the air, and cried, "To arms — down with the foreign regiments — Vive Necker!"

He struggled to where the orator was being carried off on men's shoulders. "What is it?" he said, in his excitement seizing the young man by the coat, — "what is it that we are to do?"

"Procure arms. Watch and wait, — and then do as other patriots do," was the reply.

The crowd surged closer about him. The coat gave way, and Tournay was left with a piece of the cloth in his hand. Waving it in the air with the cry of "Patriots, to arms!" he was forced onward by the crowd.

CHAPTER II

A LITTLE BREAKFAST AT ST. HILAIRE'S

THE Marquis Jean Raphael de St. Hilaire was giving a breakfast-party. It was not one of those large affairs for which the marquis was noted, where a hundred guests would sit down in his large salon to a repast costing the lavish young nobleman a princely sum. This being merely the occasion of a modest little déjeuner, the covers were laid in the marquis's morning cabinet on the second floor, which was more suitable for such an informal meal.

There were present around the table the Count and Countess d'Arlincourt; the old Chevalier de Creux; the witty Madame Diane de Rémur; the Count de Blois, dressed in the very latest and most exact fashion; and the Marquis de Lacheville, with the pallor of recent illness on his face. At the lower end of the board sat a young poet who was riding on his first wave of popularity; and next to him was a philosopher.

The guests, having finished the dessert, were lingering over a choice vintage from the marquis's cellar.

The host, leaning back in his chair with half-closed eyes, listened carelessly to the hum of con-

versation while he toyed with a few sugared al-
monds.

"And so you think, chevalier," said the Countess d'Arlincourt in reply to a remark by the old
nobleman, "that our troublesome times are not yet
over?"

"Not yet, my dear countess, nor will they be
over for a long time to come."

"Oh, how pessimistic you are, chevalier; for
my part I do not see how affairs can be worse
than they have been for the last year."

"For a longer period than that," remarked her
husband, the Count d'Arlincourt.

"Well, I remember particularly, it was a year
ago when you first told me that you could not afford to make me a present of a diamond crescent
to wear in my hair at the Duchess de Montmorenci's fancy dress-ball. You had never used that
word to me before."

"You have been extremely fortunate," said the
Chevalier de Creux, turning a pair of small, bright
eyes upon the countess and speaking with just the
slightest accent of sarcasm. "Even longer ago
than a year, many persons were in need of other
necessities than diamonds."

"Oh, yes, I know," interrupted the countess
hastily, anxious to show that she was not as ignorant as the chevalier's tone implied, — "bread.
Why don't they give the people enough bread?
It is a very simple demand, and things would then
be well."

"My dear child," put in Madame de Rémur,

"it would do no good to give them bread to-day;
they would be hungry again to-morrow. The
trouble is with the finances. When they are set
right everything will go well; and the people can
buy all the bread they want, and you can have
your diamond crescent," and the speaker smiled
at the chevalier and shrugged her white shoulders.

"Yes, but," persisted the countess, raising her
pretty eyebrows, "when *will* the finances be set
right? The people cannot go forever without
bread."

"Nor can women go forever without diamonds,"
laughed Madame de Rémur.

"Women with your eyes, fair Diane, have no
need of other diamonds," said the Marquis de St.
Hilaire debonairely. The lady smiled graciously at
the compliment. She was a young and attractive
widow and she looked at St. Hilaire not unkindly.

"We have frequently had financial crises in the
past," said d'Arlincourt, "and gotten safely over
them; and so we should to-day, were it not for
the host of philosophical writers who have broken
loose; who call the people's attention to their
ills, and foment trouble where there is none. Of
course you will understand that I make the usual
exception as to present company," he added, bowing slightly to the philosopher. But the latter
seemed lost in thought and did not appear to hear
the count's remark. The poet took up the conversation in a low tone.

"Should we not look to these very men, these
philosophers, these encyclopædists, to point the

way out of the difficulty?" and he turned from one to the other with a shrug.

"Bah, no! They are the very ones to blame, I tell you," repeated d'Arlincourt.

"My dear count," cried Madame d'Arlincourt, "I cannot permit you to speak slightingly of our philosophers. They are all the fashion now. The door of every salon in Paris is open to them. The other night, at a great reception given by the Duchess de Montmorenci, half the invited guests were philosophers, poets, encyclopædists. They say that even some of the nobility were overlooked in order to make room for the men of letters."

The Marquis de St. Hilaire threw a small cake to the spaniel that sat on its haunches begging for it.

"We cannot very well overlook this new order of nobility of the ink-and-paper that has exerted such an influence during the last generation," he said carelessly.

"I should not overlook them if I had my way," cried the Count d'Arlincourt. "I should lock them safely up in the Bastille."

"Oh!" cried the ladies in one breath; "barbarian!"

"These men are doubtless responsible for the inflamed state of the public mind," said St. Hilaire, again taking up the conversation.

"Of course they are," agreed the count.

"And so are Calonne and Brienne," continued the marquis. "They mismanaged affairs during their terms of office."

Here the philosopher smiled an assent.

"But the blame rests more heavily upon other shoulders than those of scribbling writers or corrupt officials," and the marquis paused to look around the table.

"I am all attention," cried the Countess d'Arlincourt, prepared for something amusing. "Upon whom does it rest?"

"Upon the nobility themselves," answered St. Hilaire.

For a moment there was silence; then came a storm of protests from all sides, only the chevalier and the philosopher making no audible reply, although the latter said to himself: —

"You are right, monsieur le marquis."

"St. Hilaire is in one of his mad fits," de Lacheville exclaimed.

"If it were not for the nobility there would be no poetry, no wit," murmured the poet.

"The nobility is the mainstay of the throne, the vitality of the country," said d'Arlincourt.

"What have *we* done?" cried the ladies in concert. "We ask for nothing better than to have everybody contented and happy." And they shrugged their pretty white shoulders as if to throw off the burden that St. Hilaire had placed there.

"Look at me," exclaimed St. Hilaire, rising and speaking with an animation he had not shown before. He was a man of twenty-five with a face so handsome that dissipation had not been able to mar its beauty. "I am a type of my class."

"An honor to it," said the poet.

"Thank you; then you will agree that the cap which I put on will fit other heads as well. I have wasted two fortunes."

"St. Hilaire is in one of his remorseful moods," whispered de Lacheville in the ear of Madame de Rémur.

"I have spent them in riotous living with men like myself." Here he looked at de Lacheville.

"I feel deeply honored, my dear marquis," said the latter, bowing.

"When I wanted more money I knew where to get it."

"Happy fellow," called out de Lacheville with a laugh.

"I went to the steward who managed my estates. I have estates, or rather had them, for they are now mortgaged to the last notch, in Normandy, Picardy, Auvergne and Poitou — I would say to my steward, 'I need more money.'"

"'Very well, monsieur le marquis, but I must put on the screws a little to get it.'

"'Put on a dozen if you like, but get me the funds.'

"'It shall be done, monsieur le marquis.'

"Again and again I went to him for money. He always responded in the same manner, but each time the screws had to be turned a little tighter. Do you suppose my peasants love me for that? No, they hate me just as yours hate you, de Lacheville, and yours hate you, d'Arlincourt."
De Lacheville laughed, and the count lifted up his

hand in denial. "I knew that the day of reckoning would come," St. Hilaire went on. "Every time I went to Monsieur Rignot, my steward, every time he put on the screws at my request, I knew it was bringing us nearer the final smash."

"Us!" repeated d'Arlincourt, with a gesture of impatience.

"Yes, us," said St. Hilaire; "we are all in the same boat, but we have all done the same thing in a greater or less degree. We shall all have to pay the penalty."

"There is where I differ with you, my dear marquis," said the Count d'Arlincourt; "I am willing to take what responsibility falls to me by right, but I emphatically refuse to pay the penalty of your follies."

"My follies are but those of my class. You may have been an exception yourself, d'Arlincourt, but that will not save you."

"What penalties must we pay? Save him from what?" demanded the pretty countess, looking at St. Hilaire with her large blue eyes.

"From the revolution," was the answer. There was a general exclamation of surprise. D'Arlincourt took up the word.

"Like all men given to excess, — pardon the remark, marquis, but you have yourself admitted it, — you exaggerate the present unquiet state of affairs. The people will not revolt. They have no real cause. If you had made such a statement twenty years ago during the ascendency of the infamous du Barry I might not have contradicted you. But now the people as a mass are loyal. They love their king."

" I still affirm," said St. Hilaire, "that the time is ripe for a revolution. Sooner or later it must come."

The chevalier from the further end of the table said quietly; " It *has* come."

"Surely you are not serious," said d'Arlincourt, turning to the chevalier, " in calling the disturbance of the past few days a revolution. Why, I have seen more serious revolts than this blow into nothing. Our Paris mob is a fickle creature, demanding blood one moment and the next moment throwing up its cap with delight if you show it a colored picture."

" The disturbance of to-day will become great enough to shake France to its centre," said the chevalier.

" One would think that you possessed the gift of second sight," laughed de Lacheville.

" I do," replied the old man impressively.

" Give us an example of it, then," demanded d'Arlincourt. " What part am I to take in the new revolution ? "

" I see behind you, my dear d'Arlincourt," replied the chevalier, leaning back in his chair and looking in the count's direction through half-closed eyelids, " the shadow of a scaffold."

Unwittingly the count turned with a start, to see Blaise standing behind him in the act of filling his glass with wine. There was a general laugh.

" Madame de Rémur will bare her white

shoulders to the rude grasp of the executioner.
De Lacheville will escape. No, he will not.
He will die by his own hand to cheat the scaf-
fold."

"And I," interrupted the Countess d'Arlincourt, "shall I share their fate?"

The chevalier looked at her with a peculiar
expression in his eyes. "My sight fails here," he
said. "I cannot foretell your fate. Yet you may
live; your beauty should save you. People do not
kill those who please them; those who bore them
are less fortunate." And he turned his snapping
brown eyes in the direction of the gentle poet and
the venerable philosopher.

"St. Hilaire's sudden and great interest in the
people's welfare may prove of service to him,"
remarked d'Arlincourt significantly.

"It will not save him," replied the chevalier.
"He will finally come to the same end. The
shadow of the scaffold is behind him also."

St. Hilaire laughed as he cracked an almond.
"Though I may sympathize somewhat with a
people who have been oppressed and robbed, I
should feel unhappy indeed to be left out in the
cold when so many of the illustrious had gone
before. But you have overlooked yourself. That
is like you, chevalier, unselfish to the last."

"Oh, I am too old to be of importance; I shall
die of gout," said the old nobleman.

"You have disposed of us effectually," said the
poet, "and I shall be greatly honored at being
permitted to leave this world in such good com-

pany.   But may I ask, are we to be the sole victims
of your revolution?"

"Far from it," answered the old chevalier, closing his eyes and speaking in an abstracted manner,
as if talking to himself, while his friends listened
in rapt attention, half inclined to smile at the
affair as at a joke, and yet so serious was he that
they could not escape the influence of his seriousness.

"I can see," he continued, "a long line of the
most illustrious in France.   They are passing
onward to the block.   They are princes of the
blood; aye, even the king's head shall fall."

"Enough!" cried out the voice of d'Arlincourt, above the general exclamations of horror
that the chevalier's pretended vision called forth.
"You overstep the line, Chevalier de Creux.   I
do not object to a pleasantry, but when you go so
far as to predict the execution of the king you
carry a jest too far.   It is time to call a halt."

"But was it a jest?" asked the chevalier dryly.

"A very poor one," said de Lacheville.

"My dear friend," said the chevalier in his
blandest tone, "I am not predicting what I should
like to have take place.   Not what ought to be,
but what will be."

The count scowled and de Lacheville turned
away with a shrug and began a conversation with
Madame de Rémur.

"We all know that the chevalier is a merry
gentleman, yet no jester," said St. Hilaire.
"What will be, will be.   I, for one, am willing

to drink a toast to the chevalier's revolution.
Blaise, bring out some of that wine I received
from the Count de Beaujeu. I lost fifty thousand
livres to him the night he made me a present of
this wine; it will be like drinking liquid gold."

Blaise filled the glasses amid general silence.

St. Hilaire rose to his feet, holding his wine-
glass above his head.

"What, my friends, you are not afraid?" he
exclaimed in a tone of surprise, looking about the
table where only the chevalier and the philosopher had followed his example. "Is it possible
you have taken the chevalier's visions so much to
heart?"

They all rose from their places, ashamed to have
it thought that they had taken in too serious a
vein the little comedy played by the chevalier.

"Any excuse to drink such wine as this," said
de Lacheville, with a forced laugh.

"We drink to the revolution!" cried St. Hilaire in his reckless manner — and he touched
glasses with Madame de Rémur and then with the
Countess d'Arlincourt. As the glasses clinked
about the table, a heavy booming sound fell upon
the ears of the revelers.

"What noise is that?" cried the countess nervously. They stopped to listen, holding their
glasses aloft. The booming ceased, then followed
a roar like that of the angry surf beating upon a
rockbound shore.

"It is the chevalier's revolution," exclaimed
Madame de Rémur.

"Are we to be frightened from drinking our toast by a little noise?" cried St. Hilaire. "What if it be the revolution? Let us drink to it. Come!" and they drained their glasses to the accompaniment of what sounded like a volley of musketry.

The ladies looked pale and were glad to quit the table for the salon, where they were joined by the poet and the philosopher, leaving the others still at their wine.

The Marquis de Lacheville took another glass, and then a third.

"You had best be careful how you heat your blood with this rich wine, de Lacheville, while that wound in your side is scarcely healed," remarked d'Arlincourt.

"Confound the wound, and curse the young villain who gave it me," growled de Lacheville. "I have been forced to lead the life of an anchorite for the past fortnight; but such nectar as this cannot inflame, it only soothes," and he reached out his hand toward the decanter. As he did so, the sound of guns reverberated again through the room, making the windows rattle and jarring the dishes on the table. The ladies in the adjoining room cried out in alarm, and d'Arlincourt rose and went to reassure them.

"I will go with you," said the chevalier, and he joined the count.

De Lacheville threw his napkin down upon the spot of wine that had splashed from his upraised glass upon the damask cloth.

"The devil take them!" he cried petulantly; then filling his glass again with an air of bravado, "will they not permit a man to breakfast in peace?"

"Your nerves must be badly shaken, de Lacheville, if you permit such a slight thing to disturb you," laughed St. Hilaire, filling a glass to the brim.

D'Arlincourt entered from the next room hurriedly. "I am going to see what all this firing means," he said. "Will you accompany me, gentlemen?"

"I make it a point never to seek for news or excitement, but rather allow them to come to me," said St. Hilaire leisurely. "You would better sit down and let me send a servant to ascertain the cause of this turmoil."

"Why leave the house in search of truth when we have with us an oracle in the shape of the chevalier?" interposed the Marquis de Lacheville.

"I shall be able to bring a more accurate account," replied d'Arlincourt with an impatient shrug.

"As you will," said St. Hilaire. "Blaise, give the Count d'Arlincourt his hat and sword. Are you quite sure you do not want some of my lackeys to accompany you?" he asked.

D'Arlincourt declined the offer and hastily left the room.

The two marquises were left in possession of the dining-room and the wine. They both continued to drink, each after his own fashion. With each successive glass, de Lacheville became louder in voice and more boastful, while as St. Hilaire sipped his wine, he became quieter and more indifferent.

Within ten minutes d'Arlincourt returned to them, his face betraying great excitement.

"A mob has attacked and captured the Bastille. The multitude is surging through the streets. They will pass before this very door."

"It is impossible that they could have taken the Bastille!" exclaimed de Lacheville, rising to his feet and steadying himself by holding to the back of his chair.

"There are thirty thousand of them," replied d'Arlincourt, "and through some treachery they have obtained arms. In order to save bloodshed Governor Delaunay surrendered the fortress on receiving the promise of the insurgents that the lives of all its defenders should be spared. They are now dragging him through the streets, crying out for his blood. The man was mad to trust the word of such a rabble."

"Let us go into the salon," remarked St. Hilaire quietly. "There we can reassure the ladies and also view this interesting spectacle."

The three gentlemen entered the room which fronted upon the street, d'Arlincourt with compressed lips and flashing eyes; de Lacheville, unsteady of gait and with wine-flushed face, murmuring maledictions against the beast multitude; and St. Hilaire, cool and calm as was his wont.

In the salon they found the chevalier entertaining Madame de Rémur with an anecdote which was the occasion of much laughter on her part.

The poet was reciting some of his own verses to the countess, while the philosopher was asleep in an armchair.

"The crowd have torn down the Bastille," cried de Lacheville, speaking in a thick voice, "and they are now coming down this street, seeking whom they can devour."

The ladies cried out in terror.

"Marquis, you have interrupted one of my best stories," said the chevalier petulantly.

"But, chevalier, the mob have taken the Bastille."

"Could n't you have allowed them two minutes more to complete their work? However, what you say is very interesting, though it does not surprise me. I have been expecting it."

"You forget that the chevalier is gifted with second sight," said the count, with a slight sneer.

"I have been expecting it for some time," continued the chevalier, "though what they wanted to take it for, I cannot imagine. If they should attack the Hotel de Ville or the Louvre, or march against Versailles, I could understand it."

Madame de Rémur and the philosopher, who had awakened from his nap, had approached to hear the news; and the Marquis de Lacheville repeated it to them as if he had been an eye-witness of the whole affair.

"For my part," he said in conclusion, "I think this disturbance amounts to very little; the Baron de Besneval has but to give the order to his troops, and the valiant mob will disperse like chaff. I have seen such fellows run before this. It is amusing to see what a steel bayonet will do toward accelerating the pace of the canaille."

"They say that the French Guards are not loyal," remarked the chevalier.

"The French Guards be hanged!" shouted the Marquis de Lacheville hotly. "I would not trust them further than the canaille itself; they are a white-livered lot in spite of their gaudy uniforms. Thank heaven, we have other troops who are good and loyal, and who will put down these disorders in a trice."

"We shall look to you, then, marquis," said the cavalier, "to restore peace and quiet for us at once."

"I would not soil my hands with such dirt," replied de Lacheville haughtily, and scowling at what he thought was a disposition on the part of the chevalier to ridicule him.

"Is there really danger?" inquired the Countess d'Arlincourt of her husband.

"The situation is grave, but I hardly think there is great cause for alarm," he answered. "The king has too many loyal subjects to permit anarchy and riot to exist for any length of time."

"Let us go out upon the balcony," interrupted St. Hilaire; "the show is about to pass under our windows." He threw open the windows and ushered his friends out upon the balcony with a gesture as if he were bidding them welcome to his box at the opera.

Down the street, with a roar that drowned all other sounds, came the surging mass like a torrent that had burst its bounds. In the front ranks, carried on the shoulders of a dozen, were two men dressed in the uniform of the French Guards. They were greeted on all sides with acclamations.

"See how the Guards fraternize with the mob," said de Lacheville. "Down with the French Guards! Down with the rabble!" he cried in his excitement, shaking his fist over the railing.

St. Hilaire gripped his arm. "I don't care how much you expose your own life, but as I do not wish to bring insult or danger upon the ladies under my roof, perhaps you had better refrain from expressing your opinions for the present."

"Do you think they would dare attack this house?" demanded de Lacheville, turning pale.

"Men who have successfully stormed a prison are not likely to hesitate before the walls of a house, even though it does belong to a marquis," replied St. Hilaire. "Look at that!" he exclaimed suddenly, pointing up the street. Then turning to d'Arlincourt, he said, "Get the ladies inside as quickly as possible." The count had no sooner followed his directions, than along the street, borne on long poles on a level with the very eyes of those on the balcony, appeared two heads dripping with blood.

"Dear me, whose are those?" exclaimed the chevalier, adjusting his eyeglasses. "By my soul, it's poor Delaunay's head. They have treated him most shabbily. Can you make out the other, St. Hilaire?"

"No," answered the marquis, "I was never good at recognizing faces," and he stepped to the window to reassure the ladies in the salon.

The chevalier leaned over the railing and called out to one of the men in the crowd : —

"My good fellow, will you have the kindness to tell me whose head they are carrying on the second pole?"

The man, thus addressed, looked up. He was tall and broad-shouldered, with face browned from exposure to the sun. With one arm he supported a member of the French Guards who had been wounded.

"Flesselle's," he answered. "He has betrayed the people again and again. He has received a terrible punishment."

The man who had given the chevalier this answer did not move on immediately, but stood looking up at the balcony. The old nobleman, following this look, saw that it rested on the Marquis de Lacheville.

The latter, meeting the man's eye at the same moment, recognized Robert Tournay. He started forward as if about to speak, then noticing the weapon in Tournay's hand and remembering the recent warning of St. Hilaire, he checked himself. Neither spoke, but the marquis could not repress a look of hatred, which was answered by a look of defiance by Tournay. Then the latter turned

away with his companion leaning on his shoulder.
The crowd closed up and he was soon lost to
sight.

"They have killed Flesselle, the mayor of
Paris," said the chevalier, as St. Hilaire joined
him a moment later. "Well," he continued, as if
in answer to St. Hilaire's shrug, "Flesselle was a
fool, but I am sorry for poor Delaunay. Come,
St. Hilaire, let us go in, the crowd is thinning out
now; in a short time the streets will be passable
and I must be going. I have to thank you for a
most enjoyable day, marquis."

"The pleasure has been mine," replied the Marquis de St. Hilaire, bowing.

"Are you going to the duchess's to-night?"
inquired the chevalier.

"No, I think not," answered St. Hilaire, putting his hand upon the window-bar. "After you,
my dear chevalier," indicating the way into the
salon. As he was about to step into the room the
chevalier turned and took a final look at the street.
The main body of the mob had passed and their
shouts were heard receding in the distance; although underneath the window were still a number of persons, coming and going in restless excitement.

"I think, marquis," he said, with his curious
smile, "that your friends need soap and water
badly."

"They do, chevalier," said the other, returning
che smile, "and the smell is sickening. Come to
my bedroom; I will give you a new perfume."

That evening, after the departure of his guests, the Marquis de St. Hilaire called in his man of affairs.

"Rignot," he demanded carelessly, "have I a single estate that is unencumbered?"

"Unfortunately no, monsieur le marquis."

"Think again, Rignot. Is there not some little estate still intact? Some small farm heretofore overlooked by us?"

"Not a cottage, monsieur le marquis."

"What bills are unpaid?"

"Some three hundred thousand livres are rather pressing."

"Is that the sum total of all my liabilities? I want a full statement to-night."

"You owe about eight hundred thousand francs, monsieur le marquis."

"Pay them at once."

"But, monsieur le marquis, it will be impossible. Where shall I get the funds?"

"You may sell my furniture, personal property" —

"What, everything, monsieur le marquis?"

"Yes, everything; and after paying all my debts, if there is anything left, take out a commission for yourself and give me the balance;" and then he turned to the window and looked out on the lights of the city of Paris, indicating that the interview was at an end. Rignot withdrew.

"Assuredly," said the Marquis de St. Hilaire with a yawn, "this revolution arrives in good time. I should soon have become a beggar."

CHAPTER III

THE BAKER AND HIS FAMILY

THE Count d'Arlincourt had just left the palace at Versailles.

He had been present at the reception to the Royal Flanders regiment. He had heard their vow of fidelity to the king. He had been among the officers and the nobles of the court who had trampled under foot the tricolor of Paris and decorated their coats with the white cockade, and now he left the royal presence with his sovereign's thanks and commendations ringing in his ears.

As he proceeded through the courtyard three gentlemen entered at the main gate. A shade of annoyance passed over the count's brow as he recognized St. Hilaire and two other noblemen, all members of the States General, and all reputed to lean somewhat too radically toward the popular side in politics. He had hardly seen St. Hilaire since the breakfast party at the house of the latter three months before. The toast of the marquis and his expressed sympathy with revolutionary orders had caused a decided estrangement.

Indeed, St. Hilaire and the two noblemen who were with him had become alienated from their order, and many of their former friends among the nobility had refused to speak or hold any relations with them whatever.

The count could not avoid meeting them, but he was undecided whether to ignore them entirely or pass them with such a slight inclination of the head as to be equally cutting.

The cordial bow of the Marquis de St. Hilaire, however, for whom he had always felt a peculiar and inexplicable regard, caused him to change his mind.

He saluted the three gentlemen politely, though with a certain reserve of manner natural to him, and addressed St. Hilaire.

"A word with you, marquis," he said, "if I may be pardoned for taking you from these gentlemen for a few minutes?"

St. Hilaire turned to his companions: "With your permission, messieurs, I will join you in five minutes in the palace."

The gentlemen bowed in assent and walked toward the palace, leaving the count and the marquis alone in the centre of the court.

"You were not present at the reception in the palace. We missed you greatly, marquis," the former began, with an attempt at cordiality of manner, having resolved to make one last appeal to his friend.

"Thank you, my dear d'Arlincourt, for your kindness in saying so," replied the marquis affably, "but I must tell you frankly that even if affairs in the Assembly had not claimed my time, other circumstances would have rendered my presence at this banquet impossible."

"The king," continued d'Arlincourt quietly, "inquired for you several times and seemed much disturbed at your absence."

"I am now on my way to wait upon his majesty," replied St. Hilaire.

The count's face lighted up. "A tardy apology is better than none at all, for I presume you are going to explain your absence."

"The two gentlemen who have left us, and myself, have been sent by the convention as a committee to urge his majesty to sanction their latest decrees, — the bill relating to popular rights," replied St. Hilaire quietly.

"For the love of Heaven, Raphael!" burst out the count, "can it be possible that you intend to persist in championing the popular cause, like the Duke d'Orleans, or the Marquis de Lafayette? Your present position is that of a madman. Come back to our side now. To-morrow it may be too late."

"For the life of me, André," replied St. Hilaire lightly, "I cannot tell you to-day what my line of action will be to-morrow, but in any case I beg you will not compare me either with the duke or Lafayette. I am neither as dull as the one nor as virtuous as the other. Why not permit me still to resemble only the Marquis de St. Hilaire?"

"Then," replied the count warmly, "I tell you that as the Marquis de St. Hilaire, your duty to the king should have brought you to the reception in honor of the Flanders regiment."

The marquis dropped his air of levity suddenly.

"Do you know, count," he said slowly, "I have just come from the Assembly, where news reached us a little while ago that a mob of forty thousand was marching from Paris toward Versailles."

The count started with surprise, but betrayed no other emotion.

"Is it a fitting time to be fêting a regiment composed of mercenaries? Is it a fitting time to be clinking glasses and drinking toasts when forty thousand men and women are approaching with their cry for bread?"

The count drew himself up as he replied, — "What more fitting time could there be for the loyal nobles to gather about their sovereign than in the hour of danger? I, for one, would not let the fear of any Paris mob keep me from the king's side at such a moment."

St. Hilaire flushed deeply. "Count d'Arlincourt," he said quickly, "I pass over that insinuation because it comes from an old friend. But know this: that I am one of the members of the Assembly who have sworn to support the constitution and enforce the rights of man. I should indeed have been false to my trust had I participated in a fête to these foreigners where oaths were openly made to defeat that constitution."

"Our ideas of duty evidently differ," replied the count stiffly. "My duty is to my king."

"They do differ," said St. Hilaire. "My first allegiance is to the nation. Count d'Arlincourt, I respect you and your opinions, but I also have a regard for my oath. I have chosen my path and I shall follow it."

" Good-day, Marquis de St. Hilaire," said the count, in his usual cold manner.

" Farewell, Count d'Arlincourt," was the polite rejoinder, and raising his hat St. Hilaire passed onward in the direction of the palace.

Forty thousand men and women were marching from Paris to Versailles. They had forced a king to recall a banished minister. They had sacked a prison fortress, — razing to the ground walls that had frowned on them for ages, wiping out in one day a landmark of tyranny that had been standing there for centuries. Now they were coming to see their king at his palace. They had heard of the banquet at Versailles, given in honor of the royal Flanders regiment, where wine had flowed like water and where food was in abundance. At such a banquet, they argued, there must be bread enough for the whole world ; and they were coming to get their share of it.

Although it was in the month of October, the sun was hot and the road dusty. In the front rank, amid all the dust and sweat and noise, walked Robert Tournay. He carried no weapon, nor did he seek to lead ; but animated by curiosity and by sympathy, he felt himself drawn into this great heaving mass of people who had decided to correct these abuses themselves, even if to do it they had to take the laws into their own hands.

Hearing a shout and rumble of wheels behind him, Tournay looked over his shoulder to see a cannon coming through the crowd, which parted on each side to let it pass, and then closed up behind it. This cannon was drawn along the road by a score of men, whose bare feet, beating the dust, sent up a pulverous cloud that blew back into the faces of those behind like smoke.

Seated upon the gun carriage, her hair streaming in the wind, was a young woman wearing the red cap of liberty, and waving in her hand a blood-red flag. The cannon stopped under the shade of some poplar trees, and men stood around it wiping the perspiration from their foreheads.

"A cheer for the Goddess of Liberty," cried a voice in the crowd. A shout went up that made the poplars tremble.

"Citizens," cried the girl, in response, standing erect and flinging her flag to the breeze, "you want bread!"

"Bread! Bread!" was the answering shout.

"The women of Paris will lead you to it. Then you shall help yourselves."

"Show us where it is and we'll take it fast enough," was the answering cry.

"Where should it be but in the king's palace? There they are feasting while the people in Paris are starving. They shall give the people of their bread!"

"What if they have eaten it all?" asked another voice.

"Then shall the king bake more," answered the girl — "enough for every one in his kingdom. He shall be the nation's baker, and his wife shall help him knead the dough, and their little boy shall give out the loaves."

There was a laugh at this and cries of " Good !
Good ! "

" My friends," she continued, taking off her cap
and swinging it by the tassel, " this marching is
hot work, and talking is dry business. Has any
one a drink for La Demoiselle Liberté ? "

A number of bottles were instantly proffered
her.

" This *eau de vie* puts new life into one," she
exclaimed, throwing back her head and putting a
flask to her lips. With an easy gesture she took
a deep draught of the liquor, to the increasing
admiration of the bystanders. On removing the
bottle from her lips, she said with a nod : " How
many of you men can beat that ? Here goes one
more." She was on the point of repeating the
act when she caught sight of Tournay, who had
drawn near and stood by the wheel of the truck
looking at her intently.

" Here, friend, you look at this liquor thirstily ;
take a good pull at it. You 're a likely youth,
and a sup of brandy will foster your strength !
What ! You will not drink ? Bah, man ! I
would not have it said that I was a little boy,
afraid of good liquor. But why do you stare at
me like that, without speaking ? Have you no
tongue ? " Tournay put aside the proffered bottle
and said : —

" I stared at you because I know you. You are
Marianne Froment, the miller's daughter, who left
La Thierry a year ago. And you should remember
Robert Tournay."

The young woman shook her head with a decided gesture.

"You mistake, friend; my name is not Marianne Froment. I know no miller, and have never heard of the place you speak of."

Tournay remembered when he had seen her last in the alley of the park. He felt no animosity toward her; instead he felt compassion for the silly girl whose head had been turned by the flattery of a nobleman who had already grown tired of her.

"It is you who are mistaken, Marianne," he replied quietly, "although when I knew you at La Thierry, drinking strong liquor was not one of your practices."

"I am La Demoiselle Liberté," replied the girl defiantly, throwing her brown curls back from her forehead and replacing her cap. "I have drunk such liquor as this from my cradle. So here's to you! May you some day grow to be a man."

Tournay stayed the bottle in its course to her lips, and took her hand in his.

"You are Marianne Froment," he persisted, "and it would be much better for you to be in the quiet country of La Thierry. Why not go back?"

"If Marianne did go back, who would speak to her? Who among all those who live there would take her by the hand?" she asked.

"Have I not taken you by the hand just now?" asked Tournay.

"I believe you would be the only one," she replied, stifling a sigh. "Not even my father would

do that. But you are no longer at La Thierry.
What are you doing here, and what sent you away
from home? Are you going back?"

Tournay shook his head. "There are reasons,"
he replied slowly, "why I can never return."

"Neither can Marianne Froment," rejoined the
girl. "Therefore, compatriot, drink with me to
our future good comradeship. And pass the bottle to your neighbor. Then let us go on together.
En avant, my friends," she cried out in a loud
voice. "The sooner we start again the earlier
we shall reach our bakery. Follow the carriage
of La Demoiselle Liberté, and she will lead you
to it."

A score of brawny arms grasped the ropes attached to the truck, and with a heavy rattle the
cannon was drawn through the crowd, which
cheered it on its way.

The forty thousand swept into Versailles in an
overpowering tide, finding nothing to stop their
triumphant course.

The crowd choked up the streets of the town,
filling the public square and invading the Assembly chamber.

The Assembly, with all the gravity and dignity
of its recent birth, rose to its feet to greet as many
of the Paris deputation as could crowd into the
room, steaming with the sweat and dust of the
march. Outside the door another crowd remained,
clamoring noisily.

The president of the Assembly addressed them
in a few words full of dignity. "I have just

learned," he said in his quiet way, "that the king has been pleased to accord his royal sanction to all the articles of the Bill of Popular Rights which was passed by your Assembly on the 5th of August."

" Will that give the people more bread ? " asked La Demoiselle, looking up at Tournay with an inquiring expression in her brown eyes. Despite her red cap, her swagger, and her boisterous talk, she was very pretty and child-like. As he looked down upon her standing by his side her brown head did not reach his shoulder.

" Whether it gives them bread or not, it is a glorious thing for the people," exclaimed Tournay with enthusiasm.

A few minutes later the demoiselle yawned. " The old fellow is too tiresome," she said ; " let us go to the palace and get our bread."

Evidently the same thought moved the rest of the deputation. They began to file out, while President Meunier was still addressing them, with a restless scuffling of their feet, and a murmuring among themselves, " To the palace ! To the palace ! "

The last Tournay saw of Demoiselle Liberté she was pushing through the crowd that made way for her right willingly, while she cried out : " I will show you the bakery, my brave people ; I am now on my way to interview the chief baker."

The forty thousand got their bread. They got their bread and more. They pressed in so close

upon their monarch, they were so menacing, so
determined in their way, that he promised to dismiss his royal Flanders regiment and go back to
Paris with his beloved subjects. And so the hungry, sullen, desperate mob became a shouting,
happy, victorious one. They cheered their monarch, who had sworn to be a father to his people;
they cheered the royal family, even the queen; but
most of all they cheered the loaves of bread which
were distributed among the eager multitude.
Every shop in the town was soon depleted of its
stock, and all the bakers were working over-time
to supply the food.

"Did I not tell you I would lead you where
bread was plenty?" demanded the Demoiselle de
la Liberté gayly of those gathered around. "The
king is a capital baker; we have only to keep him
with us and we shall have food at all times." And
she dipped her crust in a cup of wine.

"We will take our baker back with us to Paris,"
cried one.

"Aye, and the baker's wife and his little boy,"
cried another. At this there was a laugh.

Tournay, who had aided in the distribution of
the food, approached the group, relieved by the
thought that all were satisfied and contented, at
least for the moment.

"Ah, there is my handsome compatriot," exclaimed the demoiselle as soon as she set eyes
upon him. "Wilt thou join us in our supper,
compatriot?" she called out. She was seated
carelessly on the truck of the gun-carriage, with a

cup of wine in one hand and a half-loaf in the other, her face flushed with excitement. Unlike most of the women who stood about her, she was of graceful form, with hands and arms unblackened by hard toil, and the skin of her throat soft and white. She wore her red cap in a rakish manner on the side of her head, its tassel falling down over her forehead between her eyes. Every little while she would throw it back by a quick toss of the head.

Tournay took the cup from her outstretched hand, and put it to his lips. "Marianne," he said in a low tone, "it would be better if you were at home among your own people."

"Why do you still call me by that name?" she asked in a tone of suppressed passion. "*My* home is Paris. *These* are my people. They never question who I am nor whence I came. There is not one in La Thierry who would deal thus with me, unless it be yourself. You took my hand this morning. And for that I will take yours and call you my compatriot." Then changing to her usual tone of gayety, she cried aloud, "Come, compatriot! This has been a glorious day. The people of Paris have captured their king and are about to take him to Paris. Give us a toast!"

Tournay felt that what she had said was true. Probably not one of those who had known Marianne in La Thierry would speak to her should she return there. He turned to those who stood around the gun. "Friends," he cried, "I drink to freedom! May all among you who love it as

I do live for it and be ready to die for it." There was a shout as he turned away and left them, and over his shoulder, looking back, he saw the demoiselle dancing on the cannon, cup in hand.

He left the crowded part of the city to find some quiet spot as a change from the noise and tumult of the past two days. Turning a corner he came face to face with a man whom he had seen among the crowd in the Assembly hall, — a man of gigantic stature with deep-set eyes. His appearance was so striking that he could have passed nowhere unnoticed, and even in the crowded hall Tournay's gaze had returned to him constantly. As they met, Tournay again looked at him earnestly. The man stopped with the abrupt question : —

"Why did you come to Versailles?"

"Because," answered Tournay, "when I saw great numbers of people in Paris starving, and heard of the banqueting here, my blood boiled. This Flanders regiment, which is feeding fat at the people's cost, must be sent away. We cannot pause on our way to freedom with the destruction of the Bastille. The king must come to Paris where the people need him, and not spend his time here under the influence of a corrupt nobility."

"The king," mused the other; "do you believe in kings?"

"How do you mean?—'Do I believe in kings'?"

"Seventeen years ago," said the giant, "when only a boy, I stood in the cathedral at Rheims while the coronation of the king was taking place.

I had never seen a king before, and moved by a
strong desire to see a being so exalted, I had
walked many leagues to gratify my curiosity.
When I saw a pale-faced stripling kneel before
the archbishop to receive the crown, I could
hardly keep from bursting into loud laughter at
the thought that such a puny creature could hold
the destiny of a great nation in his hands. I have
often thought of it since, and to this day it is as
absurd as it was then."

"I think a nation should have a king," said
Tournay, after a few moments' thought. "But
he should reign in the interests of his people.
And of all the people, not a small part."

"And so you came down here to see that our
little king did his duty," suggested the large man,
smiling.

"I came here, as I have already said, because in
my humble way I wanted to do something for my
country."

"For your country?" repeated his companion
interrogatively; "for the people?"

"Yes," answered Tournay, "the people, — the
common people, to whom I belong; those who
have never had a voice lifted up to speak for them,
nor a hand to fight their battles."

"There is a voice to speak for them at last,"
replied the giant, his eyes shining with a fierce
light. "France is full of them. From north to
south, from east to west, they have been called
and are answering. In the Assembly their voices
are heard. In every street in Paris their voices

are heard. I can speak for them and I will; aye
and fight for them too," and he lifted his massive
arm with a gesture which in its force seemed to
indicate that alone he could fight for and win the
people's cause. "Throughout France there are
millions of arms which like mine are ready to
strike down tyranny. Have no fear, my friend.
The nation has found a champion in itself! The
people have taken up their own cause!" The
power of the man, his earnestness and energy,
stirred Tournay to the depths of his soul. He
looked with admiration at the lion-like figure
standing before him. Then grasping the man's
hand he said with earnestness : —

"I too am one of them, — I may not be of much
use, still I am one. Will you show me how I can
be of more service ? "

"A stout arm and a brave heart are always
worth much," replied the giant. "I like you,
friend ; your voice has the true ring in it. And
where Jacques Danton likes he trusts. Come
with me and I will tell you more."

CHAPTER IV

THE " BON PATRIOT "

COLONEL ROBERT TOURNAY of the Republican army sat over his coffee in the café of the " Bon Patriot " one December morning in the year 1793 of the Gregorian Calendar, and the year 2 of the French Republic.

The four years that had passed since the July afternoon, when he first entered Paris through the southern gate, had been full of stirring events in which Tournay had taken such an active part as to make the time equal to many years of an ordinary lifetime, — years which had drawn lines upon his forehead that are not usual upon the brow of twenty-six. His figure was considerably heavier, but even more elastic and muscular, telling of a life of constant bodily exercise.

Shortly after his return to Paris from Versailles on the eventful day when the Demoiselle de la Liberté, accompanied by her forty thousand, brought the baker and his family back to their people, Tournay had enrolled himself in the National Guard to protect Paris and the country against foreign invasion.

From Paris to the army at the front was the next step, where he served with such bravery as to gain promotion to his present rank. Promotions were rapid in those days, and men rose from the lowest social ranks to the highest military positions, if they proved their fitness by valor and ability.

By the winter of '93 Tournay had won the shoulder-straps of a colonel, and had now been sent to Paris by General Hoche with dispatches to the National Convention. His dispatches had been delivered and he was waiting impatiently for the reply which he was to take back to the front. More than eighteen months had passed since he had been in Paris, and the scenes in the city streets had a new charm for him. It was with a feeling of pride that he looked out from the windows of the "Bon Patriot" and saw the active, bustling crowds on the boulevards and realized that the Republic was an accomplished fact and that he had done his part toward creating it. And yet there was some sadness mingled with his pride. Although an ardent Republican he could not sympathize in all the horrors of the Revolution, — indeed he had been greatly shocked by them. Yet his long absence from Paris had prevented him from witnessing the worst phases of the reign of terror, and thus he could not fully realize them. He was, moreover, first of all, a man of the people. He had resented from childhood the cruelty and oppressions under which they had suffered, and his joy at the abolition of unjust laws, his pride in the assertion of equality for all men, overweighed his regret for the bloodshed that had accompanied

the triumph of their cause and the gaining of the
Republic.

Sitting over his coffee, he recalled his early life
at La Thierry. Since the day of his flight, he
had never returned there, and with the exception
of an annual letter from his father, who although
a Royalist could not quite make up his mind to
cast off his only son, he had no communication
with the inhabitants of the château. From these
occasional and brief epistles he had learned that
the Baron de Rochefort had gone to England almost at the outbreak of the Revolution. In a
more roundabout way he learned the cause of the
baron's departure to be a secret mission to the
Court of St. James on behalf of the tottering
French monarchy. The mission had come to
naught; the baron had fallen ill in London and
died there a few months after his arrival.

Edmé, his only child, was therefore left at La
Thierry, where she lived in great seclusion, with
Matthieu Tournay still in faithful attendance.
The marriage with the Marquis de Lacheville had
never taken place. As the Revolution progressed
and the de Rochefort fortune dwindled, the marquis's ardor, never at glowing heat, cooled percep-
tibly, and during the past two years nothing had
been heard of him at the château. It was thought
that he had either gone abroad or was living in
seclusion in Paris.

Tournay had sometimes felt a little anxious as
to the safety of Mademoiselle Edmé and his father,
but the letters he received from old Matthieu were

reassuring, and as the place was a secluded one
and the family not known to have shared actively
in the royalist cause, his anxieties had for some
time been allayed and he thought of them now as
likely to escape suspicion and to remain there in
quiet obscurity.

Tournay was roused from his reverie by the conversation of two men at an adjoining table, or,
more strictly speaking, a man and a boy, for the
younger was not over seventeen years of age. His
face was quite innocent of any beard. On his
yellow curls he wore the red nightcap of the Jacobins and his belt was an arsenal of knives and
pistols. Taking up a glass of beer he blew off
the froth with a quick puff of the lips.

" Thus would I blow off the heads of all kings,"
he said in a voice that courted attention; " I give
you a toast, comrade : death to every tyrant in
Europe."

" I 'll drink that toast willingly," answered the
other, a big fellow, who despite his swagger and
insolent manner, had a face bearing considerable
traces of good looks. " But I should prefer to
drink confusion to each in a separate glass, seeing
that you are standing treat for the day," and he
laughed at his own wit.

" The Revolution does not march quick enough
to suit my fancy," he went on, turning his glass
upside down to indicate that it needed replenish-
ing, and then wiping the froth from the ends of
his drooping brown mustache. " The convention is too slow in its work of purging the nation.

Were it not for Robespierre we should make no progress. Why are there still aristocrats walking in the broad light of day?"

"Very few come out in the daylight, citizen," remarked the boy. "They creep out at night generally."

"Well, why are they allowed to live at all, young friend?" said the elder man, striking the table with his fist.

"Be patient, good Citizen Gonflou; the Committee of Public Safety has sent out a good batch of arrests within the last twenty-four hours," said the lad knowingly. "I have it from my brother, who has been charged with the execution of one."

"Your brother, Bernard Gardin?" inquired the other as he drained his glass. "Who is it now?"

"Bernard has gone down to our old home in the village of La Thierry to arrest a young aristocrat by the name of Edmé de Rochefort," replied the boy.

"Oh, oh, a woman!" laughed Gonflou. "Well, I'm glad I've not got your brother's work. I'm too tender-hearted when it comes to be a question of women."

Tournay uttered an exclamation of surprise. The next instant he tipped over his coffee-cup with a clatter to cover up the betrayal of interest in the conversation, and in replacing it, managed to draw his chair nearer to the two men.

"When did he start?" was the inquiry of Gonflou.

"This morning at six. He will return in four days."

Recovered from the first shock, Tournay's resolution was immediate. Edmé de Rochefort must be saved from arrest — and from the death that was almost certain to follow.

He was a man of action, accustomed to think quickly, and he began at once to devise means to save her. His first thought was of Danton. On this man's friendship he felt sure he could rely. His ability and willingness to assist him he resolved to test immediately.

The conversation between the two men at the adjoining table took another turn and he saw he was likely to hear no more on this subject, so he rose from his seat and hurried from the café. Ten minutes later he climbed the dark stairway that led to Danton's lodging. Here he found the Republican giant in his shirtsleeves, — a short pipe between his lips, bending over his writing table. He did not look up as Tournay took a chair at his elbow, but a nod from the massive head showed that he was aware of his presence.

"Jacques," asked Tournay abruptly, "was an order for the arrest of a certain Citizeness Edmé de Rochefort signed by the committee last night?"

Danton looked at him for a moment while he stroked his chin thoughtfully.

"Hum — de Rochefort? A daughter of the Baron Honoré who went to England as emissary from the late monarchy? Yes, I believe the woman is to be arrested," was the reply.

"If I furnish you with abundant reason for it will you have the order rescinded at once?"

"I cannot," was the answer.

"Is there any other charge against the Citizeness de Rochefort except that she is the daughter of her father?"

"None that I know of."

"Why arrest a young woman merely because her father went to England as an emissary of Louis Capet more than three years ago?"

Danton shrugged his shoulders. Tournay continued.

"In view of the length of time which has elapsed, in view of the absolute lack of result from the baron's mission, in view of the youth and innocence of this girl, will you not endeavor to have this order rescinded?"

"Why do you desire it so strongly?" demanded Danton, laying down his pen for the first time.

"Because I have known her from a child. I was born on the de Rochefort estate," was the prompt reply.

"Is that all?" asked Danton.

"No, it is not the only reason. I abhor this dragging of the weak and innocent into the political whirlpool. We do not need to make war upon women. I have protested against this before now, and I tell you again that we are disgracing the Republic by the crimes committed in its name. You are all-powerful with the masses, Jacques, your voice is always listened to, — why do you not put an end to the atrocities, which instead of decreasing, are growing worse daily? Where is your eloquence? Where is your power? How can you sit passively by and see these horrors? Are they done with your sanction? Can it be that a man with your strength can take a pleasure in crushing the weak and defenseless?"

"Would to God that I had the power to stop it," cried Danton. "Do you think that I take pleasure in the arrest of innocent young women? Do you think that it is with delight that I see our prisons crowded with thousands whose only crime is to have been born among the aristocrats?" He rose and paced the floor savagely. "You talk of my power with the people. You say they listen to my voice. To keep that power I must remain in advance. If once I lag behind it is gone forever. We have given life to this terrible creature the Revolution, and we must march before it. If we falter it will crush us too."

"Let it crush us then," cried Tournay, springing to his feet. "I will no longer be driven by it."

Danton looked at him a moment with kindly eyes, then shook his head and said mournfully: "And France, what would she do without me? All I have done has been done for her sake. And I do not regret what has been done," he continued, resuming his former manner. "No, when I see what we have done I regret nothing. That the innocent have perished, I know, and I deplore it. That the innocent must still perish is inevitable. But what is the blood of a few thousand to wash

out the cruelty of ages? What are the cries of a
few compared with the groans of millions throughout the centuries! Even now the allied armies of
all Europe are thundering at the doors of France.
We cannot pause now. They have dared us to
the combat, and in return, as gage of battle, we
have hurled them down the bleeding head of a
king. We must go on."

Then sinking into his seat, he said quietly, "No,
Robert, my friend, let Robespierre and his followers have their way in these small matters for a
little while longer. What are the lives of a few
peachy-cheeked girls weighed against the destiny
of a nation?" And he took up his pen.

Tournay sat in silent thought for a few minutes.
He saw that it would be useless to say more.
After Danton's pen had labored heavily over a
few pages, he exclaimed, "Jacques!"

"Well?"

"Will you procure me a passport from the
Committee of Public Safety which will take me to
the German frontier?"

"Are you going to run away?" asked Danton,
still busy over his work.

"Whatever happens, I shall never leave France,"
replied Tournay quietly.

"Very well," said Danton, ringing a bell. "I
never shall suspect your patriotism, but there are
those who might if you talked to them as you
have to me."

As his secretary appeared in answer to the summons, he took up a sheet of paper to write the
order.

"Make it for Colonel Robert Tournay and wife," said Tournay carelessly, leaning over his shoulder.

Danton looked up at him suddenly. "I did not know you were married," he said.

Tournay made no reply.

Danton wrote a few lines rapidly. "Take this to the secretary of the Committee of Public Safety," he said to his clerk, "and return with an answer in half an hour."

In less than that time the man returned with the information that the secretary was away and would not return until two o'clock that afternoon.

"Will that do?" asked Danton, turning to Tournay.

"And it is now ten," said Tournay rather impatiently. "It will have to do, I am afraid."

"I will send it to your lodgings the moment it comes in," said Danton, resuming his work.

"Very well, do so, and many thanks. If I am not there have it left with the friend who shares my lodgings." Tournay quitted the office and hastened home, stopping on the way at a stable where his horse was quartered, to give instructions that the animal be saddled and brought to his door without delay.

Reaching his house, he ran up the four flights of stairs that led to the little suite of rooms which he was sharing with his friend Gaillard.

Gaillard was a versatile fellow; he had been a poet, an actor, and a journalist. Sometimes

the one and sometimes the other, as inclination
prompted or destiny decreed.

Shortly after Tournay's first arrival at Paris,
he had met Gaillard, who was then a journalist,
at a public meeting. The chance acquaintance
led to friendship. He had found the young writer
in some financial straits and had rendered him
such assistance as his own slender purse could
afford.

Gaillard, who never forgot the favor, was devoted to his friend. He watched his career as a
soldier with interest and pride, and now that Tournay had come to Paris for a few days, Gaillard
had insisted that his small chambers should have
the honor of sheltering the gallant officer of the
Republic.

Gaillard was at present amusing crowds nightly
at the Theatre of the Republic, where he was playing a series of comedy rôles.

It was with satisfaction that Tournay, as he
ascended the stairs, heard Gaillard's voice in the
room, repeating the lines of his part for that evening's performance.

"Well, my brave colonel, how goes the convention to-day?" said Gaillard, as Tournay entered
the room. "Has the Tribunal done me the honor
to request that I be shaved by the guillotine?"

"I have not been to the convention to-day.
Other business has prevented," replied Tournay,
going into his bedroom and taking a pair of pistols from his wardrobe.

"No? then I must wait until I get to the club

before I learn the exact number of the nobility who are to patronize the national razor to-day."

"Are you in the piece for to-night, Gaillard?" asked Tournay, hardly hearing what his friend was saying.

"I am."

"That's unfortunate, for I wanted to ask a great service of you," said Tournay, as he proceeded to clean and load the weapon.

"Tell me what it is; I may be able to help you."

"I am going at once to La Thierry."

"La Thierry?" inquired Gaillard.

"Yes. It is my birthplace. I am going there on an important errand. I must start instantly. I cannot even wait for a paper which is to be sent to me here by Danton. I am perfectly willing to let you know that it is a passport to the frontier, for myself and one other. The paper will not arrive until two o'clock, several hours after I am on the way. I must have a swift messenger follow with it and join me at the inn in the village of La Thierry."

"I will see that this is done," replied Gaillard. "Is that all?"

"That is all," said Tournay, hurrying from the room. On the threshold he turned. "Are you positive that you will be able to find a trustworthy messenger? Failure would be fatal."

"I swear to you to have it there," cried Gaillard, lifting up his arm and striking a dramatic attitude.

Tournay knew that, despite his apparent frivolity, Gaillard possessed not only a loyal heart, but a clear head, and he felt that he could trust him thoroughly. Much relieved in mind, he descended the stairway and sprang upon his horse at the door. Since leaving Danton he had been thinking out a plan which he hoped would successfully save Mademoiselle Edmé de Rochefort, but to carry it into effect he must reach La Thierry before Gardin. So putting spurs to his horse, he dashed through the streets at a pace which threatened the lives of a number of the good citizens. In a short time he was out of the gates, galloping along the road toward La Thierry at a tremendous pace. Then suddenly recollecting that the road to be traveled was a long one, he drew a tighter rein on his horse and slackened his speed.

"Thou must restrain thy ardor," he said, leaning forward and stroking the sleek neck of the animal affectionately; "thou hast a long journey before thee and must not break down under it."

At ten o'clock that night he drew up before the inn at Vallières, just half the distance to La Thierry. He reluctantly saw that his horse had entirely given out. As for himself, he would have gone on if he could have obtained a fresh beast. He looked critically at those in the stable of the inn, and realized that with four hours' rest his own horse would bring him to his journey's end more readily than any of the sorry animals the landlord had to offer. Having come to this decision he threw himself fully dressed on a bed for a short sleep. He slept until two in the morning. Then, after a hasty cup of coffee, he was again in the saddle and continuing his journey.

He rode steadily on with the advancing day, passing some travelers, none of whom he recognized. At noon he entered the village of Amand. Thence there were two roads to La Thierry. One, the more direct, led to the right over the hill; the other, to the left and along the river, was the longer but the better road. If his horse had been fresh, Tournay would have taken the short-cut, going over hill and dale at a gallop, but his tired beast decided him to choose the river road.

Toward the end of the afternoon he saw in the distance the spire of the church of La Thierry. He felt positive by this time that Gardin must have taken the upper road or he should have overtaken him before this, so rapidly had he traveled.

Every step of the way was familiar to him. Every bend in the river, every stone by the wayside was associated with his boyhood. Just before he came to the village of La Thierry, he left the main road and turning to the right followed a lane that made a short cut to the château de Rochefort. It was about two miles long and in summer was an archway of shaded trees and full of refreshment. Now the branches were bare, and the flying feet of his steed sank to the fetlocks in the carpet of damp, dead leaves.

As he approached the château on the right he heard a sound that caused him to draw rein in consternation. Springing from his horse he fas-

tened him to a sapling by the wayside, seized his
pistols from his holsters, and hurried forward on
foot. At every step he took the sounds grew
louder. There was no mistaking their meaning.

The lane terminated about a hundred yards
from the house. Tournay threw himself flat upon
the earth and working his way to a place where
he was sheltered by the overhanging branches of
some hemlock trees, looked cautiously out toward
the château.

An attack was being made on the château at
the front. Half a score of men armed with clubs
and various other weapons were endeavoring to
break down the iron - studded oaken door. A
gigantic figure with shirt open to the waist, whom
Tournay recognized as the blacksmith of La Thierry, was dealing blow after blow in rapid succession with a huge sledge-hammer. The door,
which had been built to resist a siege during the
religious wars of the sixteenth century, groaned
and trembled under the blows of the mighty Vul-
can, but still held fast to the hinges. A man,
standing a little apart from the others and directing their movements, Tournay knew to be Gardin.
Seeing that they were making little headway, the
latter ordered his men to desist, evidently to form
a more definite plan of attack. In the mean time
Tournay was working along the line of the hem-
locks towards the rear of the house. Suddenly
three or four men detached themselves from the
attacking party and approached him. Fearing
that he had been discovered, he lay perfectly quiet.

He soon saw that they were making for the trunk of a sturdy ash-tree which had been recently felled by a stroke of lightning. This they soon stripped of its branches, and hewing off about thirty feet of the trunk they bore it back on their shoulders with shouts of triumph. Here was a battering-ram which would clear a way for them.

Seeing them again occupied with the assault, Tournay continued to crawl cautiously along the edge of the grove until he was in a line with the rear buildings. Here were the servants' rooms, the business offices of the estate, and at one corner the office and the rooms occupied by Matthieu Tournay, the steward. This, the oldest part of the building, was covered thick with old ivy, by whose gnarled and twisted roots he had climbed often, when a boy, to the little chamber in the roof which had been his own. From this he knew well how to reach the apartments in the main building. The repeated blows of the ash-tree against the doors warned him that they could not resist the attack much longer. He climbed quickly up until he reached the well-known little window under the eaves. Dashing it open with his fist he swung himself into the attic-room which he had known so well in his boyhood.

CHAPTER V

A BROKEN DOOR

"Open, in the name of the Republic."

No answer.

Crash! Crash! Blow followed blow upon the door of the old château.

"Again, citizens, once again! Brasseur! bring fagots, we 'll fire the old trap. Forgons, take this sledge-hammer in your big hands. At it, man! — we 'll soon have the lair of the aristocrats down about their ears. Defour, Haillons, and you others, take up that ash-tree and let it strike in the same place as before."

Amid a pandemonium of shouts and curses the blows continued to rain upon the iron-studded outer door of the château de Rochefort, and the tree, used as a battering-ram, poised upon the shoulders of a dozen men, was dashed forward with a force that made the hinge-bolts start from their sockets and the oaken panels fill the air with splinters.

The besieged had taken refuge in one of the large salons on the second floor. There were only four of them: an old man, a priest, and two women.

"They have nearly forced the outer door," cried old Matthieu Tournay, wiping the perspiration from his brow with trembling hand.

"But the inner one," exclaimed the priest, laying his hand on Matthieu's arm. "How long will that keep them off?"

"They 'll break through that easily. Nothing can save us now; we are all lost," replied the old man.

"May the Blessed Virgin preserve us from the monsters," murmured the priest, looking towards the woman.

Edmé de Rochefort stood near the window. The terrifying sounds which echoed through the lower part of the building would have unnerved her, had not anger supplied a sustaining force, and brought a deep flush to supplant the pallor on her cheeks. The spirit of her race was roused within her. Had she been a man she would have charged alone, sword in hand, against the mob; but being only a woman she stood waiting the issue. Trembling slightly, she stood with her small hands clenched and white teeth firmly set. At her elbow was Agatha, her maid. She was paler than her mistress, but it was not for herself she feared. Her devotion made her fear more for Edmé's safety than for her own.

As the shouts redoubled Edmé saw the two old men turn, pallid and trembling, towards her.

"They seek me only," she said resolutely. "Why should I endanger your lives by remaining here? I will go to meet them!"

"You shall not go!" cried Agatha, placing herself in front of her mistress.

"It can only be a question of a few minutes at the longest. Let me go, Agatha."

"Listen," cried the priest, "they are in the house! They are coming up the stairway now!"

"No," cried old Matthieu, "I can still hear them down there in the courtyard."

Nevertheless a quick footstep was heard approaching from the corridor. The portières at the further end of the room were thrown apart, and a man, wearing the uniform of the Republican army, entered the salon.

"Robert!" came in a glad cry from old Tournay's lips.

Tournay did not wait to exchange words with his father, but approached Edmé.

"I have ridden from Paris to prevent your arrest, mademoiselle; thank God I have arrived in time. Only do as I direct and I shall be able to save you."

"How are we to know that we can trust you?" she said, looking at him fixedly.

He caught his breath as if unprepared for such a question. "You *must* trust me, mademoiselle."

Edmé laughed scornfully.

The color which rose to his cheek showed that her laugh cut even deeper than her words.

"Mademoiselle," he began, "if you" —

She interrupted him passionately. "Are not those men below who seek to destroy my château your friends? They have been clamoring for admittance in the name of the Republic." And she looked significantly at the tricolored cockade in his hat.

"And because I am a Republican and wear the

uniform of the nation do you really think that I could have anything in common with those ruffians? You do me great injustice; I am here with one object, to protect this household."

Edmé continued to look steadily at him.

"You say nothing, mademoiselle. You condemn me by your silence. I will prove to you how deeply you wrong me even if it take my life. I would give that gladly only to prove it to you. But there is more than my life at stake. There is your safety — and the safety of these, your servants. My father — mademoiselle!"

Edmé's look softened a little as she answered: —

"Although since you left our house we have only thought of you as an enemy, still I believe your father's son would be incapable of treachery. As for saving us, listen to the mob below. One man is helpless against so many."

"I can save you — but it depends upon yourself. No matter what I may say or do, you must trust me implicitly."

"Oh! do as my son says, mademoiselle!" interposed old Matthieu, joining his hands beseechingly. "For your sake, for all our sakes, listen to and be guided by him."

"If you can really protect us in this dreadful hour I should be guilty if I risked the lives of those who have faithfully remained at my side, by refusing your aid. I will follow your father's and your counsel," said Edmé quietly.

"Is the door of the salon barred?" asked Tournay of his father.

"With such slight fastenings as we have," answered the old man.

"See that it is fast," said Tournay. "It will give us a few minutes. Then listen to me."

There was a crash — louder than any that had yet been heard, and the mob poured into the lower part of the château.

Here they paused for a moment to recover breath and wipe the perspiration from their brows. Then some of the party began again their work of destruction among the pieces of furniture, while others brought up wine from the cellar to refresh themselves and their thirsty companions.

Gardin, anxious only to make the arrest, stormed at this slight delay.

"Cannot you leave your wine until your work is done, citizens?" he called out impatiently. "The aristocrat is above stairs — follow me!"

Through the large hall of the château and up the broad staircase, on the heels of their leader, swarmed the mob, yelling and cursing.

Gardin and Forgons, like bloodhounds who scent their prey, made direct for the door of the great salon, where the little party awaited them. Gardin shook the door violently, then threw himself against it to force an entrance.

"Here, citizen, we have already proven that two pair of shoulders are better than one at that game," laughed Forgons, adding his strength to that of Gardin. Under their combined weight the door yielded with a suddenness that precipitated both men into the room, — Gardin on his hands and face while Forgons fell over him, — and the two rolled together in the middle of the floor. Amid a shout of rough laughter from the men in the rear the two leaders regained their feet.

The scowl on Gardin's face vanished in a look of astonishment when he found himself face to face with a man in the uniform of a colonel of the French army.

Matthieu and the old priest had retreated to the corner of the room at their entrance. Beside the chimney-piece stood Edmé de Rochefort. The sight of the frenzied mob, the knowledge that it was her arrest alone they sought; the shrinking dread which the thought of their rude touch inspired, made her heart sink with sickening terror. Yet beyond trembling slightly, she gave no sign of fear.

Gardin had expected to find a frightened girl, surrounded possibly by a few servants who remained faithful. The sight of Tournay's tall figure, his resolute face, above all his uniform, standing between him and the object of his search, made him hesitate.

"There she is! That's the aristocrat!" exclaimed Forgons, as Gardin hesitated. "Let me get my hands upon her." He rushed forward, but before he could touch Edmé, Tournay pushed him backward with a force that sent him reeling into the group of men behind.

"A thousand devils," cried Forgons, when he regained his equilibrium, "what is the meaning of this, citizen colonel? Are you defending the little aristocrat?"

"Keep back, will you, Forgons," interposed Gardin, fearing that his dignity as leader would be usurped. "Leave me to manage this affair. I am here," he said, addressing Colonel Tournay, "to apprehend the person of an aristocrat, and shall brook no interference on the part of any one."

"Let me look at your warrant," demanded Tournay, in a tone of authority.

"I am not obliged to show that to you," replied Gardin doggedly.

"Let me see it, I say!" was the determined rejoinder.

Gardin slowly drew a document from the breast of his coat and handed it over with a sullen "Well, there's no harm in your seeing it."

Tournay read it carefully. Then folding it up with great deliberation he returned it.

"It seems quite regular."

"Regular," repeated Gardin, with a laugh,— "well, I like that. Of course it's quite regular, — signed and stamped by the Committee of Public Safety. Then with a show of mock politeness: "Now if the citizen colonel will condescend to step aside I will conduct this young citizeness from the room."

"That order of arrest calls for a certain citizeness de Rochefort, does it not?" asked Tournay, without moving.

"Certainly it does. The Citizeness Edmé de Rochefort who stands there, right behind you."

"You will not find her here," replied Tournay.

"None of your jests with me, citizen colonel; why, as I said before, she's standing behind you. I should know her for an aristocrat by the proud look on her face if I had not seen her a hundred times here in La Thierry."

"This is not Citizeness de Rochefort."

"That's a lie," replied Gardin bluntly, "and in any case she is the woman I am going to arrest."

"That woman is Citizeness Tournay, my wife. You cannot arrest her on that warrant, Citizen Gardin."

As the colonel spoke these words, which he did slowly and deliberately, Mademoiselle de Rochefort drew a quick, short breath.

"It is a trick," cried Gardin savagely; "you are trying to save her by a subterfuge."

Tournay repeated coolly, "She is my wife, and I am Robert Tournay, colonel in the Army of the Moselle. Again I advise you not to try to arrest her without a warrant."

"And I say again it is a lying trick," cried Gardin, beside himself with rage. "You cannot save your aristocratic sweetheart this way, citizen colonel. The Republic demands her arrest and I mean to take her."

"Citizen Ambrose," said Tournay, turning to the priest, "is not this woman my wife?"

"Most certainly," said the old priest, coming forward with dignity; "this lady is Madame Robert Tournay."

"Madame!" cried Gardin, repeating the word in a rage. "There are no ladies in France now,

and all priests are liars.   This is a trick, and you,
citizen colonel, shall answer for it.   Out of my
way!"   He grasped Tournay by the lapel of his
coat, and twisting his fingers into the cloth endeavored to force the colonel to one side.   There was
a sharp struggle, then Tournay threw him off with
such violence as to send him staggering across
the room.   His head struck the sharp edge of a
mahogany cabinet as he reeled backward, and he
rolled senseless to the floor.

With a shout of rage at the assault upon their
leader the mob rushed forward to close about
Tournay.   But he was too quick for them; the
muzzles of a pair of pistols met them as they advanced, one covering Forgons, who was in front,
the other leveled at the men behind him.

The mob cowered and fell back a little.   Clubs,
hammers, and knives were their only weapons,
which they still brandished threateningly.   If Tournay had shown the least sign of flinching he would
have fallen the next moment, beaten and crushed
to death.   He advanced a step forward.   Before
the threatening muzzles of the steadily-aimed pistols, the men recoiled still further, and were quiet
for a moment.   Tournay seized the opportunity to
speak.

"This fellow," he cried in a loud voice, pointing to Gardin, "has dared to lay hands upon an
officer of the Republican army.   In doing so he
has insulted the nation and deserves death.   Is
there any man here who would repeat this insult?"

The mob, taken by surprise, looked at their fallen leader and then at the two shining pistol-barrels that confronted them, and remained irresolute. Tournay thought he heard Edmé catch her breath quickly when the answer from the mob drowned everything.

"No, no! There are none here who would insult the nation!"

"Citizens, I am of the people, like yourselves. I am also a soldier of France. I have fought its battles, I wear its colors. See!" he went on, taking off his hat and pointing to the tricolor cockade — "here is the tricolor. If you do not respect that, you insult the Republic. Is there any one here who would dare to insult the Republic?"

"No, no!" came in quick response. "Long live the Republic!"

"But all who wear the tricolor are not our friends," muttered Forgons uneasily.

"Citizens," continued Tournay, affecting not to hear, "Gardin has no warrant to arrest this woman, who is not an aristocrat, since she has become my wife, the Citizeness Tournay. As for Gardin, he has insulted the Republic. He has forfeited the right to lead you. In the name of the Republic I appoint you, Forgons, the secretary of this section. To-night I return to Paris and will see that the confirmation of your appointment is sent you at once. Now, citizens, take up this fellow," he said, pointing to Gardin. "He shows signs of returning consciousness. A little cold water pumped over his head will bring him back to life. Come, follow me, I will be your leader for the present."

The mob took up the body and bore it off, cheering loudly for the Republic. Forgons went with them slowly, shaking his head, with a puzzled expression on his face.

CHAPTER VI

A MAN AND A MARQUIS

COLONEL TOURNAY accompanied the crowd of zealous Republicans who had been the followers of Gardin, until he saw them dispersed to their various homes or noisily installed in the wine-room of the village inn. Then he rapidly retraced his steps to the château.

He found Mademoiselle Rochefort seated in the salon, contemplating half mournfully, half disdainfully, the evidences of the mob's incursion, which surrounded her in the shape of costly pieces of furniture from the drawing-room, now marred and broken; and bottles from the wine cellars, shattered and strewn upon the floor.

She did not make any movement as Tournay entered the room, but seemed occupied with her own thoughts; and for a few moments he stood in silence, hesitating to speak, as if the communication he had to make required more tact and diplomacy than for the moment he felt himself master of.

Finally, approaching her, he said : " Mademoiselle, the immediate danger is past. You have nothing to fear for the present. As soon as you have recovered sufficiently I would like to speak with you."

She let her hand drop from her forehead and looked up at him. Her face was very pale, but she was quite composed and the voice was firm with which she answered : —

"I am able to hear you now, Robert Tournay."

He drew a sigh of relief. "She has the de Rochefort spirit," he thought.

"All is quiet now," he said. "But when Gardin fully recovers consciousness I fear he will excite his followers to further violence. It will be unsafe for you to remain here." As she did not answer, he continued, — "I have made arrangements, mademoiselle, to conduct you to the German frontier. Can you prepare to accompany me at once ? "

"I am prepared to leave here at once — but — I cannot go with you. It is better that I go alone," Mademoiselle de Rochefort replied.

"Alone ! It would be folly in you to attempt it. Do you suppose that I could stand quietly by and see you incur such a danger ? "

Mademoiselle de Rochefort's eyes, at all other times so frank and fearless, did not meet his earnest gaze ; she answered him hastily, as one who would have an unpleasant interview come to a speedy end : —

"You have saved me from a great danger. Believe me, I am not ungrateful. You have already done too much. I cannot accept anything more from you. Pray leave me now to go my own way."

"That is impossible, mademoiselle ; I shall only

leave you when you are across the frontier. Traveling as my wife, under the passports that I have secured, the journey can be made in comparative safety, provided always that we start in time."

At the words " my wife " Mademoiselle de Rochefort started, but she only repeated : —

" I cannot go with you."

" But," ejaculated Tournay, " I don't understand ; it was agreed " —

She looked up at him. " I agreed to permit you to tell those wretches that I was your wife, Father Ambrose, your father, and you, all protesting that it was the only way to prevent them from destroying the château and those within it. But you also said that the marriage would not be considered valid, and as soon as the danger was over you would go away."

" I said," answered Tournay quietly, " that I should in no way consider the marriage valid ; that when I had once taken you to a place of safety I should leave you. But until then I shall remain by your side."

" Some one said you would go away at once, either your father or the priest, and so I yielded. Now you tell me I must go away with you, and " — she hesitated at the words, " be known as your wife."

" But no one will know who you are," said Tournay earnestly. " The carriage will be a closed one — you shall have Agatha with you. No one shall be allowed to intrude upon you. Three or four days will bring us to the frontier.

As soon as you are there, and in the care of some of your friends who have already emigrated, I will leave you. Cannot you trust me three days ? " he asked sorrowfully.

" I cannot go with you," she repeated. " You are of the Republic — I have already accepted too much from your hands. Can I forget that those hands which you now stretch out to aid me have helped to tear down a throne ? that like all the Republicans, you share the guilt of a king's murder ? "

" I am only guilty of loving France more than the king. I did help to destroy a monarchy, but it was to build up a Republic."

" Then, instead of aiding, you should denounce me. I am of the Monarchy and I hate your Republic," she said defiantly. " I will accept protection from one of my own order or trust to God and my own efforts to preserve me."

" Where are those of your own order ? " demanded Tournay bitterly. " They are scattered like leaves. Some have taken refuge in England or in Prussia. Some are hiding here in France. Your own class fail you in the time of need."

" They do not fail," cried Edmé. " If none are here it is because they are risking their lives elsewhere for our unhappy and hopeless cause ; or languishing in your Republican prisons where so many of the chivalry of France lie awaiting death."

As if the thought goaded her to desperation she added fiercely, " Where I will join them rather than purchase my freedom at the price you propose."

"Mademoiselle," said Tournay calmly but with great firmness, "listen to reason. There is no time for lengthy explanation. I am actuated only by a desire for your safety. You must accompany me hence. I shall take you away with me."

Edmé arose and confronted him with a look of scorn. "I stood here a short time ago," she said, "and before all that rabble heard myself proclaimed your wife; I, Edmé de Rochefort, called a wife of a Republican — one of their number. Oh, the shame of it! What would my father have said if he had heard that I owed my life to a man steeped in the blood of the Revolution? That his daughter consented to be called the wife of her steward's son! a man of ignoble birth, a servant" —

"Stop!" cried Tournay, the blood mounting to his forehead. "Stop! It is true that those of my blood have served your family for generations. It was one of my blood, I have heard it told, who in days gone by gave up his life for one of your ancestors upon the field of battle. Was that ignoble? My father served yours faithfully during a long life; was that ignoble? So have I, in my turn, served you. I was born to the position, but I served you proudly, not ignobly. In speaking thus, you wrong yourself more than you do me, mademoiselle."

The suddenness of his outburst silenced her. He saw that her bosom heaved convulsively. He

"STOP!" CRIED TOURNAY

could not guess the conflicting emotions in her
breast; her pride struggling with her gratitude;
her horror and detestation of the Republic contending with her admiration for his brave bearing
in the face of danger; but as he looked at her,
slight and girlish, standing there before him with
flushed cheeks, as he saw the fire flash in her eyes
although her hands trembled, he realized keenly
how young, how defenseless she was, and his sudden burst of anger subsided.   Her very pride
moved him to pity by its impotence, and his heart
yearned to be permitted to protect her from all
the dangers which threatened her.

In a voice that trembled with emotion he went
on : —

"Mademoiselle, I have known you since you
were a child, and I have served you faithfully.
Your wishes, your caprices have been my law.   It
was no galling servitude to me, mademoiselle, for
mine was a service of love."   He uttered the last
words almost in a whisper, then stopped suddenly,
as if the avowal had slipped from his lips unwittingly.

Mademoiselle de Rochefort started; while he
spoke she had turned away; so he could not see
her face, but he could imagine the look of disdain
and scorn with which she had listened.

"Yes, I dared to love you," he continued.   "I
never meant to tell you, but now that the avowal
has slipped from my lips I would have you know
that I always loved you.   That is why I am here
now, pleading with you, not for your love, for that

I know never can be mine, but for your safety, your life." She remained silent, and he continued, speaking rapidly, — "You have said that a king's blood is upon my hands. His death was necessary and I do not regret it." Edmé shuddered and letting herself sink back into a chair sat there with her head resting on her hand, while she still kept her face turned from him. "I do not regret it, because it has given us the Republic. I glory in the Republic which has made me your equal." Bending over her, he said in a low voice, "I love you and am worthy of your love. Mademoiselle, listen to me. Come with me while there is yet time. Give me but the right to be your protector. I will protect you as the man guards the object of his purest, his deepest affection." In his fervor he bent over her until his lips almost touched her hair. "I will win a name that even you will be proud to own. Edmé, come with me. It is the love of years that speaks to you thus — Come!" and he took her hand in his. As his fingers closed upon hers she sprang to her feet.

"Do not touch me," she cried, with a tone almost of terror. "I will hear no more. I cannot bear it. I cannot bear to see you. Go! for the love of heaven, leave me."

For a moment Tournay stood still. Her words wounded him to the quick, yet as they stabbed deepest, he loved her the more. Without speaking again he turned and left her. As he descended the stairs and passed out through the broken doorway he vowed within himself that despite her pride, despite what she might say or do, he would yet find means to save her.

An hour passed, and Edmé remained in the salon where Tournay had left her. The spirit she had shown a short time before seemed much subdued. Darkness had settled down over the room, and she felt herself alone and deserted. A current of air, coming through the broken doorway, swept up the stairs into the apartment, chilling her with its cold breath. She wondered what had become of Father Ambrose and old Matthieu, and whether Agatha had deserted her. Yet she did not seek for them. Indeed, she did not know where to find them, for the house had all the silence of emptiness.

She tried to plan what she should do in case she had been entirely abandoned, but her brain, usually so active, seemed benumbed. She could not think. Conscious that she must shake off this feeling of helplessness, she was about to rise and go in search of a light, when she heard a footstep outside in the corridor. " Agatha has come back," she thought, and stepped forward to meet her maid. The sound of footsteps approached until they reached the door of the salon ; there they seemed to hesitate.

Edmé was on the point of calling Agatha by name, when the door was pushed open and a man entered and passed stealthily across the floor of the salon into the ante-chamber without noticing her presence. Edmé thrust her hand over her mouth to stifle the cry that was upon her lips.

The man was evidently familiar with the surroundings, for almost immediately the light of a
candle shone out from the ante-room, throwing
a faint glow upon the polished floor of the salon.
Edmé had seen him very imperfectly in the darkness. She was uncertain whether he was one of
the mob, returned alone for plunder, or one of the
lackeys of her household who had got the better
of his terror and returned to the château.

Unable to bear the suspense, she advanced toward the door of the ante-room. Her heart beat
rapidly as she placed her hand upon the door, which
had been left ajar. She hesitated one moment, then
summoning up the courage that had sustained her
during the whole of that terrible afternoon, she
boldly pushed the door open and looked into the
room. To her amazement she saw, bending over
a cabinet, her cousin, the Marquis de Lacheville.
The marquis held a candle in one hand while he
searched hurriedly for something in the drawer of
the cabinet. In his haste and anxiety he threw
out the contents of each drawer as he opened it
till the floor was littered with papers. So intent
was he upon his search that he did not hear
Edmé's approach.

"Monsieur de Lacheville!" she said in a low
tone. Upon hearing his name, the marquis uttered
a cry like that of a hunted animal, and turning,
confronted her.

"Mademoiselle de Rochefort, you here! How
you startled me!" he exclaimed, endeavoring to
control himself; but his knees shook, and his lips
twitched nervously.

" Your coming gave me a start also, monsieur.
You glided across the floor of the salon so like a
phantom, I did not know who it was, nor what
to think."

" I have just arrived from Paris, where I have
been in hiding for months," he stammered. " Upon
seeing the doors all battered down and the fright-
ful disorder in the lower halls, I thought the château
must be deserted and that you had sought some
place of refuge. Knowing that in times past the
baron, your father, was in the habit of keeping
money in this old secretary, I have been ransack-
ing it from top to bottom. I have need of a considerable sum; but I find nothing here — not a
sou."

Edmé noticed that his dress was in great disorder and that his face was pale and haggard.
Every few moments he put up his hand in an attempt to stop the nervous twitching of the mouth
which he seemed unable to control.

" My nerves have been much shaken lately," he
said, as she looked at him with wonder. And then
he laughed discordantly. The sound of the mirthless laughter, accompanied by no change in the
expression of his face, was painful to Edmé's ears.

" I have been pursued," he said, " hunted in
Paris like a dog, but I have given them the slip;
they shall not overtake me now." The wild look
in his eyes became more intense. " I am going
to leave France; I have a friend whom I can trust
waiting for me near at hand. Together in disguise we are going to the frontier — either to Bel-

gium or Germany. We shall be safe there. But
I must have some more money, money for our
journey." His fear had so bereft him of his reason
that he apparently forgot the presence of his cousin,
the mistress of the house, and turned once more
to the old writing-desk to recommence his search
with feverish haste.

"To Germany!" cried Edmé joyfully. "You
are going to Germany? then you can take me with
you. We can leave this unhappy bloodstained
country for a land of law and order."

The marquis turned upon her sharply.

"Why did not your father take you with him
to England?" he demanded.

"Why? You have no need to ask the question.
He went upon some secret business for King Louis.
He went away unexpectedly. When he left he
imagined that I, a woman, living in quiet seclusion, would be perfectly safe, notwithstanding the
disordered state of the country even at that time."

"Can you not find a place of refuge with some
friend here in France?" asked de Lacheville.
"The journey I am about to undertake will be
full of danger and fatigue."

"I am not afraid of danger," replied Edmé,
"and as for fatigue, I am strong and able to support it."

"But," persisted de Lacheville, "if you could
find some suitable refuge here it would be so much
better."

"I cannot," retorted Edmé, in a decided tone
of voice, "and I prefer to accompany you to Ger-

many, although it seems to me that you offer your
escort somewhat reluctantly."

"The fact is, Cousin Edmé," replied the marquis, "I cannot take you with me. Alone, my
escape will be difficult; with you it will be impossible."

Edmé looked at him for a moment with open-
eyed wonder, then she repeated the word. "Impossible! Do you mean to tell me that you, a kinsman,
are going to leave me here to meet whatever fate
may befall me, while you save yourself by flight?"

"No, no, you do not understand me," the marquis replied, his pale face flushing. "It is for
your own sake that I cannot take you. It will mean
almost certain capture. If, as I said before, you
could remain in some place of safety in France
for a little while " —

"I am ready to run whatever risk you do," replied the girl coolly. "When do you start?"

"Mademoiselle, this is madness," exclaimed de
Lacheville, pacing the floor. "Can you not listen
to reason?"

The sound of shouting in the distance caused
him to stop suddenly and run to the window. The
candle had burned down to the socket and went
out with a few last feeble flickers. The cries of
Gardin's ruffians were borne to him on the wind.

The slight composure which he had managed to
regain during his talk with Edmé left him again,
and he turned toward her, the trembling, shaking
coward that he was when she had first discovered
him.

"Do you hear that?" he whispered, his hand shaking as he put it to his lips.

"I have heard it in this very room to-day," replied Edmé, looking at him with disdain.

"They are coming here again," he whispered hoarsely. "But they shall not find me," he exclaimed fiercely, clenching his fist and shaking it in a weak menace toward the spot whence the sound came. "I have a swift horse in the court-yard beneath. In an hour I shall be safe from them," and he prepared to leave the room.

The ordeal of the afternoon had told on Edmé's nerves and the thought of being left alone again made her desperate.

"You shall not leave me here alone," she cried, seizing his arm. "You were born a man — behave like one. Devise some means to take me from this place at once. Do not leave me alone to face those wretches again, or I shall believe you are a coward."

De Lacheville roughly released himself from her grasp.

"I care not what you think of me," he snarled. "It is each for himself. I cannot imperil my safety for a woman. I must escape." And he rushed from the room.

She heard the crunching of his horses' feet upon the gravel, and going to the window saw him ride rapidly away. The remembrance of the young Republican leader offering to risk his life for her, and the cowering figure of her cousin, indifferent to all but his own safety, flashed before her in quick contrast. She turned away from the window to find herself in the arms of Agatha, who had at that moment returned.

"Agatha," she exclaimed, "do your hear those hoof-beats? Monsieur de Lacheville is running away. He, a nobleman, is a coward and flies from danger, while another man, a Republican — oh, Agatha, Agatha, what are we to do? whom are we to believe; in whom should we trust?"

"Calm yourself, mademoiselle," replied Agatha, "and think only of what I have to tell you. Listen to me closely. We must leave at once. I have a plan of flight. I have been making a few hurried preparations."

"True, Agatha, in my bewilderment and anger, I forgot for the moment the danger we incur by remaining here. Where are Father Ambrose and Matthieu?"

"Matthieu is here in the château; he says he will never desert you as long as you can have need of his poor services. Father Ambrose has disappeared, but I think he is in a place of safety. But now you are to be thought of. Will you trust me?"

"How can you ask that, Agatha? Have you not always proved faithful?"

"I mean, can you trust me to lead, and will you follow and be guided by my suggestions?"

"I will do just as you may direct. I know you have a wise head, Agatha."

"This is my plan, then," continued the maid; "listen carefully while I tell it to you."

An hour later the two women, dressed as peasants, with faces and hands brown from apparent exposure to the sun in the hayfield, left the park behind the château de Rochefort, and made their way along a hedge-bound lane that wound through the fields. As they reached the crest of a hill they stopped and looked back at the château. A red glow appeared in the eastern sky.

"Look, Agatha," said Edmé, "morning is coming, the sun is about to rise."

Suddenly the glow leaped into a broad flame which lit up the whole sky.

"'T is the château on fire!" cried both women in one breath, and clinging to each other they stood and watched it burn.

CHAPTER VII

THE first object that Robert Tournay saw as he rode into the inn yard at La Thierry was a horse reeking with sweat. The next moment he was greeted by the smiling face of Gaillard, who came out of the inn. "Have you brought the passport?" cried Tournay eagerly, as he grasped his friend by the hand.

For reply Gaillard took a paper from his pocket, unfolded it, and disclosed the seal of the Committee of Public Safety. "Am I in time?" he asked. "I have ridden post haste to get here with it. Can I serve you further?"

"Come into the inn, and I'll tell you," replied Tournay. "I am almost exhausted and must have something to eat."

Ordering some supper and a bottle of wine, which were brought at once, Tournay helped Gaillard and himself bountifully. They ate and drank for a few minutes in silence, Gaillard waiting for him to speak.

Gaillard was rather short in stature, with a pair of broad, athletic shoulders. His face was freckled, and animated by a pair of particularly active blue eyes. A large mouth, instead of adding to his plainness, was rather attractive than otherwise, for on all occasions it would widen into the most encouraging, good-natured smile, showing two rows of regular, white teeth, firmly set in a strong jaw.

After he had partaken of a little food and drink, Tournay recounted to Gaillard the substance of what had taken place at the château, leaving out most of his final interview with Edmé de Rochefort, but dwelling on her flat refusal to accept his escort to the frontier.

The actor listened to him intently and in silence; his face, usually humorous, expressive of deep and earnest thought.

" Now what do you advise ? " asked Tournay, as he pushed back his plate and emptied the last of the wine into Gaillard's glass.

" What plan have you ? " questioned Gaillard.

" I mean to take her away from here at all hazards," answered Tournay.

" Quite right," nodded Gaillard.

" But I can't very well pick her up and carry her off bodily," continued Tournay. " And if I did she would be quite capable of surrendering herself into the hands of the first committee in the first town where they stop us to examine our passport."

" Then we must induce her to go of her own free will."

" Which she will not do," replied Tournay gloomily.

" It seems to me," said Gaillard, speaking

slowly, while he held his glass of wine to the light and inspected it minutely, "that if some one should approach Mademoiselle de Rochefort, purporting to come from some of her friends who have already gone abroad, and should say he was sent secretly to conduct her to them, she would be willing to go with him."

"Unless she suspected him to be an impostor, she might possibly go," replied Tournay.

"He will have to convince her that he is not an impostor, and after a night spent in the château alone she is more likely to believe in him," was Gaillard's reply. "How about Gardin," he asked suddenly. "Do you anticipate any further trouble from that quarter?"

"I hardly think so," replied Tournay. "I shall go back to the château at once and remain in the vicinity all night unknown to Mademoiselle de Rochefort. See if you cannot procure a carriage here suitable for a long journey. Then come up the château road. I shall be in waiting for you at the entrance to the park. We will confer together as to a plan of action to be carried out at daylight."

"Good," replied Gaillard; "I will set about my part of the work at once."

The two men rose from the table; Gaillard went to the inn stables and Tournay mounted his horse and rode toward the château.

He had not made half the distance between the village and the château when he heard a footstep crunch on the gravel of the road, and reined in his horse just as the figure of a man crept by him.

"Who is there?" cried Tournay, clicking the hammer of his pistol.

"A good citizen," was the reply in a timid voice.

"Father, is it you?" exclaimed Tournay, springing from his horse and approaching the figure. "Is all well at the château?"

"It is my son Robert," cried the old man. "I did not recognize your voice until after I had spoken; but I am no good citizen of your present disorderly Republic."

"Is all well at the château?" repeated Robert Tournay.

"Well? How can we all be well when the doors are broken in and the furniture strewn about the place in pieces? Can I call all well when " —

"Mademoiselle Edmé?" interrupted Robert, with impatience, "how about her?"

"She has gone," said Matthieu Tournay.

"Gone!" cried Robert, clutching his father by the shoulder. "Gone — how and where?"

"You need not be alarmed for her safety," said the old man; "she is with Agatha, — a brave, clever girl, capable of anything. They set out this very night to seek a refuge with some relatives of Agatha who will keep them in safety."

"And you permitted them to go?" demanded the younger Tournay, almost shaking his father in his excitement.

"Permitted them? Yes, and encouraged them. I would myself have gone with them if I had not feared that my feebleness would impede rather than assist their flight. As it is, you need have no apprehension; when Agatha undertakes a thing she carries it through, and mademoiselle also is resolute and strong - willed. They will be safe enough, I warrant."

"Where did they go?" asked Robert.

"I've promised not to tell," said the old man doggedly.

"Father," exclaimed young Tournay, "do you not see how important it is that I should know where they have gone? If you have any affection for mademoiselle you will tell me. Cannot you trust your own son?"

"Will you promise not to prevent their going?" replied the old man.

Tournay thought for a moment. "Yes."

"To La Haye, in the province of Touraine, near the boundary of La Vendée."

"Will they reach there in safety?" inquired Tournay, half to himself.

"You need have no alarm on that score. They have disguised themselves as peasants; no one will be able to recognize them. Look!" he added suddenly, pointing in the direction of the château.

A tongue of flame shot into the night air, then another and another followed in quick succession.

"Is the château on fire?" cried Robert in consternation.

As if in answer the flames burst fiercely forth,

and the noble old pile stood revealed to them by
the light of the fire that consumed it.

The surrounding landscape became brilliant as
day, and the great oaks of the park waved their
bare branches frantically in the direction of the
edifice they had sheltered so many years; seeming
to sigh pityingly as one turret after another fell
crashing to the ground.

Young Tournay looked around to see if any of
the attacking party were still lurking in the vicinity; but with the exception of himself and his
father, no human eye was witness of the burning.

" Gardin's men must have ignited that during
their drunken invasion of the wine-cellar," he
exclaimed excitedly.   Then in the next breath
he added, " Thank God! Mademoiselle has been
spared this sight."

Old Tournay stood looking at the conflagration
in silence; then turning away with a sigh, he said
simply, " There goes the only home I have ever
known; where my father lived before me and
where you were born, Robert. I must now find a
new place to pass what few days of life remain to
me."

Tournay laid his hand on his father's arm.
" Will you come with me to Paris? " he asked.

" No, no," replied his father. " I am not in
sympathy with Paris, Robert, nor with your ways.
I don't understand them, boy. It may be all right
for you. I know you are a good son, you have
always been that, but I shall find a shelter in La
Thierry. None will molest an old man like me."

Leading his horse by the bridle, Tournay walked back to the village with his father. On the way they were met by Gaillard, who had seen the flames and had guessed their meaning.

Robert Tournay explained the situation to him as they all went back to the inn. Greatly in need of rest, Robert threw himself down to wait until the morrow.

They were up with the dawn, when Gaillard had a new suggestion to offer.

"You must return at once to Paris, my friend, for you must arrive there before Gardin. You will need all the influence of your own military position and the aid of your most powerful friends to enable you to meet the charges that man will bring against you for frustrating the arrest. I will try to find mademoiselle at La Haye, and will meet you at our lodgings as soon as possible."

Robert grasped his companion's hand warmly.

"I shall never forget your friendship, Gaillard."

"You may remember it as long as you like if you will not refer to it. I can never repay you for your many acts of friendship toward me."

"But your profession," interrupted Tournay, "how can you leave the theatre all this time? How will your place be filled?"

"Oh, it will be filled very well. I arranged all that before leaving; whether I shall find it vacant or not when I return is another matter. But it does not trouble me; let it not trouble you, my friend." And with a cheerful wave of the hand, Gaillard departed.

CHAPTER VIII

PÈRE LOUCHET'S GUESTS

In the southern part of the province of Touraine, in the village of La Haye, lived Pierre Louchet, or as his neighbors called him, Père Louchet.

Logically speaking, Louchet, being a bachelor, had no right to this title, but as he took a paternal interest in all the young people of the village, they had fitted him with this sobriquet, partly in a spirit of gentle irony and partly in affectionate recognition of his fatherly attitude toward them.

Père Louchet lived alone in a little cottage that was always as neat and well-kept as if some feminine hand held sway there. Indeed, if he fell sick, or was too busy with the crops on his small farm to pay proper attention to his household duties, there were plenty of women from the neighboring cottages who were glad to come in and make his gruel or sweep up his hearth, so it was not on account of any unpopularity with the gentler sex that he lived on in a state of celibacy.

In a society where marriage was almost universal, such an eccentricity as that exhibited by Pierre Louchet in remaining single did not escape comment. Indeed at the age of fifty he was as often bantered on the subject as he had been at thirty.

But neither the raillery and innuendoes of the neighbors nor the entreaties, threats, and cajoleries of his sister, Jeanne Maillot, had ever moved him to take a wife.

" It 's a family disgrace," said Jeanne, putting her red hands on her hips, and regarding her elder brother with a look of scorn. " Here am I ten years younger than you, and with five children. And Marie who lives at Fulgent has eight. And you, the only man in our family, sit there by the chimney and smoke your pipe contentedly, and let the young girls of La Haye grow up around you one after another, marry, settle down, and have daughters who are old enough to be married by this time ; and you do nothing to keep up the name of Louchet."

" 'T is not much of a name," replied Pierre.

" It is one your father had, and was quite good enough for me, until I took Maillot."

" If I should marry, there would be less for your own children when I am gone."

" I 'm sure it was your happiness I was thinking of before all," replied Jeanne, mollified at this presentation of the case.

" If it 's my happiness you are thinking about, let me stay as I am. I and my pipe are quite company enough, and if I want more I only have to step across a field and I can find you and your good husband Maillot." And Père Louchet's eyes would twinkle kindly while his pipe sent up a thicker wreath of smoke.

One young woman once declared maliciously

that Père Louchet squinted. But those who heard
the remark declared that it was because he was
always endeavoring to look in any direction except
towards her who sought to attract his attention,
and after that the slander was never repeated.

One morning in December the neighborhood of
La Haye was set all in a flutter of curiosity by a
sudden increase in the family in Père Louchet's
cottage.

As an explanation of it he remarked with his
eyes twinkling more than usual: " I am getting
old and need help about the place, and that is why
a nephew and a niece of my brother-in-law Maillot
have come to live with me."

Paul and Elise Durand were natives of " up
north " and had never before been as far south as
La Haye. The woman was about twenty-five years
old, brown as a berry, with a sturdy figure and
strong arms. Her brother was tall and slender.
He said he was nearly twenty, yet he was small
for his age and his entire innocence of any beard
gave him a still more boyish appearance. He
spoke with a softer accent than most country lads
in those parts, but that was because he came from
the neighborhood of Paris; and then he and his
sister had both been in the service of a great
" Seigneur " before the Revolution.

In the neighboring province of La Vendée the
peasants, led by the priests and nobles, were threatening to take up arms in support of the monarchy.
But the inhabitants of La Haye took little interest
in political affairs, and although they shared some-

what the sentiment of opposition in La Vendée to the new government in Paris, they busied themselves generally with their vineyards and their crops and took no active part in politics. Paul and Elise were content in the fact that their new home was so quiet and so remote from the strife that was raging so fiercely all about them.

One morning, shortly after her arrival, Elise was resting by the stile which divided the field of Père Louchet from that of his brother-in-law. She had placed on the stile the bucket containing six fresh cheeses wrapped in cool green grape leaves, while she herself sat down upon the bottom step beside it, to remove her wooden sabot and shake out a little pebble that had been irritating her foot. The wooden shoe replaced, she took up her pail and was about to spring blithely over the stile, when she drew back with a little cry of surprise mingled with alarm. Standing on the other side, his arm resting on the top step, leaned a young man who had evidently been watching her closely.

Drawing a short pipe from between a row of white teeth, his mouth expanded in a wide grin.

" Did I frighten you ? " he said, in a slight foreign accent but with an extremely pleasant tone of voice.

" Not at all," answered Elise, looking at him frankly. " I 'm not easily frightened. If you will move a little to one side, I can cross the stile and go about my affairs."

" What have you in the pail ? " asked the man, as he complied with her request.

"Cheeses," she answered, as he came lightly over the wall. "It's clear you're not of this part of the country or you would never have asked that question."

"I am not from this part of the country," said the stranger. "You ought to know that by my accent."

"Where is your native place?" asked Elise, her curiosity aroused.

"A long distance from here — Prussia. Have you ever heard of that country?"

"Yes."

"We are most of us against the Republic — there," said he. "I am, for one," and he looked at her out of the corner of his eyes. She made no reply. "Let me carry your cheeses," he said, laying his hand upon the bucket.

"They are not heavy," said Elise, "and I must hurry home."

"All ways are the same to me and I will go along with you," he said, taking the bucket from her. "It's heavy for you."

"It's no burden for me, and as I don't know you I prefer to go home by myself," she said frankly.

"Oh, I'm a merry fellow — you need not fear me. I am your friend."

"I have no way of being sure of that," was the reply, "though you don't look as if you could be an enemy."

"I should be glad for an opportunity to prove myself your friend. And I could prove that I am

no stranger by telling you a good deal about yourself and your brother Paul."

"Indeed," was all Elise vouchsafed in reply,
but she looked a little uncomfortable.

"I might tell you of an order of arrest that was
not carried out; of a château burned; of the
midnight flight of two women and the arrival at
La Haye of a woman and her younger brother;
all this I might tell you, with the assurance that
these secrets are safe in the keeping of a friend."

"How will you prove that you are a friend?"
Elise said in a low voice with apparent unconcern,
although she felt her heart beating with fear.

"The fact that I have just told you what I
know and shall tell no one else, should be one
proof," he said. Elise did not answer, but looked
at him with a keen expression as if she would read
his thoughts.

He had a frank, open face, the very plainness
of which bespoke the honesty of the man.

"Suppose I should say that I came from Hagenhof in Prussia and that I was sent here by friends
of your brother who have gone there. Suppose I
should say that they wanted you to join them and
that I could take you there with little risk to yourselves, would you be inclined to trust me then?"

"What risk do we incur by remaining where
we are?" inquired Elise, without answering his
question.

"You will always run the risk of discovery
while in France," he replied. "But tell me, are
you inclined to trust me?"

"Yes," answered Elise, stopping and looking him full in the face. "I am."

"Good," he cried, setting down the pail and extending his hand.

"I am disposed to trust you," she went on, "but in order to do so fully I should wish to see a letter from the friend you speak of."

"It is dangerous to carry such a writing," he replied significantly.

"True, but you can mention names."

"I can, and will, — names your brother will know well. The Baron von Valdenmeer, for instance. Besides, if I were your enemy I need not come thus secretly. Your enemies can use open means."

"I said" — Elise hesitated — "I am disposed to believe you are what you claim to be, but I can do nothing without the consent of my brother."

"Good! will you obtain his consent?"

"I will try."

"Good again. You will succeed. Talk with him and get his consent to leave here. And as soon as possible I will make all the arrangements for the journey so that we may leave in a week or at the latest a fortnight. Then if you have not persuaded your brother that it is for his interest to go with me, I will try and add my arguments to yours."

"I trust you will find us ready," said Elise; "but in the mean time shall you remain here?"

"No, I must go to Paris," was the Prussian's answer. "If you should have occasion to communicate with me, a word sent to Hector Gaillard, 15 Rue des Mathurins, will reach me. But do not send any word unless it is of the greatest importance, and then employ a messenger whom you can trust."

" Is that your name ? " asked the woman.

" That is my name while in France. Can you remember that and the address ? "

" I can."

" Then good-by. And a word at parting," he said — turning after he had leaped the fence. " It is perhaps needless to caution you, but my advice would be that your brother should not go too often to the village. His hands are too small. Good-by." And he walked off up the lane smoking his short pipe, and whistling gayly.

Two days later Gaillard joined his friend Tournay in Paris. He found Tournay much more hopeful than when he had left him, and his spirits rose still more as he heard Gaillard's news.

" It is Wednesday," Tournay said. " On Saturday the convention has promised to send me back with my dispatches. Can you be ready for La Haye by Saturday morning ? "

" Yes," said Gaillard, " twelve hours earlier if necessary."

" It is agreed then for Saturday, unless the convention delays."

Three days after her meeting with Gaillard, Elise, on returning from a neighboring town where she had gone to dispose of some butter, found the kitchen deserted and the fire out. She had ex-

pected to find a bowl of hot potato soup and a
plate of sausage and garlic.   Instead she found a
cold hearthstone and an empty casserole.

As usual, the first thought of the devoted sister
was of Paul, and she called his name loudly.   It
did not take long to ascertain that the house was
empty, and with her heart beating wildly with
anxiety she ran outside the cottage crying, " Oh,
Paul, my child, — my brother, Paul ! "   There was
no answer save from the cattle in the outhouse
who shook their stanchions, impatient for their
evening meal.   She looked about for Père Louchet.   He also was absent.   Evidently he had
driven in the cows and had been prevented from
feeding them.   Something serious had happened,
and it must have occurred within an hour, for at
this time the cattle were usually feeding.

Elise sat down for a moment on an upturned
basket to collect herself.   Her first thought was to
go to Maillot's in search of them.   They might be
there, yet it would take an hour to go to Maillot's
and return.   And then what if Louchet and Paul
were not there !   What if the couple had been
murdered and the bodies were still on the farm ? "
Elise shuddered at the thought, and called loud
again, "Paul, Paul, my brother, art thou not
here ? "

From the hay in the loft above came a smoth-
ered sound.   With a glad cry Elise sprang up the
stairs, to see Père Louchet's head and shoulders
emerging from under a pile of clover.

"Where is Paul?" cried Elise, pouncing upon

him before he had freed himself from the hay, and almost dragging him to his feet. He blinked at her for a moment while he picked the stray wisps of straw from his hair and neck.

" Gone," he said laconically.

" Gone! Where? " cried Elise, frantically taking him by the shoulders and shaking him so that the hayseed and straw flew from his coat. " Père Louchet, what is the matter? I never saw you like this before; have you been drinking? "

" No," he said slowly, and then as if the thought occurred to him for the first time, he went toward a cask of cherry brandy which stood in a corner of the granary and drew almost a tin-cupful.

With blazing eyes Elise saw him measure out the liquor slowly, with a hand that trembled slightly, and put the cup to his lips. She felt as if she must spring upon him and dash the cup from his hands, but she controlled herself with an effort. Louchet drained off the brandy to the last drop, straightened up, and looked at Elise. He acted like a different man.

" Paul was taken from here about an hour ago by three men. They had papers and red seals and tricolor cockades enough to take a dozen."

" And you let them take him? " cried Elise.

Père Louchet looked at his niece quizzically with his twinkling eye.

" There were three of them, Elise, my child, and they had big red seals and swore a great deal."

" Of course," admitted the woman hastily, " you could do nothing by force."

" I did try to prevent them from going upstairs where Paul was," the old man replied, " but one of them knocked me on the head and into a corner where I lay like a log."

" Oh that I had been here," moaned Elise, as she and Louchet went toward the house. " If I could only know where they have taken Paul ! "

" To Tours," replied Père Louchet with decision.

" How do you know ? " asked Elise quickly.

" I remember it plainly now. When I lay in the corner with a kind of dazed feeling in my head, not wishing to get up and stir around, I saw one of the men —not the one who hit me, but a smaller man with a larger hat and more cockades and more seals, take a paper out of his pocket and read it to Paul. I tried to make out what it said, for although I could hear every word that was uttered, I could not get an idea in my head that would hold together ; but I was able to catch the word Tours ; I am sure they have gone to Tours."

" How is your head now, Père Louchet ? " asked Elise with feverish eagerness.

" As clear as a bell," was the reply. " Let me have one little nip more of that brandy and it will be clearer."

" Can you ride ? "

" Like a boy."

" Good ! Make up a bundle of food and clothing for a two-days' journey and I 'll have a horse at the door by the time you are ready."

Ten minutes later Père Louchet, with a bundle of necessities strapped on his back, was mounted on one of his best horses which Elise had saddled for him.

"Now, where am I to ride to?" he demanded, directing his twinkling eye down upon his niece.

"Ride to Paris. Seek out Gaillard, 15 Rue Mathurins; give him this letter. That is all I ask of you."

"And you — what are you going to do?" said Père Louchet, putting the letter in his inside breast pocket with a slap on the outside to emphasize its safety.

"I ride toward Tours," replied the intrepid woman.

CHAPTER IX

PRISON BOAT NUMBER FOUR

PAUL DURAND was confined in the prison at Tours. The prison was so crowded that he had to be placed in a small room at the top of the building adjoining the quarters occupied by the jailer and his family.

Paul was paler than usual, the result of fatigue from the long, rapid ride from La Haye, but he showed no signs of fear and held up his head bravely as the jailer entered the room. The latter carried a bundle under his arm.

"You are to take these clothes," he said, "go into the adjoining room, and put them on in place of the garments you have on."

Paul took the bundle and went into the next room. For fifteen minutes the jailer sat upon the one chair the room contained, humming and jingling his bunch of keys. Then the door into the outer corridor was thrown open and a large man entered. The jailer sprang to his feet with alacrity.

"Where's the prisoner, Potin?" demanded the newcomer in a harsh voice.

"In the next room, Citizen Lebœuf," replied Potin.

Lebœuf strode toward the door and laid his hand upon the latch.

"I beg your pardon, Citizen Lebœuf, but the prisoner may not be ready to receive you."

"Well, there's no particular reason to be squeamish, is there?" asked Lebœuf, screwing his fat face into a leer.

"If you will wait another minute I think the prisoner will come out," suggested Potin deferentially, jingling his keys.

"Bah, you show your lodgers too much consideration, citizen jailer; you spoil them." Nevertheless Lebœuf allowed his hand to drop from the latch and took a few impatient strides across the floor.

The door opened and, turning, Lebœuf saw Mademoiselle de Rochefort standing on the threshold. She was thinner than when she left La Thierry: but her eyes had lost none of their fire, and she looked Citizen Lebœuf in the face without flinching. His dull eyes kindled while he looked at her some moments without speaking.

"Do you know who I am?" he inquired in his thick, husky voice.

"Yes, I overheard the jailer call you Citizen Lebœuf."

"Right. I am Citizen Lebœuf; and do you know why you have been brought here?"

"A paper was read to me last night which pretended to give some explanation," was her quiet rejoinder.

"In order to save time and expense your trial

will take place at Tours, rather than at Paris. I am one of the judges of this district."

Mademoiselle Edmé looked at him with an expression of indifference.

" You do not appear to be afraid."

" I am not afraid," was the quiet reply.

Lebœuf eyed her with evident admiration.

" Why did you put on boy's clothes?" he asked abruptly.

" In order to avoid detection," she answered frankly, coming forward and seating herself in the chair which Potin had vacated upon her entrance. Lebœuf was standing before her, hat in hand, an act of politeness he had not shown to any one for years.

" And you did it well," he said. " You threw them off the track completely. Had it not been for me, your hiding-place would never have been discovered. It was a splendid trick you played upon those bunglers from Paris." And he slapped his thigh in keen appreciation of it, and laughed hoarsely.

" I will take your boy's clothes with me," he continued as he prepared to leave the room, " lest you should be tempted to put them on again from force of habit. We don't want you turning into a boy any more. No, you make too pretty a woman." Then going up to the jailer he said something to him in a low voice which Edmé could not hear. Potin seemed to be remonstrating feebly. Lebœuf scowled, and from his manner appeared to insist upon the point at issue.

" Are you sure you are not afraid ? " he said
again abruptly to Edmé as he went to the door
and stood with one hand on the latch looking back
into the room.

" No ! "

He looked at her admiringly.

" Remember you are a woman now and have a
perfect right to be afraid ; also to kick and scream
when anything is the matter."

Edmé made no reply.

" In case you should ever feel afraid," he said
significantly, " just send for Lebœuf, that 's all,"
and with this he left the room.

Edmé remained in Potin's charge for two days.
The jailer treated her with great consideration,
and she congratulated herself upon having fallen
into such kindly hands. She momentarily expected to be summoned before the Tribunal. She
did not know what the result would be ; but she
looked forward to her trial with impatience. In
any event it would end the suspense in which she
was living.

On the afternoon of the second day Potin entered her room, accompanied by one of his depu-
ties.

" You must prepare to go with this man, citizeness, " said the little jailer.

" Has the Tribunal sent for me ? she inquired.

" Not yet. But you are to be transferred to
another prison."

" I prefer to stay here," she said. " Cannot
you ask them to allow me to remain ? "

"You have no choice in the matter, nor have I; I have only my orders."

"From whom did the order come? From that man Lebœuf who came here the other day?" she demanded quickly.

"I am not at liberty to say," replied Potin, shifting his feet uneasily.

"Are you forbidden to tell me where I am to be taken?" was her next question.

"To prison boat Number Four. The city prisons are so full," he continued, in answer to her look of surprised inquiry, "that great numbers have to be lodged in the boats anchored in the river. Number Four is one of the largest," he added as if by way of consolation.

In company of the deputy Edmé was conducted to the floating prison on the Loire. As they stepped over the side they were met by a little round-shouldered man with splay feet. His face was wrinkled and brown almost to blackness; his dress showed that he had a fondness for bright colors, as he wore a purple shirt with a crimson sash, a bright yellow neckcloth, and a red cap. The deputy turned over his charge to him, received his quittance, and went away.

Edmé was conducted to a room in the stern of the vessel. It was a small room and to her surprise she found it furnished comfortably, almost luxuriously. On a table in the centre stood a carafe of wine and a basket of sweet biscuit. Two or three chairs and a couch completed the equipment of the room. At the extreme end, the porthole had been enlarged into a window which looked out over the river. This window was closed by wooden bars. Otherwise the place looked more like the comfortable quarters of some ship's officer than a jail.

"Is this where I am to remain?" she asked of her new jailer.

The man nodded and withdrew, locking the door after him.

Edmé threw herself into a chair. It was intended that she should at least be comfortable while in prison, and this thought helped to keep up her spirits. She rose, took a glass of wine and some of the biscuit, and then after finishing this refreshment, feeling fatigued, she lay down upon the couch and fell asleep.

It was nearly dark when she awoke. Lying on the couch she could see the dying light of the short December day shining feebly in at the window, reflected by the metal of a swinging lamp over the table. As she lay there she became aware of a noise that had evidently awakened her. It was the sound of wailing and lamentation, accompanied by the creaking of timber and the swash of water.

Rising from the bed she went to the window and looked out over the river.

Going down the stream were two other prison boats. They were scarcely fifty yards away and proceeded slowly with the current, the water lapping against their black sides. They were old vessels, and creaked and groaned as if they were about to fall apart from very rottenness. From between their decks came the sound of human voices raised in cries of fear, despair, and lamentation; all mingled in a strange, horrible medley, which, borne over the water by the sighing night wind, struck a chill into Edmé's heart.

The vessels, stealing down the river with their sailless masts against the evening sky, looked like phantom ships conveying cargoes of unrestful, tortured spirits into darkness. The sight so fascinated Edmé that she stood watching them until they drifted out of sight and the cries of those on board grew fainter and fainter in the distance. So absorbed had she been as not to hear the lock click in the door and a man enter the room. She only became aware of his presence on hearing a heavy sigh just behind her, and turning her head she saw Lebœuf's heavy face at her shoulder. She gave a startled cry and stepped nearer the window.

"It is a sad sight, is it not," he remarked, with a look of sympathy ill-suited to the leer in his eyes, "and one that might easily frighten the strongest of us."

"It is your sudden appearance, when I thought I was entirely alone, that startled me," replied Edmé, regaining her composure with an effort. "I was so intent upon looking at those boats that I did not hear you come in."

"I see you did n't. I may be bulky, but I 'm active and can move quietly," and he gave a chuckle.

Edmé thought him even more repulsive than
at the time of his visit to the prison. His face
seemed coarser and more inflamed, and his eyes,
so dull and heavy before, shone as if animated by
drink.

"Where are they taking those poor people?"
she asked; "for I presume those are prison boats."

"They are," was the reply in a thick utterance.
"Just like this. Are you sure that you want to
know where they are being taken?"

"Would I have asked you otherwise?"

"Are you sure you won't faint?"

Edmé gave a shrug of contempt. She saw that
he was trying to work upon her fears, and felt her
spirit rise in antagonism.

The look of admiration that he gave her was
more offensive than his pretended sympathy. Leaning forward he whispered, "They are going down
the river for about two miles. There they will
get rid of their troublesome freight and return
empty."

"What do you mean?" asked Edmé. "Where
do they land the prisoners?

"They don't land them, they water them," and
he gave a low, inward laugh. "They drown every
prisoner on board. Tie them together in couples,
man and woman, and tumble them overboard by
the score."

Edmé gave a cry of horror. "It is too horrible
to be true. I don't believe it!"

"Why not?" asked Lebœuf; "drowning is an
easy death, and every one of them has been fairly

and honestly condemned." This boat is to follow
in its turn. Every prisoner here has looked upon
the sun for the last time, though not one of them
knows just when he is to die."

The idea of such wholesale murder seemed so
utterly impossible to her that in her mind she set
down Lebœuf's whole account as a fiction of his
drink - besotted brain, called up to frighten her.
Yet at the moment when she turned from him in
disgust to look out of the window, she saw that
their own vessel had begun to move slowly through
the water.

" We have started," said Lebœuf, as if he were
mentioning a matter of the smallest consequence.

" You say that every one upon this boat is a
condemned person," said Edmé quietly, repressing
her terror with an effort.

Lebœuf nodded.

" But I am not. I have not even had a hearing."

"No?" exclaimed Lebœuf in a tone of surprise. " Then those jailers have made another
mistake."

Edmé advanced toward him one step, and in
a tone which made the huge man draw back,
said : —

" I was brought here by your order ! "

" Oh, no, I knew nothing of the change. It was
that villain Potin."

"I was brought here by your order," she repeated. " I demand that I be taken where I can
have a trial."

"Potin has made another mistake," was all Lebœuf would vouchsafe in reply.

"If there has been any mistake, it is yours. I
demand that you set it right."

"It is too late!"

"There must be some one aboard this vessel
who has the power to do it, if you have not. I
will go and appeal for aid," and she took a step
toward the door.

Lebœuf interposed his bulky body between her
and the means of exit; closed and locked the door
on the inside.

"I will cry aloud. Some one will hear me," she
said in desperation.

"Who will hear you above all that noise?" he
inquired tersely.

The prisoners on the boat, now fully aware that
their time of execution had come, were crying out
against their fate, — some praying for mercy, some
calling down the maledictions of heaven upon their
butchers, while others wept silently.

"Merciful Virgin, protect me. I have lost all
hope," cried Edmé, turning from Lebœuf and
sinking despairingly upon her knees.

"Ah, now you are frightened!" exclaimed Lebœuf, "admit that you are frightened!"

"If it is any satisfaction to have succeeded in
terrifying a woman unable to defend herself, I
will not rob you of the pleasure, but know that it
is not death, but the manner of it, that I fear."

"But you are afraid; you have confessed to it
at last, and now Lebœuf will see that they do not

harm you." He gave a grim chuckle as if he enjoyed having won his point. Rapidly pushing the
table to one side, turning back the rug that covered
the floor, he stooped; and to Edmé's astonished
gaze lifted up a trap door in the floor of the cabin.
Edmé drew back from the black hole at her feet.

"It is large enough to afford you air for several
hours," Lebœuf said. "By that time I will get
you out again. Quick, descend the steps."

Edmé, fearing further treachery, drew back in
alarm. "I prefer to meet my fate here."

Lebœuf struck a light and by the rays of the
lamp a ladder was revealed.

"I tell you it is certain death to remain here
fifteen minutes longer. Even I could not save
you then. The more they throw into the water
the more frenzied they become for other victims.
They will ransack the entire boat; but they won't
find you down there. Lebœuf alone knows this
place. Quick! If you would live to see the sun
rise to-morrow, go down the steps of that ladder."

He took her by the shoulder to assist in the
descent. His touch was so distasteful to her that
she threw off his hand and went down the ladder
unaided. "Make not the slightest sound, whatever you may hear going on up here above you,
and wait patiently until I come to release you."

With these words the door was shut down and
Lebœuf went out and up to the deck alone.

The vessel had reached a point in the river just
outside the city. Here the stream narrowed and
ran swiftly between the banks.

The sky was windy; and between the rifts of
the high-banked clouds the moon shone fitfully.
To the east lay the city of Tours, its spires standing out in sharp silhouette against the sky. On the
river bank the wind swept over the dead, dry grass
with a mournful, swaying sound and rattled the
rotting halyards of the old hulk, which with one
small sail set in the bow to keep it steady, made
slowly down the river with the current, hugging
the left bank as if fearful of trusting itself to the
swifter depths beyond.

A rusty chain rasped through the hawse-hole,
and the vessel swung at anchor.

In a small and close compartment in the ship's
depths, totally without light, and with her nerves
wrought upon by Lebœuf's appalling story, Edmé
could only guess at what was happening above her
head.

She knew that something terrible was taking
place. She could hear a confusion of cries and
trampling of feet; of hoarse shouts and commands;
and she pictured in her imagination scenes quite
as horrible as were actually taking place above
her. In every wave that splashed against the vessel's side she could see the white face of a struggling, drowning creature, and every sound upon
the vessel was the despairing death-note of a fresh
victim. Through it all she could see the large face
of Lebœuf leering at her with his bleary eyes. To
have exchanged one fate for a worse one was to
have gained nothing, and in her mental agony she
almost envied those who a short time ago had been

struggling helplessly in the hands of their executioners, and whose bodies now were quietly sleeping in the waters of the flowing river.

A quiet fell upon the vessel. The last cry had been uttered, the last command given, and no sound reached Edmé's ears but the soft plash of the water as it struck under the stern of the boat.

Then the remembrance of Lebœuf's face and look became still more vivid. She feared him in spite of all her courage; in spite of her pride that was greater than her courage, she feared him. The knowledge that he was aware of his power and took delight in it made the thought that she would soon have to face him there alone more terrible than her dread of the worst of deaths.

A footfall sounded on the floor above her head. That it was not Lebœuf's heavy tread, Edmé was certain. Rather than fall into his hands again she would trust herself to the mercies of the worst ruffian among the executioners, and she struck with her clenched hand a succession of quick knocks upon the trap.

The footsteps ceased, and in the stillness that followed Edmé called out to the man above her and told him where to find the opening. In another instant the door was lifted up and she came up into the cabin.

"Kill me," she cried out; "throw me into the river if it be your pleasure, but I implore you, do not let " —

The man's hand closed over her mouth, and lifting her in his arms he carried her across the cabin.

The room was dark; either Lebœuf had put out
the light when he left, or the newcomer had extin-
guished it, but Edmé saw that he bore her toward
the window from which the lattice had been removed.   She closed her eyes to meet the end.
She felt herself swiftly lifted through the window,
and then instead of water her feet struck a firm
substance.

"Steady for one moment," said a voice in her
ear as she opened her eyes in bewilderment to find
herself standing on the seat of a small skiff, a man
supporting her by the arm.   Her face was on a
level with the window, and looking back into the
cabin she saw a light at the further end, as the
bulky form of Lebœuf appeared at the door, lantern in hand, his heavy countenance made more
ugly by an expression of surprise and rage.

Voices were heard in hot dispute, then came two
pistol shots so close together as to seem almost one.
A figure leaped through the smoke that poured
from the window, and Edmé from her seat in the
skiff's bow where she had been swung with little
ceremony, saw a man cut the line, while the other
bent over his oars and made the small craft fly
away from the vessel, straight for the opposite
shore.   The man who had leaped from the window took his place silently in the stern.   Placing
one hand on the tiller, he turned and looked intently over his shoulder at the dark outline of the
prison ship, which was rapidly receding into the
gloom.

His hat had fallen off, and in the uncertain light

Edmé saw for the first time that it was Robert Tournay.

Before a word could be uttered by any of them, a tongue of flame shot out from the vessel behind them, followed by a loud and sharp report. The dash of spray that swept over the boat told that the shot had struck the water close by them.

The man at the oars shook the water from his eyes and redoubled his efforts. " Head her down the river a little," he said.

" But the carriage is at least two miles above here," replied Tournay.

" No matter," answered Gaillard. " The shore here is too steep. We must land a little further down."

Tournay altered their course and steered the boat slantingly across the current.

They were now nearing the right-hand shore, which rose abruptly from the river to a height of some twenty feet. The current here was swifter, and the greatest caution had to be exercised. A second flash flamed out from the prison ship, a sound of crashing wood, and the little skiff seemed to leap into the air and then slide from under their feet, while the icy water of the Loire rushed in Edmé's ears, — strangling her and dragging her down, until it seemed as if the water's weight would crush her. Then she began to come upward with increasing velocity until at last, when she thought never to reach the surface, she felt her head rise above the water and saw the cloudy, threatening sky, which seemed to reel above her as she gasped for breath.

Another head shot to the surface by her side, and she felt herself sustained, to sink no more. The words: "Place your right hand upon my shoulder and keep your face turned down the stream away from the current," came to her ears as if in a dream. Instinctively she obeyed. With a few rapid strokes Tournay reached the shore. The bank overhung the river and under it the water ran rapidly.

With only one arm free he could not draw himself and Edmé up the steep incline. Twice he succeeded in catching a tuft of grass or projecting root, and each time the force of the current broke his hold upon it, and twirling them round like straws carried them on down the stream.

Gaillard, who had been struck by a splinter on the forehead, was at first stunned by the blow, and without struggling was swept fifty yards down the river. The cold water brought him back to consciousness, and he struck out for the shore. He noticed, some hundred yards below, a place where the river swept to the south and where the bank was considerably lower. Allowing himself to be borne along by the current, he took an occasional stroke to carry him in toward the shore, and made the point easily.

Drawing himself from the water by some overhanging bushes, he shook himself like a wet dog, and sitting on the river's edge proceeded to bind up his injured eye, while with the other he looked anxiously along the river-side. Suddenly he bent down and caught at an object in the water.

" Let me take the girl," he said quickly. " Now your hand on this bush — there ! " And with a swift motion he drew Edmé up, and Tournay, relieved of her weight, swung himself to their side.

For a short time they lay panting on the bank. Gaillard was the first to get upon his feet.

" We shall perish of cold here," he exclaimed, springing up and down to warm his benumbed blood, while the wet ends of his yellow necker-chief flapped about his forehead.

" Can you walk, Mademoiselle de Rochefort ? "

Edmé placed her hand upon her side to still the sharp shooting pain, and answered " Yes."

" Good ; the road is only a few rods from here, but we must follow it at least two miles to the west."

" I shall be able to do it ! "

As she uttered these words the pain in her side increased. She felt her strength leave her, and but for the support of Tournay's arm she would have fallen to the ground.

" She has fainted," cried Tournay in consterna-tion.

" No," she remonstrated feebly, struggling with the numbness that was overpowering her. " It is the cold. Let me rest for a moment ; I shall be better soon."

" Mademoiselle, you must walk, else you will die of cold," exclaimed Tournay. " Take her by the arm, Gaillard."

Instead of complying with the request, Gaillard

stood with head bent forward peering up the road
into the night gloom.

"Gaillard! man, do you not hear me?"

"The carriage! I hear the rattle of its wheels,"
cried Gaillard joyfully. "Agatha can always be
depended upon to do the right thing at the right
moment!"

"Hurry to meet her," cried Tournay; "tell her
we are here!"

Gaillard sprang rapidly forward, shouting as he
ran.

"Courage but a little moment longer," whispered
Tournay, and taking Edmé in his arms he followed
Gaillard as fast as his burden permitted.

She had not entirely lost consciousness, but cold
and fatigue had combined to enervate and render
her powerless of motion.

In a half swoon she felt herself carried she knew
not whither. She felt Tournay's strong arms
about her, and a sense of security came over her
as she faintly realized that each step took her
further away from the dreaded Lebœuf.

Tournay hastened toward the carriage. The
wind swept freshly over the marshes, and he held
Edmé close as if to shield her from the cold. Her
hair blew back into his face, covering his eyes
and touching his lips. As he felt her soft tresses
against his cheek his heart throbbed so that he
forgot cold, fatigue, and danger. . . . Where they
blinded him he gently put the locks aside with one
hand in a caressing manner and looked tenderly
down into the white face pressed against his wet
coat.

The sound of wheels upon the frozen road came nearer. Lights flashed around a turn in the road, and Tournay staggered to the carriage door as the vehicle drew up suddenly.

"Hurrah!" cried Gaillard from the box, where he had taken the reins from the driver. "We have won!"

CHAPTER X

In the carriage Agatha related to her mistress what had occurred after her disappearance from La Haye. How she had sent Père Louchet with the message to Gaillard at Paris, and then had followed on to Tours and discovered where her mistress was imprisoned. Tournay and Gaillard, coming post haste to Tours, had reached there on the same day that saw the transfer of Mademoiselle de Rochefort to the prison-ship upon the Loire. Together with Agatha, they had formulated a plan of rescue and put it into immediate execution.

The two men had approached the vessel in a small skiff on the river, while Agatha had awaited them in a carriage on the other side. The moving of the prison ship down the river might have disconcerted their plans had not the watchful Agatha seen the movement, and following along the shore reached them when they had almost succumbed from the exposure and cold.

The carriage was a commodious one and well equipped for the long journey, and in a few minutes Agatha had her mistress in a change of warm clothing. As soon as Edmé was able, she bade Agatha call Tournay to the carriage door.

"Thanks are a small return for what you have done," she said as he rode by her side, "yet they are all I have to give." Then she stretched her hand out to him with an impulsive gesture, — "Robert Tournay, I misjudged you when you were last at La Thierry. Will you forgive it?"

It was the first time she had spoken to him as one addresses an equal, and it moved him greatly. He leaned forward and took the hand she gave him, looking down at her with a smile that lit up his face, as he said : —

"Mademoiselle, I forgave the words you spoke as soon as they were uttered. It is happiness enough to know that I have saved you." Before he released it, he thought he felt the hand in his tremble a little.

The remembrance flashed through her mind, how, years before, she had once noticed Tournay's manly bearing as he rode into the château-court upon a spirited horse. She had at that time thought him handsome, with an air about him superior to his station, and then had dismissed him from her thoughts. As he rode before her now, the water still dripping from his clothing, hatless, with damp locks clinging to his forehead, she thought she had never looked upon a nobler figure among all the gentlemen who in the old days frequented the château of the baron, her father.

"Where are we going?" she asked, with more emotion than such a simple question warranted.

"To the German frontier," was the reply. "We must travel rapidly night and day. I shall

hardly dare to stop for rest until you are safely
over the border."

" I leave myself in your charge," she said, leaning back in the carriage.

He gave a word of command and the coach
rushed forward through the night.

Tournay's words had recalled vividly to Edmé
her unhappy situation. Although innocent of all
crime, she was proscribed and forced to fly from
her own country to take refuge among those who
were invading it. And the man who rode by the
side of her carriage, and had undertaken to con-
vey her in safety across the border, was a soldier,
fighting for the government that persecuted her.
Laying her head upon Agatha's shoulder she felt
her heart swell with bitterness. For hours, during
which Agatha imagined that she slept, she watched
in silence through the window the dark outlines of
the swiftly moving landscape. Finally long after
Agatha's regular breathing announced her slumber,
Edmé, worn out by the excitement and fatigue,
leaned back in the opposite corner and slept like
a tired child.

For five days the coach rolled toward the frontier, Tournay and Gaillard riding on horseback.

Through Blois, Orleans, Arcis sur-Aube to Bar-
le-Duc and on toward Metz they went, stopping
only to exchange their worn-out horses for fresh
ones, and for such few hours of rest as were absolutely indispensable.

During all the journey, Tournay saw little of
Mademoiselle de Rochefort, although her comfort

and her safety were his constant care. The passport with which he was provided prevented all
delay ; and it was thought best that mademoiselle
should remain as secluded in the carriage as possible. When she did step out for a breath of air
or a few hours' rest at some inn she always wore
a veil to hide her features. Whenever he approached her to inform her as to the route they
traveled he always did so with the greatest deference, showing marked solicitude for her health
and comfort ; expressing deep regret that the nature of their journey rendered the great speed
imperative.

One afternoon as they crossed the little stream
of the Sarre, Tournay, who had been riding some
fifty yards in advance, drew rein and waited for
the carriage to come up to him.

"In an hour, mademoiselle," he said, as in obe-
dience to his signal the vehicle drew up by the
roadside, "we shall be across the frontier, and in
Germany. At Hagenhof resides the Baron von
Waldenmeer, who I think is known to you as
your father's friend."

"He was one of my father's friends," Mademoiselle Edmé acquiesced.

"I remember having often heard his name
mentioned at La Thierry," said Tournay. "So
I took this direction rather than further south,
which would have been somewhat shorter. A few
hours will bring us to Hagenhof, where you will
be able to put yourself under the baron's protection."

" And you ? " inquired Edmé, " what are you going to do ? "

" I shall return to France."

.   .   .   .

The armies of Prussia and Austria, three hundred thousand strong, were drawing in on France, to help to crush out the Republic and restore the old régime.

The Baron von Waldenmeer's division was already on the frontier, quartered at Falzenberg — waiting for other troops to come up before joining the Austrian army at Wissembourg, near which the French had concentrated a large force.

On a cold December afternoon two batteries of Prussian heavy artillery were proceeding through the wood on the road going east from Inweiler, whence they had been sent to join the main body of troops at Falzenberg. It was snowing and at five o'clock darkness was already settling down on the woodland road. Over the snow-carpeted leaves the wheels of the gun carriages rolled almost noiselessly.

" Paff," growled Lieutenant Saueraugen, wiping the flakes from his eyelashes for the twentieth time, as he thought of the hot sausages at that moment being devoured in the mess-room at Falzenberg, and ten miles between it and him. " A pest on such weather and such slow progress! at this rate we shall not be at Falzenberg before midnight."

" *Donnerwetter!* what is this?" he cried with his next breath, as along the road that crossed from the north came a two-horse carriage at a rapid gait. The driver of the vehicle saw the battery on the other road, and tried to check the speed of his horses. The rider on the nigh leader of the caisson whirled his horse to the left, but it received the carriage pole on the right foreleg and went to the ground, dragging its mate with it. Then followed a snorting of frightened animals and a rattling of harness, flavored with the shouts and oaths of the lieutenant and his men as they tried to bring order out of the entanglement.

Two men on horseback rode up from behind the carriage, and with their assistance the fallen horses were brought to their feet and the broken harness repaired.

" Who the devil are you that tear through these woods like this?" demanded the German, examining the abrasure on the leader's leg. " Come, give account of yourselves." The two riders had remounted and seemed anxious to be off.

" We are bound for Hagenhof," replied one of them. " We are in a great hurry, and regret this accident, for which we are entirely to blame. Name the amount which you think a proper compensation for your injured horse and broken harness and we will gladly pay it."

He had spoken in German and in the easy, careless manner of one who deemed the matter too trivial to be the cause of any controversy.

" You are French!" exclaimed the lieutenant, looking at the party closely.

" We are," replied the man who had spoken before.

"You must accompany me to Falzenberg," said the German officer, "and interview the general there."

"What does he say?" inquired the second Frenchman of his companion.

"Come, you had best not chatter your French before me," put in the surly lieutenant, as one of the Frenchmen proceeded to interpret to the other. "You may be spies for all I know, but that we shall find out when we get to Falzenberg."

The dark eyes of the second Frenchman looked inquiringly at his comrade. The other again translated the officer's words.

"We are most unfortunate, Gaillard, to have fallen in with this imbecile," was the reply.

"My friend commends your prudence and judgment," repeated the interpreter, his mouth widening and showing his white teeth, "and desires me to tell you that we have important business at Hagenhof. If you will send us there under an escort, we shall be able to prove that we are not spying upon the movement of your troops."

The lieutenant scowled. "Can so few words of your language stand for all that in German?" he demanded.

The Frenchman laughed lightly as he replied, "Our language is very flexible."

"So perhaps may be your necks," said the officer brutally, a suspicion entering his mind that he was being laughed at. "But you must come with me to Falzenberg, and there's an end of it."

"Why not to Hagenhof?" persisted Gaillard with perfect good-humor.

"To Falzenberg!" roared the Prussian officer, swearing roundly, "and before we start, let me see what sort of freight you are carrying along the road." He approached the carriage with the intention of opening the door.

Tournay wheeled his horse between him and the coach with a suddenness that made the German jump aside to avoid being trodden upon by the animal.

"We are going to General von Waldenmeer at Hagenhof," he said, speaking his own language, "and if you prevent or delay our journey you may rue it."

The lieutenant, infuriated at this interference, caught Tournay's horse by the bridle with one hand, while the other flew to his belt; but the mention of General von Waldenmeer's name and the ring of decision in the speaker's voice caused him to pause.

"General von Waldenmeer at Hagenhof," repeated Tournay slowly and distinctly, as if he were speaking to a person of defective hearing.

"Who is making so free with the name of Waldenmeer?" cried a voice in the French tongue but with a strong German accent; and half a dozen Prussian officers came riding out of the wood, the fresh-fallen snow flying from the evergreen branches like white down as their horses drove through them.

They circled round the group by the carriage, drawing their animals up with a suddenness that threw them on their haunches.

"Who is it that claims the friendship of von Waldenmeer?" repeated one of the number, this time speaking in German. He was a young man about twenty-two, with short, dark red hair, and a small mustache. He rode a black horse that pranced and curvetted nervously.

"These people, my colonel," said the lieutenant, growing suddenly polite. "I was about to tell them" —

"Never mind what you were about to tell them, Lieutenant Saueraugen," replied the colonel haughtily, "but inform me as briefly as possible what has occurred."

Confused by the thought that possibly he had been rude to friends of General von Waldenmeer, the lieutenant stammered through a recital which was far from clear.

While the lieutenant was speaking, the young Prussian colonel was slapping his boot sharply with his riding-whip, or checking the impatient pawing of his horse.

"*Potstausend!*" he exclaimed, interrupting the unhappy lieutenant in the middle of his story. "I cannot make head or tail of your account, Saueraugen. Broken harness, and French spies, closed carriage, and injured horses." Then, turning to Tournay, he addressed him in French: —

"I understand you are on your way to find General von Waldenmeer, — he is in the field, quartered at present at Falzenberg. You can accompany me there."

"We are bound for General von Waldenmeer's

castle at Hagenhof," replied Tournay politely,
" and with your permission we will proceed there."

" Do you know the general?" inquired the
Prussian colonel.

" I have not that honor."

" I am his son, Karl von Waldenmeer, and I
think it would be best for you to accompany me
to Falzenberg, where I am going to join my father."

" Perhaps if the baroness is still at Hagenhof it
would better suit the inclination of the lady whom
I escort, Mademoiselle de Rochefort, to go forward
rather than be compelled to go to Falzenberg."

Colonel von Waldenmeer sat in thought during
the long space, for him, of five seconds. " I
think you would better come with me as far as
Falzenberg," he said.

" As you command," answered Tournay.

" Did I understand you to say that the occupant
of that carriage was a Mademoiselle de Rochefort?" asked the young von Waldenmeer, as Tournay spoke aside to Gaillard.

" Yes."

" What is the nature of your business with the
baron my father?" was the next question, abruptly
put.

" Will you permit me to discuss that with the
baron himself?"

" As you will," answered the Prussian colonel
with hauteur. Then turning to the group of officers who had sat motionless upon their horses, he
said : —

"Gentlemen, you will please accompany this carriage to Falzenberg. Lieutenant Saueraugen, bring up your batteries with all possible speed and report to me. Franz von Shiffen, you will please come with me." He gave his black charger a slight touch with the spur, the spirited animal sprang forward, and he was seen galloping down the road, with Franz von Shiffen riding hotly after him.

Baron von Waldenmeer, general of the division of the Rhine, was seated with a beer mug before him and his pipe freshly lit, enjoying his evening smoke, when word was brought to him that the party of Frenchmen, encountered by his son and some other members of his staff on the road from Inweiler, had arrived at Falzenberg, and was now awaiting his pleasure in the room below. His son, who had come in some time before, had told him of the incident of the meeting.

The baron blew a cloud of smoke out of his capacious mouth.

"Show the entire party up here at once. We can then hear their story and decide as to the probability of it. You, Karl, send word to General von Scrappenhauer that I shall have to defer our party of Skat for an hour. Ludwig, have your father's beer mug replenished. Would you have his throat become like the bed of a dried-up stream? And now send up your Frenchmen; I am waiting for them."

Ludwig von Waldenmeer, who was the picture of his younger brother Karl, except that he was

heavier in build and larger of girth, passed the
beer flagon from his end of the table to his father.

Karl gave a few commands to an orderly, then
took a seat by the general's side.   The latter was
a man of about sixty.   Around his shining bald
pate was a fringe of grizzled hair that had once
been red.   His mustache was a bristling, scrubby
brush of the same color.   Although not of great
height he was broad of chest and still broader
about the waistband; and even in his lightest
boots he rode in the saddle at two hundred pounds.

An orderly opened the door and ushered in the
four French travelers.   Mademoiselle de Rochefort entered first.   She paused for a moment at
the sight of a room full of officers.   Then she took
a few steps into the room and stood awaiting the
baron's command.   The baron took one look at
the figure before him, then rose suddenly to his
feet and came toward her; the other officers took
the signal and rose from their places at the table
and stood beside their chairs.

"You are the daughter of Honoré de Rochefort.
One has no need to ask the question, it is answered by your face."   And General von Waldenmeer took Edmé by the hand and led her to a
seat by his side.   Agatha kept at her mistress's
elbow like a faithful guardian.

Tournay and Gaillard, travel - stained and
splashed with mud from head to foot, remained
standing by the door.

"If you have come, as I surmise, to find in
Prussia a home denied you by your native land,

let me say that nowhere will you find a warmer
welcome than under the roof of von Waldenmeer," and the general put her hand to his lips.

"I have come," she replied, "to find a refuge
from the persecution which follows me in my own
unhappy country. Thanks to the devotion of
these friends," and she turned toward Tournay
with a look of gratitude, "I have been able to
reach here in safety, to throw myself upon your
protection, and to ask your advice as to my future
movements."

"If you will pardon this reception in a rough
soldier's camp, mademoiselle, and can put up with
such poor accommodation as this house affords,
to-morrow you shall be escorted on to Hagenhof,
where my wife will receive you as one of her own
daughters." And he bent over her hand for the
second time.

This unusual show of gallantry on the part of
their general caused Franz von Shippen to place
his hand before his mouth to hide a smile, while
Ludwig von Waldenmeer looked up at the ceiling.

"Franz," called out the general, "interview the
good lady whose house we occupy and see that the
best room she has is prepared for Mademoiselle
de Rochefort. Ludwig, to-morrow you shall have
the honor of escorting this lady to Hagenhof.
There you shall be welcome, mademoiselle, as long
as you choose to honor us with your company.
But rest assured it will not be long before your
own country will be rescued from the miscreants
who are devouring it. All Europe is in arms

to avenge outraged royalty ; the Prussian army of
two hundred thousand men is now prepared to
march on Paris. With us are thousands of your
own nobility. We make common cause against
anarchy and murder. We shall not rest until we
have restored the monarchy and chastised these
insolent Republicans."

Edmé looked quickly in the direction of Tournay, fearful lest the baron's words should stir him
to make a reply, but he and Gaillard stood listening imperturbably. From their quiet and unob-
trusive demeanor the general had taken them for
servants of Mademoiselle de Rochefort and had
not given them a second look.

" But you are fatigued, mademoiselle," said von
Waldenmeer. "To-morrow morning will be a more
fitting time to discuss your affairs. The good haus-
frau by this time is preparing your quarters. I
will conduct you to them. Your followers will be
comfortably cared for outside."

Edmé, glad of an opportunity to escape further
conversation, was about to thank the general for
his permission to retire to her room, when the
outer door opened and a number of French noblemen, officers of the general's staff, entered the
room.

Among them was the Marquis de Lacheville.
His quick roving eye caught sight of Edmé instantly. He stopped in the middle of a conversation with a companion and looked over his shoulder hastily as if he would retrace his steps without
attracting attention ; but it was too late. The

deep voice of General von Waldenmeer sounded
in his ears.

"Ah, here are some of your brave countrymen,
mademoiselle, who deem it no disgrace to serve
under the flag of Prussia in order to reconquer
the throne for their rightful sovereign."

The door behind de Lacheville was closed by
the Count de Beaujeu, who was the last to enter,
and the marquis, drawing a deep breath between
his set teeth, stepped forward as one who suddenly
resolves to take a desperate chance.

"Cousin Edmé!" he exclaimed, coming up to
where she was seated and endeavoring to take her
hand. "Thank Heaven you have escaped!"

"Yes, I am in a place of safety, thanks to a
brave gentleman," she replied, drawing back her
hand. "But do not call me cousin. I ceased to
be your kinswoman when you deserted me at
Rochefort. There are no cowards of our blood."
And she turned from him with a look of unutter-
able contempt as if he were too mean an object to
deserve her passing notice. She had spoken in a
low voice, yet so distinctly that all in the room
heard what she had said. A murmur of surprise
ran round the entire group of officers. The marquis drew back under the rebuff, his face deadly
pale, while he darted at Edmé a look of hatred as
if he could have killed her.

"What's that?" roared the general as soon as
he could master his astonishment. "One of my
aides a coward?"

De Lacheville gave a quick glance around the

room, as a hunted man, brought suddenly to bay,
might seek some weapon to defend himself. As
he caught sight of Tournay, his eyes gleamed
wickedly.

"This mad girl," he exclaimed, pointing to
Mademoiselle de Rochefort as soon as he could
control his voice, " was once my affianced bride,
but she has found a mate better suited to her lik-
ing. She has been traveling with him throughout
France, and now she seeks to extenuate her own
conduct by slandering me, whom she has wronged."

" If you are not the coward mademoiselle has
called you, you will answer to me for that lie,"
said Tournay, throwing Gaillard's restraining hand
off from his arm and advancing toward the marquis threateningly.

De Lacheville drew back. He remembered the
duel in the woods at La Thierry. He looked again
into the dark eyes of the stern man who confronted
him, and his mouth twitched nervously. Then
with an effort he turned to the French gentlemen
at his side and said, speaking rapidly, " This fellow is a Republican, one of those who clamored for
King Louis's death. Shall we forget our oath to
kill these regicides wherever we may find them ? "

Before he had finished speaking, three swords
were out of their scabbards and three infuriated
French noblemen sprang at Tournay.

" Gott in Himmel ! " shouted General von Waldenmeer, as his Prussian officers beat down the
points of the excited Frenchmen, "will you spill
blood here under my very nose ? Colonel Karl

von Waldenmeer, place those French gentlemen
under restraint, and let there be quiet here while
I examine into these charges."

The Marquis de Lacheville had taken up a position near the door.

" He is Robert Tournay, an officer of the Republican army! " he cried out as he sheathed his
sword. " While he is here in the disguise of a
lackey in waiting to Mademoiselle de Rochefort,
his intention is to play the spy and return with his
information to France. For your own sake, General von Waldenmeer, you should place him where
he can do you no such injury."

" What answer have you to make to this ? "
said the old general, addressing Tournay. " Are
you a servant of Mademoiselle de Rochefort, or
are you a spy of those Republican brigands?
Speak! I condemn no man unheard."

Tournay looked round the room before replying.

" I am a colonel in the Republican army," he
said quietly. " But I came here solely to bring
mademoiselle to a place of safety ; not to spy
upon your army, which as a matter of fact I
thought twenty miles further east."

General von Waldenmeer broke the silence that
followed this avowal.

" You admit that you are an officer in the Republican army. You are within our lines under
very peculiar circumstances. You may have taken
advantage of Mademoiselle de Rochefort's confidence in you to play the spy. Until it is proven
to the contrary, I must take the ground that both

you and your companion are spies, and treat you accordingly. Colonel von Waldenmeer, you will send for a file of soldiers and place these two men under arrest."

" General von Waldenmeer ! " said Edmé de Rochefort, turning toward the old baron with an appealing gesture, " you are about to commit an act of grave injustice. Colonel Tournay is guiltless of the charge of being a spy. The charge was brought against him out of malice and revenge by the man who has just slandered me so basely."

She did not look at the Marquis de Lacheville, but under the general gaze which was directed toward him as she spoke, he quailed and shrunk from the room, shivering as with ague.

" This gentleman," she went on, looking at Tournay gratefully, " has incurred great danger and endured much privation in order to bring me here in safety. He has been brave and devoted when others cravenly deserted me ; and if he should be treated by you as a spy it would be as if I had decoyed him here only to destroy him."

" No, mademoiselle, no," said Robert Tournay in a low tone.

By a quick gesture she bade him be silent.

" General von Waldenmeer, you are a brave soldier. You have professed the greatest friendship for your old friend's daughter. She now asks you to release these gentlemen. As a soldier and a gentleman you are bound to grant her prayer."

She spoke the words simply and in the tone which was natural to her, as if the request admit

ted of no denial ; and laying her hand upon the
general's arm looked into his rough face.

For a moment he sat in silence. His heavy
brows came down until they shaded his eyes completely. Then taking the hand that rested on his
sleeve, he said : —

"At the risk of neglecting my duty as a soldier,
I will grant your request. These men shall go
free, but," he added hastily, as though his consent
to their liberation had been given too quickly,
"they must be kept under surveillance here until
to-morrow, and then they shall be escorted back
over the frontier. Colonel von Waldenmeer," he
continued, addressing his son," "I leave you to
conduct these French gentlemen to their quarters.
I make you responsible for their keeping."

Edmé held out her hand to Tournay. "Good-
night, Colonel Tournay," she said. "It is a great
joy and relief to know that you are to come to no
harm through having brought me here. And you,
who have done so much for me, will surely overlook this last and slight indignity which you are
called upon to endure for my sake."

"Mademoiselle," he replied, bending over her
hand and speaking in a tone so low that none
other in the room could hear, "there is nothing in
the world I would not endure for your sake. To
have you speak to me like this repays me a thou-
sand-fold. Adieu, mademoiselle. Now, Colonel
von Waldenmeer, I am ready ;" and with Gaillard at his side he followed young von Waldenmeer
from the room.

CHAPTER XI

UNDER WHICH FLAG?

As the three men came out into the corridor, the large outer door opened and a sergeant of artillery stepped over the threshold, saluted the colonel, and stood awaiting orders. The fine snow drifted past him into the hall, stinging the faces of von Waldenmeer and his two prisoners.

The colonel turned toward the Frenchmen, and addressing them in his quick way, said : —

"It is a vile night. Give me your word not to leave the quarters to which I assign you until sent for, and I will permit you to pass the night more in comfort under this roof."

Tournay gladly assented, the young von Waldenmeer spoke a few words of command to the sergeant, who turned on his heel and repeated the order in guttural tones to some snow-covered figures behind him. The door closed with a loud bang and the escort was heard marching away.

Colonel Karl then led the way up a broad oaken staircase to a room at the end of a long corridor on the upper floor.

"My own room is just opposite," said he with a gesture of the head, as he threw open the door. "You will be more comfortable here than in the guard-house."

The house which General von Waldenmeer had
chosen for his headquarters at Falzenberg was a
commodious one, built around an open court, where
in summer a fountain played in the centre of a
green grass plot. Tournay stepped to one of the
windows and looked out upon the scene. The
bronze figure in the fountain was draped with ice,
and a great mound of snow filled the centre of the
square, where the soldiers had cleared a passage
for themselves. On the opposite side were the
stables, and from the neighing and stamping of
hoofs, Tournay judged more than a dozen horses
were kept there. Lights flashed here and there as
a subaltern or private moved about in the performance of the night's duties.

The first thing which had struck Gaillard's eye
on entering was a large canopied bed. This
reminded him too forcibly of his fatigue to be
resisted. He threw himself down upon it, boots
and all, and was asleep as soon as his head touched
the pillow.

Von Waldenmeer stood in the centre of the
room, slapping his hessians with a little flexible
riding-whip. Tournay began to thank him for
the courtesy he had shown them, when the latter
stopped him in his abrupt way, saying : —

"I was watching the Marquis de Lacheville's
face while he was denouncing Mademoiselle de
Rochefort, and if ever I saw liar written upon a
man's countenance it was on his then. I wish that
he had lied when he accused you of being a colonel
in the Republican army." And Colonel Karl
strode toward the door impatiently.

"Why should you have wished that?" demanded Tournay. "I am proud of my position."

"Bah!" exclaimed the German, with his hand on the latch, "you should be in the Prussian army. It is an honor to serve in the army that was built up by the great Frederick. A man of your courage should not be content to serve among those Republican brigands. Good-night," — and he disappeared rapidly through the door, slamming it behind him.

Tournay roused Gaillard from his slumber. Both men were numb with fatigue. They had not taken off their clothes and slept in a bed since leaving Paris, and five minutes later they had thrown off their garments and sunk into a deep sleep in the large, white bed.

For ten hours Tournay slept without moving. Then he yawned, threw out both arms, opened his eyes a little, and was preparing to sleep again when he became conscious that a man was standing beside the bed. Opening his heavy eyes a little further, he recognized Gaillard and said to him drowsily: —

"Well! What is it, Gaillard? Can't I get a few minutes' sleep undisturbed?"

"The forenoon is half gone," replied Gaillard; "you 've slept enough for one man."

"You don't mean to say that it 's morning already!" exclaimed Tournay, leaning on one elbow and blinking at the light.

"Morning! The finest kind of a morning," replied Gaillard gayly. "I 've been up these two hours. I gained permission to go to our carriage, and I have taken out a change of linen from our equipment in the boot."

Tournay sprang from the bed and looked out of the window. The sun was high in the heaven, and the day was bright and cold.

"That Lieutenant Sauerkraut, or whatever his name may be," said Gaillard, "has just come up to say that the general would like to see you at your convenience. The lieutenant was particularly civil, for him, so I surmise nothing will interfere with our early departure. It's astonishing how quickly an underling takes his tone from his superior officer. I suppose it will be better for you to wait upon the general at once, while the old gentleman is in a good humor," continued Gaillard, "and as I have been given the liberty of the courtyard, I will employ the time in looking after our horses."

"Very well," said Tournay. "I will go to General von Waldenmeer. I hope nothing will interfere with our immediate departure."

General von Waldenmeer was seated at his table with a pile of maps and papers before him. At Tournay's entrance the two officers who were standing at the general's side withdrew to the further end of the room. It was the same room in which the scene of the previous evening had taken place. On the table at the general's elbow stood his beer-mug, filled with his morning draught. The old soldier was evidently very much absorbed in the work before him, for his heavy brows were drawn over his eyes and his lips were moving as he studied the papers. From time to time he reached out his left hand mechanically and took up the beer-mug, refreshing himself with a long pull. With the exception of the two officers, there were no other occupants of the room.

The picture of Mademoiselle Edmé, as she had appeared when pleading to the general in his behalf, was so vivid in Tournay's mind that he stood silently before the table, oblivious to his surroundings. He remained in this position for some minutes when the general, upon one of his searches for inspiration at the bottom of the beer-mug, glanced over the rim and saw the Frenchman standing like a statue before him.

"*Potstausend!*" he exclaimed, as soon as he had set down the mug and wiped the white froth from his mustache. "You were so quiet that I forgot your existence and have been studying out a plan of campaign against General Hoche under your very nose. He's a clever little man, is Hoche," continued the old German musingly. "There is some sport in beating him."

Tournay smiled quietly at hearing his idol patronizingly spoken of by an officer who had not won half his fame.

"I wish you better success than your predecessor in the attempt, General von Waldenmeer," he said.

The general smiled grimly at this hit and then changed the subject by saying: —

"Last evening I told you that I would send you back to France with an escort to the frontier."

Tournay bowed affirmatively.

"Since then, Mademoiselle de Rochefort has told me in full the story of her escape from Tours, recounting your part in it, and dwelling most flatteringly upon your bravery and discretion."

Tournay bowed again in acknowledgment.

"The service you have rendered the daughter of my old friend, by effecting her rescue and bringing her here in spite of such great obstacles, makes my obligation to you deep, very deep. My honor and my inclinations are one, when they move me to accord you, not only your freedom, but to offer you a commission in my son's regiment, the Tenth Prussian heavy artillery."

If the general had ordered him out to instant execution or conferred upon him in marriage the hand of his daughter Gretchen, Tournay could not have felt more surprise. For a few moments he could find no words in which to answer, and the general turned to the papers he had just laid down.

"Is my entry into your service made a condition of my freedom?" he finally found breath to inquire.

The Prussian general looked up from the map he had been studying, pressing his fat finger upon it to mark the place.

"Certainly not," he replied, "I make no conditions in paying a debt."

"Then I will take my liberty, which you have promised to restore to me," answered Tournay, "and return to France."

It was now the general's turn to be surprised.

"You mean to say that you will go back to Paris?"

"I shall return to the French army at — It is needless to tell you where, as you have been studying the map so attentively."

"But," interrupted General von Waldenmeer, "within six months our allied armies will be in Paris. There will be no more Republic, and every one who has been instrumental in the death of King Louis XVI. and the destruction of the monarchy will have to pay the penalty. You are a young man. You have been led into this republicanism by older heads. I offer you an opportunity — not only of escaping the consequences of your folly but the chance of redeeming yourself by fighting on the right side — and you refuse?" and the general reached out for the beer-mug to sustain himself in his disappointment. He was so sincere in his offer and in his amazement at its refusal that the angry color on Tournay's cheek faded away and a smile crept to his lips.

"Come," said the old general, putting down his mug after an unusually long pull at the contents, "you are thinking better of it. I can understand a soldier's disinclination to desert his colors, but this is not as if I were asking you to be a traitor to your country. A von Waldenmeer would cut out his own tongue rather than propose that to any other soldier. I am putting it in your way to leave the service of a faction who by anarchy and rebellion have gained control of France. Under

the banner of the allies are the true patriots of
your country. You have only to throw off that
red, white, and blue uniform and put on the colors
of Prussia and you are one of them."

Again the flush of resentment rose to Tournay's
cheek, but as he looked down upon the German
general who in perfect good faith and seriousness
made him such a proposal, and as he realized the
utter impossibility of either of them ever seeing
the subject in the same light, his look of anger
changed to one of amusement, and a grim smile
twitched at the corners of his mustache.

"I appreciate the honor you would do me,
General von Waldenmeer, but I prefer to pay the
penalty of my folly and remain loyal to the French
Republic."

The general took up his papers again. "Very
well," he said gruffly. "I will provide you with
an escort over the frontier. It will be ready to
start within the hour." His eyebrows came down
and he became deeply immersed in the study of
the map.

Tournay stood for a few moments looking at
the fat forefinger of the old soldier as it traced its
way over the surface of the map. His thoughts
were of Mademoiselle de Rochefort. He wondered
whether she had set out on her way to Hagenhof.
He almost hoped that she had left and that he
would be spared the pain of parting from her.
Yet if she were still at Falzenberg he knew he
never could force himself to leave and not make
an attempt to bid her good-by.

It was with these conflicting emotions, mingled
with a reluctance to mention her name to the gruff
old general, that he said in a low voice: —

"Has Mademoiselle de Rochefort started on her
journey to Hagenhof?"

He received no answer.

There had been a slight tremor in his voice as
he spoke Edmé's name. Hesitating for a moment,
he stepped to the table and placing one hand on
it he asked again in a steady tone, "When does
Mademoiselle de Rochefort go to Hagenhof?"

The one word "To-morrow" came abruptly out
of the large head buried in the papers before him.

Tournay drew a sigh of relief. If she had
gone away, leaving him no word, he would have
been the most miserable of men. Without further words with the general he turned and left the
room.

As he went along the hallway he heard the
rustle of a woman's gown behind him, and turning,
saw to his great satisfaction the figure of Agatha
hurrying toward him.

"Agatha," he exclaimed, as she came up to
him, "where is mademoiselle? Can I see her?"

"Mademoiselle is in Frau Krieger's apartment
at the further end of the east wing. If you will
come with me I will show you where it is. It is
fortunate that I have met you as I do, else it
would have been difficult to find you in this large
place."

"Then you were sent to fetch me?" inquired
Tournay eagerly.

"I did not say that," replied Agatha with a quiet smile.

"But you evidently were in search of me," persisted Tournay.

"I have no time to answer questions now," she replied, with a laugh. "Here is the room," and she ushered him into a long old-fashioned salon, whose uncomfortable pieces of furniture looked as if they had stood for generations staring at their own ugly reflections in the polished surface of the floor.

At one end of the room stood a porcelain stove in which a fire was burning ; but the large white sepulchral object seemed to chill the atmosphere more than the fire could warm it. Two high windows hung with heavy curtains faced the square in front of the house, while in the rear two other windows looked out upon the courtyard.

Frau Krieger, the widow of a Prussian officer of high rank, had reserved the salon and one or two adjoining rooms for her own use, and saw with pride the remainder of her domicile turned into barracks by General von Waldenmeer and his staff.

"Wait here a moment and I will tell mademoiselle," said Agatha, traversing the salon and disappearing through a door in the further side. Tournay walked to the front window and glanced out on the street.

The sentinel at the porte-cochère was on the point of presenting arms to Ludwig von Waldenmeer, who rode out; and two of the general's staff officers stood smoking and chatting in front of the building. Tournay's alert ear caught the sound of light footsteps, and he turned just as Edmé crossed the threshold from the inner room.

He had told himself many times within the last few minutes that the interview must be a brief one if he were to retain complete mastery over his feelings. As he approached her, his face, in spite of his efforts to control it, expressed some of the emotions which the sight of her awakened.

She extended her hand to him in her graceful, natural way, and he bent over it, mechanically uttering the words he had been repeating over and over to himself.

. " I have come, mademoiselle, to say adieu."

At this, the color which had mantled her cheek as he touched her fingers disappeared.

" You have not seen General von Waldenmeer, then ? " she asked quickly.

" Yes, mademoiselle, and because I have seen him I intend to start at once."

" General von Waldenmeer says that in less than three months' time the Prussian army will be in Paris," said Edmé.

A slight smile of incredulity was Tournay's only reply.

" The monarchy will be restored," she continued ; " little mercy will be shown the Republicans. They will have justice meted out to them by their conquerors."

" The allied armies will never reach Paris, mademoiselle, and before they restore the mon-

archy they must kill every Republican who stands
between them and the throne."

"I do not want them to kill you," she said
simply.

His heart beat wildly. For an instant he did
not speak. When he could trust his voice to answer he said : —

"I thank you deeply for your solicitude, mademoiselle, but whatever happens I must go back to
my duty."

Edmé hesitated a moment, then spoke, at first
with evident effort; then warming into a tone
of almost passionate entreaty.

"You have done much for an unhappy woman,
Robert Tournay. The remembrance of the loyalty
and devotion with which you watched over and
protected me shall never pass out of my memory.
The de Rocheforts do not easily forget such a debt
as I owe you. In an attempt to repay it in some
measure, I persuaded General von Waldenmeer to
offer you an honorable position in his service. I
am a proud woman, Monsieur Tournay, and it cost
me something to make such an appeal to the Prussian officer, and now you reject his offer and present yourself before me so coolly and say carelessly,
'I have come, mademoiselle, to bid you adieu.'"

"You think it easy for me to say those words?"
replied Tournay vehemently.

She did not wait for him to finish, but went
on : —

"I place it in your power to serve the rightful
cause, honorably and loyally, — the cause of the

king; *my* cause, Robert Tournay, and you refuse to do so."

"Do you not see that what you propose would be my dishonor?" he asked gently.

"No," answered Edmé firmly. "You are a brave but obstinate man, who madly pursues a wicked course; because, having once espoused it, you think to desert it would be disloyal. You are mad, Robert Tournay, but I will rescue you from your folly. I will save you in spite of yourself. I command you to stay here!" and with the same imperious gesture which he knew so well of old, she stood before him, her dark blue eyes, as was their wont under stress of excitement, flashing almost black. The tone was one of command, but there was in it a note of entreaty that went to his heart. He caught the hand which she held out to him, and exclaimed fervently: —

"I would give ten years of life to be able to obey you, but it cannot be. You do not know what you are asking of me or you would not put my honor thus upon the rack. It is cruel of you, mademoiselle, but I forgive you. You cannot understand. How should you — you are of the Monarchy, and I am of the Republic. The Republic calls me and I must go."

"The Republic!" repeated Edmé, "Oh! execrable Republic! It has robbed me of everything in the world — family, estate, friends, and now" — She paused, the sentence incomplete upon her lips, and looked at him with an expression of pain upon her face as if some violent struggle were taking place within her. " And now you are going back to it. You may become its victim ; you, who are so brave and strong and noble. Yes," she continued, " I will give the word its full meaning, Robert Tournay, you are noble — too noble to become a martyr in such a cause. I entreat you not to go. I fear for your safety."

Tournay's head swam. For a moment he felt that he must fold her in his arms and tell her that for her sake he would give up everything in the world for which he had striven, — country, liberty, and honor ; the Republic itself.

With a mighty effort he threw off the feeling of weakness, passionately crying, " For God's sake, mademoiselle, do not speak to me like that. You will make me forget my manhood. You will make me act so that your respect, which I have been so fortunate as to win, will turn to contempt. You could almost make me turn traitor to the Republic."

" What is this Republic? this creature of the imagination which you place above all else in the world? " she asked impetuously. " What has it done for France? What has it done for you? "

Before Tournay could answer, the sound of martial music was heard outside, and the measured tread of passing troops shook the room. He stepped to the window and drawing aside the curtains motioned Edmé to come to his side.

Wonderingly she approached and saw a brigade of infantry passing in review of the general of division. They marched with absolute precision,

the sun reflecting on the polished barrels of their
guns as on a solid wall.

"There go the best troops in the world," said
Tournay. Edmé looked up in his face with surprise at his sudden change of manner.

"The soldiers of Prussia: at the command of
their officers they will march like that to the batteries' mouth, closing up the gap of the fallen men
with clock-work movements. There are two hundred thousand of them, and they are preparing to
attack France. Joined with them are the tried
veterans of Austria. On the sea," he continued,
"the fleets of England are bearing down upon
the ports of France. In the south, Spain is pouring her soldiers over the Pyrences. These allied
armies have banded together to destroy France.
Yet we shall throw them back again, as we did
at Wattignes and at Jemappes. There the flower
of the European armies was scattered by our raw
French troops. Although outnumbered and out-
manœuvred, the *men* of France hurled back their
foes in broken and disordered array. And why?
Because in the heart of every Frenchman burns
the new-born fire of liberty. He is fighting for
the freedom he has bought so dearly. He is
fighting for that Republic which has made him
what he is — a *man!* It is France against the
world! and by the Republic alone will she triumph
over her enemies. That is my answer, mademoiselle. The Republic has made a new France, and
I am part of it. At her call I must leave everything and go to her defense."

While he spoke thus, Edmé saw his face animated with a light she had learned to know so well, — the same light that had shone from his eyes when he confronted the mob in her château ; the same fire that flashed as he defended himself before General von Waldenmeer.

" You say I place my duty to the Republic above any earthly consideration," he said. " Let me tell you that I hold your respect still dearer. If I should desert my cause, the cause for which I have lived, should I not lose that respect? Ask your own heart, mademoiselle, would it not be so? "

She stood in silence. Then her eyes met his. He read her answer there before she spoke, and in the look she gave him he thought he read still more — something he dared not believe, scarcely dared hope.

" You are right," she replied, speaking slowly and distinctly. " Go back to France! It is I who bid you go."

" I knew you would tell me to go," he replied.

The sound of voices in the corridor outside fell upon their ears.

" There are Gaillard and the escort," said Tournay, sadly. " Mademoiselle, good-by! I may never see you again. But I thank God that you are here in safety, and I shall find some happiness in the thought that I have been an instrument in your deliverance."

She did not answer, but stretched out her hand to him. He took it, and dropping on one knee, put it to his lips. " It is for the last time," he said, looking up at her. His face was deadly pale, and there was a look of pleading in his brown eyes.

She placed her other hand upon his head. It was but the slightest touch, as if she yielded to a sudden impulse, and then with the same swift movement she drew away from him.

"As it *must* be, I pray you to go quickly," she said, and without waiting for a reply she turned and left him.

Tournay rose to his feet, — " I swear to you now, mademoiselle, that some day I shall see you again," and he rushed from the room to the court-yard below.

"Are the horses ready?" he whispered hoarsely, grasping Gaillard by the arm.

"At the door with an escort of Prussian officers," was the reply.

"What time is it?"

"Three hours before dark."

"We must be over the frontier and well into France by to-night," was Tournay's rejoinder. "Come!"

Standing by the window, Edmé saw him leap into the saddle. He gave one look in her direction, but could not see her, concealed as she was by the heavy curtains.

She heard the officers laughing and talking among themselves. She saw one of the men jump from his horse, tighten a saddle girth, and remount with an agile spring. Then Colonel von Walden-meer approached and addressed some remark to

Robert Tournay. The latter, who had been sitting erect and motionless upon his horse, turned slightly in the saddle to answer the Prussian officer.

Edmé could see that his features were set and their expression stern.

Colonel von Waldenmeer mounted his own horse, gave a word of command, and the party started forward.

Edmé watched them as they went up the road. Ten horses riding two abreast, the snow flying out from under the heels of the galloping hoofs. She watched them until the square shoulders of Colonel Tournay were hardly distinguishable from those of Colonel Karl who rode beside him. The cavalcade disappeared around a bend in the road, and Edmé turned from the wintry aspect without to the dreary salon with a heavy heart.

CHAPTER XII

THE FOUR COMMISSIONERS

UNDER the escort of Karl von Waldenmeer and half a dozen of his French officers, Tournay and Gaillard rode rapidly toward the French boundary.

It had stopped snowing during the night, and the weather was clear and cold.

They rode in silence, no sound being heard but the regular dull beating of their horses' hoofs on the snow-covered ground.

They drew out of the wood and saw the frozen surface of the Rhine before them, the sun dazzling their eyes with its reflected light upon the ice.

With one accord the party reined in their horses and sat motionless, looking at the glorious sight of the ice-bound river.

Karl von Waldenmeer was the first to break the silence. Pointing with his gloved hand toward the opposite shore he said : —

"There, gentlemen, is France, and my road ends here."

Tournay merely made an inclination of the head in assent. He was thinking sadly of Edmé standing by the window in the cheerless old salon at Falzenberg ; but as he looked out over the river

towards his own land he remembered the army on
the other side of the Vosges; the prospect of the
impending campaign caused his spirits to revive,
and he replied : —

"We owe you thanks, Colonel von Waldenmeer, for the kindness you have been pleased to
show us. When we meet again it will doubtless be
upon the field of battle, but I shall not even then
forget your courtesy of to-day."

"It will always give me pleasure to meet you
again, under any circumstances, Colonel Tournay," said the Prussian, "and if it be on the field,
to cross swords with you. A brave foe makes a
good friend, and I shall be glad to count you as
both of these. And now, gentlemen, we will relieve you of our escort; there lies your way over
that bridge, just below here. We return to Falzenberg."

"Let us cross upon the ice," said Gaillard to
Tournay; "it will bear our weight easily."

They rode down the bank. At the brink their
horses drew back, but being urged by their riders,
went forward, feeling the ice daintily with their
forefeet with cat-like caution. Seeing that the
ice was quite safe, the Frenchmen put spurs into
their horses and the animals swung into a gallop,
their iron-shod feet cutting into the ice with a
pleasant, crunching sound.

Reaching the further side, they rode up the
steep bank, then reined in their horses and looked
back. The declining rays of the sun tipped the
snow-clad hemlock trees on the other side of the

river with crimson, and against the dark outline of
the forest behind, the figures of Colonel von Waldenmeer and his officers sat motionless as statues.
Each party gave the military salute, and the Prus-
sians rode back into the wood, while Tournay and
Gaillard sat looking after them until they were no
longer in sight.

"We are on French soil once more," exclaimed
Tournay, "and now to join General Hoche and
fight for it."

"I had best return to Paris," said Gaillard.

"I fear to have you return there now, after
having put your head in danger by assisting me,"
said Tournay anxiously.

"I shall be as safe in Paris as anywhere in the
world," replied his friend. "Nobody will suspect the actor Gaillard of having any connection
with the flight of Mademoiselle de Rochefort. I
cannot do better than to return to Paris and re-
sume my usual mode of life there. While, if you
are suspected, as is more likely, of instigating or
effecting Mademoiselle de Rochefort's escape from
Tours, you must look to your military reputation
and your influence in the convention to protect
you from an inquiry on the part of the rabid revo-
lutionists."

"What you say, Gaillard, is sound reasoning.
I will follow your advice. Embrace me, my
friend, and let us part here."

"Good-by until we meet again, my colonel!"
was Gaillard's only audible reply, and then he
rode off toward the west, while Tournay turned

his horse in the direction of the north, where the French troops lay encamped.

It was about noon of the next day when he reached the French army, and stopping only at his own tent to put on his uniform he hurried to the headquarters of General Hoche and reported for duty. He had traveled so rapidly from Tours that he reached the army almost as soon as General Hoche expected him, and the general attributed the delay of a day or so to the bad condition of the roads.

Tournay hesitated to set him right in the matter, as he deemed it more prudent to refrain from mentioning to any one his part in Mademoiselle de Rochefort's escape.

" What news do you bring from the convention ? " was the question of the general as they were seated alone.

" Bad ! " replied Tournay, " as you can tell by the tone of these dispatches. The convention has many able men in it, but they are dominated too entirely by the Revolutionary Tribunal, and that body is dominated too much by one man. His power is ruining the Republic. Unless we get rid of Robespierre, we might as well go back to the monarchy."

After a few moments spent in reading the papers Tournay had put in his hand, General Hoche looked up with an expression of annoyance on his brow.

" Yes; the insulting tone of this dispatch is almost beyond endurance. I am glad after all

that my business is out here fighting the external
enemies of France.   Were I at Paris, I should be
embroiling myself daily with some of those who
are in power.   If we meet with the slightest re-
verses here at the front there is a howl from St.
Just and that crowd that we are betraying the
Republic.   Meanwhile they furnish us with a beg-
garly equipment.   It is they who are betraying the
Republic.   Were it not for Danton we should get
nothing.   He alone makes success against our enemies possible.   And we must be successful, Colonel
Tournay ; look here at the plan of campaign."

And the young general, in his military ardor,
forgetting entirely the insulting dispatch, turned
with enthusiasm to the maps which lay spread out
on the table.

" Here are the bulk of the Austrian forces at
Wissembourg.   That old German beer-barrel von
Waldenmeer is at Falzenberg.   He intends to
concentrate his troops there and then bring them
up to join the Austrian general, Wurmser."

Tournay started at his own general's accurate
information in regard to the enemy's position and
plans.

" We must attack Wurmser at once before he
can receive reinforcements, and then proceed to
Landau.   They have beaten us once at Wissembourg and will not be looking for us to take the
offensive again so soon.   I have already given the
order to mobilize the troops.   I and my staff will
ride forward this evening.   By to-morrow night
we shall have retaken Wissembourg."

" One moment, general," interrupted Tournay, as Hoche took up another map. " I wish to tell you that I have just seen General von Waldenmeer at Falzenberg."

Hoche looked at his officer with surprise.

" I went to the Prussian frontier on an errand, the nature of which I should prefer to keep secret for the present. I was suspected of being a spy, taken prisoner, and brought before General von Waldenmeer. He listened to my explanations and released me under circumstances no less peculiar than those which brought me within his lines." Here Tournay stopped, the blood coming to the surface under the bronze of his cheek at the steady gaze of General Hoche.

" Is that all ? " inquired the latter.

" That is all," answered his colonel, " except that had I not made this détour I should have been here twenty-four hours earlier, and that as I got within the Prussian lines by mistake and did not go as a spy, I can give you no information which you have not already obtained."

" If you had arrived twenty-four hours later you would have missed the grandest opportunity of your life ; I intend to give you, Colonel Tournay, the command of a brigade in the approaching battle."

" A brigade ? " echoed Tournay in surprise.

" You shall atone for your breach of discipline by bearing great responsibility in the attack. I intend your brigade to be where the fight is hottest, and if there is anything left of it after the engagement, and of you, colonel, you shall continue to command it and I will recommend you for promotion."

Tournay grasped his chief by the hand.

" You may be sure, General Hoche, that I shall do my utmost to deserve the honor you have done me."

" I was persuaded of that before I determined to give you the command," replied Hoche ; " now go forward and join your regiment. By midnight I shall be at Wissembourg and shall have one last word with all of my generals. I do not believe in protracted councils of war."

That evening Colonel Tournay was encamped before the field of Wissembourg. He sat in his tent waiting for the summons that should bring him to General Hoche's council board.

An orderly entered with the word that a commission of four men from the Committee of Public Safety at Paris wished to speak to him.

Tournay started from the reverie into which he had fallen. His thoughts had been dwelling upon the events of the past week, and the announcement struck a discordant note in his meditation. " Show them in," he replied briefly.

In another moment the four commissioners stood before him. Three of the men were unknown to him, but the fourth was Gardin. The latter, as spokesman, stood a little in advance of the others. On his face there was a look of mingled insolence and triumph.

Tournay's gorge rose at sight of the man, but

remembering that he was the recognized emissary from the committee he controlled his impulse to kick him from the tent.

" Will you be seated, citizens ? " he said, rising and addressing his remark more to the three commissioners who were not known to him than to Gardin. " Orderly, bring seats."

" Our business with you will be of such short duration that we shall have no need to sit down," answered Gardin curtly.

" Orderly, do not bring the seats," was Tournay's quick order, as he resumed his former place on a camp-chair and sat carelessly looking at the four men standing before him. This placed Gardin in just the opposite rôle from that he had intended to assume. He saw his mistake at once, and hastened to recover his lost ground.

" Citizen colonel," he said, drawing a paper from his pocket and putting it in Tournay's hands, " here is a document from the committee which even you cannot question. It is addressed to Robert Tournay."

Tournay broke the large red seal of the letter and read : —

CITIZEN COLONEL ROBERT TOURNAY; with the Army of the Moselle, Citizen General Lazare Hoche commanding : —

The Citizen Colonel Tournay is hereby summoned to appear before the Committee of Public Safety to answer charges affecting his patriotism and loyalty to the Republic. He will resign his

command at once, and return to Paris in the company of the four commissioners who bring him
this document.

Signed : For the Committee of Public Safety,

COUTHON,
ST. JUST.

This 5th Pluviose, the year II. of the French
Republic one and indivisible.

When he had finished reading the document
Tournay folded it carefully and placed it in his
pocket.

" Well ? " demanded Gardin impatiently.

" I cannot at present leave the army," was the
reply.

The four commissioners exchanged looks.

" We are on the eve of a decisive engagement
with the enemy. When that is over — in a few
days, if I am alive, I will answer the committee's
summons."

" We were instructed to bring you back with us
at once," said one of the commissioners.

"And we 'll do it, too," muttered another under
his breath.

The fourth pulled Gardin by the sleeve and whispered something in his ear.

"I regret, citizen commissioners," repeated Tournay, " that I cannot at present leave the army."

Then rising suddenly and confronting Gardin
he said passionately : —

" Tell your masters that it is not necessary to
drag Robert Tournay to Paris like a felon, that he

will appear before the committee of his own free
will; that he regards the welfare of France as
paramount to everything else, and that his duty to
her will take him to the field to-morrow."

"Your answer is not satisfactory to us," persisted Gardin, "nor will it be to the committee.
Once more, and for the last time, citizen colonel,
will you obey this summons as it is written?"

"No!" thundered Tournay.

"Then in the name of the Republic I suspend
you from your command, and arrest you as a traitor. Lay hands upon him!"

Gardin himself, remembering his previous encounter with Tournay in which he had come off
so poorly, merely gave the command, leaving the
others to execute it. Two of them stepped forward with alacrity, one upon each side of Tournay,
and grasped him by the arms.

He offered no resistance, but raising his voice a
little called out : —

"Officers of the guard!"

Half a dozen of his Hussars who were in the
adjoining tent hastened in at his call.

"Arrest these four men!" commanded Tournay
quietly.

"Stop!" cried Gardin; "arrest us at your
peril. We are the authorized emissaries of the
Committee of Public Safety," and he flourished
his commission in the soldiers' faces. "We are
but carrying out our strict orders. To lay hands
upon us will be to bring down upon your heads
the vengeance of Robespierre."

The Hussars stood still. The name of the man who governed France under the cloak of the Republic made them hesitate.

" Conduct the prisoner away with as much dispatch as possible," said Gardin in a quick, low tone to his companions.

" Lieutenant Dessarts, arrest these four men instantly," repeated Tournay. There was a ring in his voice which his subordinates well understood, and without further hesitation they laid hands upon the Paris commissioners and proceeded to drag them from the tent by force.

" He has been relieved of his command and therefore has no right to give you orders. Are you slaves that you obey him thus ? " yelled Gardin, struggling with the big corporal who held him.

" See that no harm is done them, Lieutenant Dessarts," Tournay called out as the men were led away. " Conduct them outside our lines and give orders that they shall not be permitted to return."

Following them to the door of his tent, Tournay coolly watched the unhappy commissioners as they were led away, protesting vehemently against the indignity of their arrest and vowing vengeance for it.

It was a cold winter night, and the wind blew down through the mountain passes of the Vosges with biting keenness. Throwing his cloak over his shoulder he strolled out through the camp. In spite of the chilling wind the soldiers showed the greatest enthusiasm. As he went down the long line of camp-fires, he was recognized and cheered roundly. Cries of " We 'll beat them at Wissembourg to-morrow, colonel ! " " Landau or death ! " greeted him on all sides.

The next day showed that they had not uttered vain boasts.

Tournay's command, sweeping through a narrow defile in the face of a destructive fire, tore through the enemy's centre, and combining with Dessaix on the left, and Pichegru on the right, sent Wurmser's troops backward before his Prussian allies could come to his assistance.

With the cry of " Landau or death ! " the victorious French dashed on toward the beleaguered city and raised the siege just as the brave garrison was in the last extremity for want of food and ammunition.

The day after the relief of Landau, Colonel Tournay entered the tent of the commander-in-chief. Hoche rose to meet him, and taking him by the hand said warmly : —

" Colonel Tournay, in the name of France I thank you for the efficiency and bravery displayed yesterday. The victory of Wissembourg will live in the annals of history, and a full share of the glory belongs to you. In my dispatches to the convention I have not omitted to mention your noble conduct."

The generous Hoche pressed the hand of his colonel in fraternal feeling. He was two years younger than Tournay, although care and fatigue gave him the looks of an older man. At twenty-

four this remarkable man had risen to be preëmi-
nently the greatest general in France, and but for
his premature death might in later years have con-
tested with Napoleon for his laurels.

"I have come, general, to ask your permission
to return to Paris," said Tournay, much gratified
by the words of praise from the lips of one whom
he regarded as the greatest military hero of the
age.

"Again?" said Hoche, in a tone of surprise.

"The Committee of Public Safety have seen fit
to summon me to appear before them," Tournay
continued. "Some one has been found to impeach
my loyalty, and I must answer the charge."

A shade passed over the face of Hoche.

"But I can ill spare you, Colonel Tournay.
What does this committee mean by suspecting
the integrity of an officer in whom I have implicit
faith? By Heaven, I will not permit it! If they
arrest you, I'll throw my commission back in their
faces before I will allow you to answer their
charges."

"That, my general, would but work injury to
France, who depends upon such a man as you to
save her. You surely will not desert her because
a few overheated brains at Paris have seen fit to
listen to some of my traducers. I will go back to
Paris and confront my enemies. My conduct at
Wissembourg will be an answer to their charge of
treason." And the colonel drew himself up with
a flash of pardonable pride in his dark eyes.

"You may be right," replied Hoche, "but I

would not trust them. The reputation which your conduct at Wissembourg will create for you will make them jealous, and they will whisper it about that your popularity renders you dangerous. I know them. They become jealous of any man's reputation. They will have me before the bar of their tribunal as soon as they feel that they can spare me."

And Hoche laughed scornfully as he uttered the prophecy which was so soon to be fulfilled.

"I have no fear but that I shall be able to satisfy them as to loyalty," replied Tournay, smiling at the absurdity of the great and popular Hoche pleading before the tribunal.

"Well, go if you will, but understand, Tournay, that if you refuse to obey this summons, I will protect you. They shall bring no fictitious charges against a trusted officer in my army without entering into a contest with me."

"I thank you again, my general, but I will not permit you to embroil yourself with the committee on my account. You are too indispensable to France. Now I will take the leave of absence you accord me. In ten days you may look for my return."

General Hoche shook his head as Tournay left his presence : —

"I fear it will be longer than that, my friend," he sighed to himself.

Colonel Tournay, accompanied by but one orderly, rode toward Paris. The feelings of pride and pleasure which his general's praise had raised in his heart were subdued by the humiliation at being summoned before the Committee of Public Safety. But there was a fire in his eye, and a hardening of the lines near the mouth which boded that he would not submit tamely to insult nor an unjust sentence.

CHAPTER XIII

THE SWORD OF ROCROY

CITIZEN ST. HILAIRE had just come in from making a few purchases at the baker's shop in the Rue des Mathurins. Shortly after dusk that evening he had recalled to mind that he was without the gill of cream for his next morning's coffee, and also that the small white loaf which formed a part of his breakfast was at that moment reposing crisp and warm on the counter of the baker's shop a few doors distant.

As Citizen St. Hilaire was very particular about his coffee and always liked to have a certain choice loaf that Jules, the baker in the Rue des Mathurins, made to perfection late every afternoon, he had braved the wind and rain of a stormy January evening, and gone out to procure his next morning's repast.

Returning to his small apartment at the top of the house, he threw off his wet cloak and was on the point of extracting from his pocket a little can of cream, when a knock sounded at the door of the chamber which served him for sitting-room, dining-room, and library. Putting the can upon the table, he took up a lamp and went to the door.

A young woman stood upon the threshold. She

had evidently come in a carriage, for the costly clothes she wore were quite unspotted by the rain.

"This is Citizen St. Hilaire," she said in a tone of conviction as she stepped into the room.

St. Hilaire bowed and stepped back to place the lamp upon a small table near at hand, and stood waiting the further pleasure of his visitor.

As he stood within the circle of light, the young woman looked from him to his modest surroundings with marked curiosity, her eyes dwelling upon each object in the room in turn. It did not take long to note every piece of furniture; the table, armchair, a few books, the violin case in the corner, with a picture or two and a pair of rapiers upon the wall. When she had completed her survey of the room her gaze returned to him once more.

He was plainly dressed in a suit of dark brown color. His linen was exquisitely neat, and his figure was so elegant that although his coat was far from new, and of no exceptional quality, it became him as well as if it were of the most costly material.

"Will you be seated?" said St. Hilaire, drawing forward the armchair from its corner.

The young woman took the seat he offered her.

"And so you are Citizen St. Hilaire," she repeated as if the name interested. "I — I am Citizeness La Liberté. I remember you well," she continued; "I saw you a number of times, years ago, at the home of the Marquis de — But why mention his name? There are no more marquises in France, and he was a worthless creature," and she tossed back her head with a gesture of careless freedom.

"No," he repeated, "there are no more marquises," and with a laugh he seated himself opposite her. The sharp end of the crisp loaf in his pocket made him aware of its presence. He took it out and put it in its place upon the table beside the cream.

"The Republic has caused many strange changes, but I should never have dreamed of finding you here like this, Citizen St. Hilaire," and again she eyed him wonderingly.

"The Republic has done a great deal for you?" said St. Hilaire, raising his eyebrows inquiringly.

"Everything," replied La Liberté with emphasis, while her eyes and the jewels on her bosom flashed upon him dazzlingly. Her look indicated that she thought the Revolution had not dealt so generously by him.

"It has done much for me too," said St. Hilaire.

"What good has it done you?" inquired La Liberté incredulously.

"It has taught me wisdom," he replied.

"Oh," she answered contemptuously, "it has brought me pleasure. Therefore I love it. But you, Citizen St. Hilaire, — will you answer me a question?"

St. Hilaire bowed in acquiescence.

"Are you satisfied with this Republic? I know it is dangerous to speak slightingly of it in these days, but between us, with only the walls to hear, do you like it?"

"I am never satisfied with anything," replied St. Hilaire with just a touch of weariness in his voice.

"I should think that you would hate it. I should were I you," and La Liberté shook her brown curls with a laugh.

"Notwithstanding," said St. Hilaire, "I would not go back to the old régime."

"I do not understand you at all," exclaimed La Liberté in despair, with a puzzled look on her brow.

"Why try?" he asked dryly. "I have given it up myself. Tell me in what way I can serve you?"

"I have come here to do you a service," she answered. The room was warm, and as she spoke she threw her ermine-lined cloak over the back of the chair.

A slight trace of surprise showed itself upon Citizen St. Hilaire's face as he looked at her inquiringly.

She had evidently found the chair too large to sit in comfortably, for she perched herself upon its arm with one foot on the floor while she swung the other easily.

"That is extraordinary!'" he exclaimed. "It is a long time since any one has gone out of his way to do me a service. May I ask why you have done so?"

"Oh, I can hardly tell you why," she replied, tapping her boot heel against the side of the chair. It was a very dainty foot and clad in the finest chaussure to be found in Paris. " You were once kind to a friend of mine," she went on to say, slowly — " and I rather liked you — and so I have come to show you this." She put a slip of paper into his hand.

It was headed, " List for the fifteenth Pluviose." Then followed a score of names. St. Hilaire saw his own among them near the end.

The young woman watched him earnestly while he read it. The careless look had quite disappeared from her face, and given place to one of seriousness.

" It is a list of names," said St. Hilaire, turning the paper over and looking at the reverse side to see if it contained anything else. " And my name is honored by being among them. Where did it come from ? What does it mean ? "

" I picked it up," replied La Liberté. " I saw it lying on a table. I did not know the other names upon it and should never have touched it had I not seen your name. And I resolved that you should see it also, and be warned in time. But you have little time to spare. To-morrow is the fifteenth."

" Warned ? " repeated St. Hilaire, " of what ? "

" Every man whose name is upon that list will be arrested to-morrow. It may be in the morning, it may be during the day, it may be late at night. But it will surely be to-morrow. Oh! I have seen so many of those lists, and of late they are longer and more frequent."

"Whose handwriting is this?" inquired St. Hilaire, looking at critically.

"I dare not tell," said La Liberté in a low tone.

"As long as you have revealed so much, why not go a step further and make the information of greater value?" he insisted quietly.

"One of the committee, I dare not mention his name even here," and she looked around the room furtively. "One of the most powerful," she went on, in a very low tone, as if frightened at her own temerity. "Cannot you guess?"

"Yes, I think I can," rejoined St. Hilaire musingly.

"Now that you have had this warning I hope you will be able to elude them. Give me the paper again, Citizen St. Hilaire, that I may replace it before it is missed. He is at the club now, but I must hurry back. Never mind the light; I can find my way well enough. My eyes are used to the dark."

St. Hilaire took up the lamp, and in spite of her remonstrances accompanied her down the four flights of stairs. At the door stood a handsome equipage.

"That is mine," she said, as St. Hilaire escorted her to the carriage; there was the same slight touch of pride in her tone that had crept out once before. "This once belonged to the Duchess de Montmorenci," she said. "It is rather heavy and old-fashioned, but will do very well until I can get a new one."

"I see that you have had the coat of arms

erased," St. Hilaire remarked. " I suppose your
new carriage will have a red nightcap on the
panel."

" Now you are laughing at me," she said, tossing
back her brown curls with a pout. " Good-night,
marquis," she added in a low voice in his ear as
he was closing the door of the carriage.

" Citizen St. Hilaire," he corrected gravely, as
she drove away. " You forget there are no more
marquises in France."

After La Liberté's departure the Citizen St.
Hilaire retraced his steps up the stairs, humming
quietly to himself. On reaching the top landing
he entered his room and sitting down by the window he looked out over the lights of Paris. For
two hours he sat thus buried deep in thought and
scarcely moving. When he finally arose from his
chair the city clock had long struck the hour of
midnight.

First drawing the bolt to the door as if to prevent intrusion even at that late hour, he opened
an old armoire in the corner of the room and took
from it an object carefully wrapped in a velvet
cover. He took from the covering a sword, with
golden hilt studded with jewels. The scabbard,
too, was of pure gold, set profusely with diamonds,
emeralds, and rubies. Unsheathing the weapon
he held it to the light. He held it carefully, almost reverently, as one holds some sacred relic.
His eye was animated and had he uttered his
thoughts he would have spoken thus : —

" This is the sword that a marshal of France

wielded upon the field of battle. He was my an-
cestor, and from father to son it has come down
to me, the last of my race. It is as bright to-day
as when it flashed from its sheath at Rocroy. I
have kept it untarnished. It is the sole remaining relic of the greatness of our name."

Replacing the sword carefully in its scabbard,
he buckled it around his waist. Then taking a
cloak from the armoire he enveloped himself in
it, so as to completely hide the jeweled scabbard.
This done, he went into his bedroom and drew
from under his couch a small chest from which he
took a purse containing some money. All these
preparations he made quietly and with great deliberation. Returning to the sitting-room he un-
bolted and opened the door. All was quiet. A
cat, that frequented the upper part of the building, and made friends with those who fed it,
walked silently in through the open door and
arching her back rubbed purringly against his
leg. He went to the cupboard, and getting out a
saucer filled it with the cream that was to have
flavored his next morning's cup of coffee, and
placed it on the floor. The animal ran to it
greedily, and for a few moments St. Hilaire stood
watching the little red tongue curl rapidly out and
in of the creature's mouth as she lapped up the
unexpected feast. Then giving a glance about
the room, but touching nothing else in it, he ex-
tinguished the light and went out into the corridor,
leaving the door ajar.

When he passed out into the street he noticed

that the rain had ceased. The wind blew freshly
from the west and the night was cool. Drawing
his cloak closer about him and allowing one hand
to rest upon his sword-hilt, he walked rapidly away,
humming softly to himself. In the room he had
just left, the cat licked up the last few drops of
cream in the saucer; signified her contentment
by stretching herself, while she dug her forepaws
into the carpet several times in succession; then
jumped into his vacant arm-chair and curled up
for a nap.

The Citizen St. Hilaire had always foreseen the
possibility of just such an emergency as now confronted him. He was quite prepared to meet it.

On the other side of the river in the small and
quiet Rue d'Arcis dwelt an old man. The house
in which he lived, number seven, was also very
old. It was large and rambling. St. Hilaire knew
it well. As a child he had played in it. It had
once belonged to him, and he had deeded it to
an old servant of his father at a time when he
regarded old houses as encumbrances upon his
estates, and when aged servants had found no
place in his retinue. If for no other reason, his
family pride had caused him to make generous
provision for a faithful retainer, and now that his
own worldly fortunes were reduced, he knew where
to find a home until he could carry out his plans
for leaving the country. For some time past he
had been forming such plans, but with his custom-
ary indifference to danger he had delayed their
execution from day to day.

Crossing the Seine by the bridge St. Michel and following the Quai, St. Hilaire remembered an unfrequented way to the house in the Rue d'Arcis. From the Quai on the left was a blind alley that ended at a row of houses. Through one of these houses had been cut an arched passage to the street beyond. The passageway came out on the other side almost directly opposite number seven, and offered a tempting short-cut.

St. Hilaire walked quietly up the alley and had almost reached the farther end, when a door on the opposite side opened and a woman came out. The lateness of the hour and the signs of timidity which the woman showed, caused St. Hilaire to stop in the entrance to the passageway and look back to observe her actions.

She peered first down the street cautiously, as if to see that there were no passers on the Quai, then up at the windows of the houses opposite to assure herself that she was unobserved from that quarter. Satisfied as to both of these points, she closed the door noiselessly, and hurriedly passed down the street. She was, however, not destined to reach the Quai unnoticed by any other eyes than St. Hilaire's, for she had not gone fifty paces when a party of four men, talking in loud voices, crossed the street on the Quai. At sight of them the woman stopped short and hesitated. The four also stopped and looked at her. One of them called out to her. Evidently frightened she turned, and crossing the street hurried back. To St. Hilaire's surprise, she passed by the house from which she had recently come, and made straight for the passageway where he stood. The four men gave chase, one of them overtaking her before she had reached the entrance. He placed his hand upon her arm, while she cried and struggled to free herself. The hood fell over her shoulders, and in the light from a lantern, hung upon a projecting crane from one of the houses, St. Hilaire recognized Madame d'Arlincourt.

The exertion to free herself from the man's grasp had caused her hair to fall down upon her shoulders. Her blue eyes had a wild look like those of a person whose mind is strained almost to madness. She fought fiercely for her freedom.

A dove striking its pinions against a lion's paw could have been able to effect its release as quickly as the poor little countess from the huge hand that held her.

St. Hilaire was as gallant a gentleman as ever drew a sword, or raised a lady's fingers to his lips. On the instant, he forgot his own danger and the cause of his flight, and stepped forward into the circle of light.

"How now, citizen? What have you to do with this young citizeness?" he cried out in distinct tones.

In his surprise at St. Hilaire's sudden appearance, the man loosened his grasp upon Madame d'Arlincourt's shoulder. With a cry she flew instantly to St. Hilaire's side for protection.

"Defend me, sir, oh, save me from them!" she cried, catching hold of his arm.

" I will not let them harm a hair of your head,"
he whispered in reply ; " calm yourself, my dear
madame."

The quiet way in which he spoke seemed to
bring back some part of her self-control.   She
ceased crying and stood by his side like a statue,
although he could feel by the pressure on his arm
that she still trembled.

" Well, citizen, what would you with this citizeness ? " repeated St. Hilaire in a loud voice, as
the other men came up behind their comrade.

" Her actions are suspicious ; she may be an
aristocrat.   We want to bring her to the Section
for examination," answered one of them.

" Let her come to the Section," echoed another.

The fellow who had first laid hands upon the
countess now recovered speech.   " If she 's an
aristocrat here 's at her ; I 've killed many an aristocrat in my day."   As he spoke he drew himself
together and raising his musket leveled it at the
woman's head.

The countess tightened her grasp on St. Hilaire's
arm with both her hands, rendering him powerless
for the moment.

St. Hilaire pushed her gently behind him, and
looking straight into his opponent's face, said
firmly : —

" She shall certainly go to the Section, citizen,
but first put down your weapon and let me speak.
I am Citizen St. Hilaire — were we in the Faubourg St. Michel almost anybody would be able to
tell you who I am."

"I know you, citizen!" exclaimed one of the men in the rear, "and you should know me also. My name is Gonflou!" and the fellow grinned good-naturedly over the shoulder of his companion, as if he recognized an old friend.

"Ah yes, good citizen Gonflou!" repeated St. Hilaire. "Restrain the ardor of this patriot who handles his musket so carelessly, while I question the little citizeness."

"Lower that musket, Haillon, or I'll beat your head with this," said Gonflou, rattling his heavy sabre threateningly.

Haillon muttered an oath and lowered the muzzle of his weapon.

"We can't be all night at this," he growled. "Better let me take a shot at the woman; she's an aristocrat, that's flat."

St. Hilaire bent over the countess.

"Release my arm!" She obeyed like a child. Stepping back with her a couple of paces, he continued: —

"Who is in the house you have just come out of? Answer me truthfully and fearlessly."

She looked up into his face, and he saw that she now recognized him as she answered in a whisper, "My husband. He is ill. I could only venture out after midnight to summon a physician who is known to us."

"Well," exclaimed Haillon, impatiently grinding the butt of his gun on the pavement, "how long does it take to find out about an aristocrat?"

"She was going to summon a doctor to attend a sick father," said St. Hilaire without looking at Haillon.

"Bah," growled the latter.

"Right behind us," continued St. Hilaire, in a very low voice, and looking into the countess' face earnestly to enforce his words, "is a passage-way that leads to the Rue d'Arcis."

Madame d'Arlincourt nodded. She understood.

"When I next begin to talk to these men, you must go through that passage to the house opposite. It is number seven. You will not be able to see the number, but it is directly opposite; you cannot mistake it. Knock seven times in quick succession. Some one will inquire from within, 'Who knocks?' You must reply 'From Raphael.' Do you understand?"

"Yes," said the countess.

"You are taking up too much of our time, citizen," interrupted Haillon, "let me take a hand at questioning."

"Be silent, Haillon;" said St. Hilaire in a tone of quick authority.

"The door will be opened without further question. Once inside you must tell them that you were sent by Raphael, and that they are to keep you until it is safe for you to return to your own domicile. Now remember!—as soon as I enter into conversation with these men."

"I can remember," replied the countess, "but what are you going to do after that? Will they not harm you?"

St. Hilaire laughed lightly. " Oh, I will take care of that. I expect to follow you in a few minutes." Then he turned and advanced a few steps in order to cover her retreat more fully.

" The citizeness has convinced me that she is nothing but a poor sewing-girl in great distress at the illness of her father. I have told her that she might continue on her errand for a doctor un-molested. You are over-zealous, good Haillon, to see an aristocrat in every shadow."

" She has disappeared," cried Gonflou.

Haillon raised his musket with finger on the trigger. St. Hilaire's hand struck upward just as the detonation echoed through the quiet street. Then the smoke, clearing away, revealed Haillon upon the pavement, while the sword in St. Hilaire's hand was red with blood.

" He has killed a citizen," bellowed Gonflou. "Comrades, cut him down. Avenge the death of a patriot."

Three sabres were uplifted against the citizen St. Hilaire. He drew back a pace or two and with a smile upon his lips warded off the blows aimed at his head and breast. Then he poised himself and set his face firmly. The sword which had first won renown on the field of Rocroy now flashed in the light of the flickering lamp of the passage d'Arcis, and another of his assailants fell to the ground.

The wrist that wielded it was just as supple and the white fingers that held the jeweled hilt just as strong as when, in the days gone by, the Mar-

quis de St. Hilaire was known as the best swords-
man in his regiment.

His two remaining adversaries hesitated in their
attack for a moment. Then Gonflou, bleeding
from two deep wounds and bellowing like an angry
bull, sprang at him again with his heavy sabre
lifted in both hands.

One of the two fallen men had half raised himself and dragged over to where Haillon lay. He
drew a pistol from the dead man's belt and, leaning forward, fired under Gonflou's arm. The blow
from Gonflou's sabre was parried, then Jean Raphael de St. Hilaire fell forward on his face and
lay without moving upon the pavement, while the
sword of Rocroy fell ringing to the ground.

One of the attacking party was still unhurt.
He raised his weapon over the prostrate body at
his feet. Gonflou pushed him aside roughly.
"That's enough, citizen. We'll take him to the
Section without cutting him up." The man who
had fired the shot had since busied himself with
tying up his own wounded arm. He now bent
over St. Hilaire. "He still breathes," he said.
"Had we not better finish him?"

"No, my little Jacques Gardin," was Gonflou's
answer, who, the moment the fight was over, became as good-natured as before; "let us take him
to the Section."

"But he has killed Haillon," persisted young
Jacques, who had reloaded the pistol and was
handling it lovingly.

"Pah," replied Gonflou, with a laugh, "Haillon

should have been careful when playing with edged tools. Come, citizens, take hold and we'll carry them both to the Section. You may take your choice, Citizen Ferrand, the corpse or the dying man. I'll carry either of them, and little Jacques shall run ahead. Forward, march, comrades."

CHAPTER XIV

SOMETHING HIDDEN

"COLONEL ROBERT TOURNAY, you are summoned before the Committee of Public Safety!" Silence followed this call. The clerk repeated his summons. Again silence.

"I move," said one of the members, "that the examination proceed. The citizen colonel was summoned and has not appeared. If he is not here to defend himself, that is his affair, not ours."

"Citizen Bernard Gardin," said the president, "repeat to the committee the result of your interview with the Citizen Tournay."

Gardin rose. "The said citizen, Colonel Tournay, refused to recognize the mandate of the Committee of Public Safety. The commissioners sent to apprehend his person were treated with marked disrespect and expelled from the camp with insult." Gardin spoke the words with bitter emphasis.

Without even looking at him, Danton interrupted the witness. "The citizen colonel pleaded that an impending battle made it necessary for him to remain in the field, did he not?"

"He did make some such excuse," sneered Gardin.

"Instead of refusing to obey the summons, the citizen colonel stated that, the battle once decided, he would hasten to Paris, did he not?" continued Danton, lifting his voice and turning his eyes full upon Gardin.

"He did say he would come at some future time," admitted Gardin, "but he refused to obey the summons which called upon him to return with the commissioners."

"And thereby insulted the committee," said Couthon.

"If the committee recalls our officers from the field upon the eve of battle they must expect our armies to be defeated," Danton remarked dryly. "Colonel Tournay refused to obey the letter of the summons and remained at his post of duty. The French armies have just won a glorious victory at Wissembourg in which the accused distinguished himself by great bravery and devotion to the Republic. I move that when he does appear he receive the thanks of this committee in the name of France."

"Do you advocate rewarding him for his disobedience and his indifference to our authority?" inquired President Robespierre.

"I believe that victories are more important to France at this juncture, citizen president, than any slight disregard of the letter of the committee's authority."

Robespierre shut his thin lips together and turned to St. Just.

"Let us proceed with the inquiry," he said after

a moment's consultation. "Clerk, call the other witnesses."

"Are you not going to give Colonel Tournay twelve hours longer in which to appear in person?" persisted Danton.

"Of what use would that be?" asked Couthon. "He will not come within twelve months."

"Let the inquiry proceed," commanded the president impatiently.

As if to show his indifference to the proceedings, Danton rose from his seat, yawned, and then strolled to the window. As he did so, a sudden shout rose from a crowd gathered below. Danton bent forward and looked out into the street to ascertain the cause.

The door swung open and Colonel Tournay entered the room. He was followed by many of the crowd. The news of the great victory of the French armies on the frontier had just reached Paris and stirred it with enthusiasm. The people in the streets had caught sight of his uniform and surmising that he had just come from the scene of war pressed about him closely, crying for details of the battle. Some had recognized him personally and called out his name. The great crowd had taken it up, and cheered wildly for one of the heroes of Wissembourg and Landau.

There was a flush of excitement on his cheek and a sparkle in his eye as he stepped forward.

"I understand that I am called before this committee to answer certain charges," he said in a clear ringing voice. "What is the accusation? I am here to answer it."

The crowd outside the door took up the shout.

" Yes, of what is the citizen colonel accused?
Who accuses the hero of Landau?"

Robespierre changed color and hesitated. Danton eyed the president with a sneer upon his lips, which he made no attempt to conceal. The breach between the two men had widened to such an extent that it had become a matter of common gossip.

" You are accused of winning a battle," said Danton with a laugh, — " a rare event in these days."

Robespierre turned and whispered to St. Just. The latter answered Tournay.

" There are three charges against you," he said. " First, you are accused of having been concerned in the rescue of a certain Citizeness de Rochefort from prison boat number four on the River Loire. Secondly, of escorting the said Citizeness de Rochefort across France under a false name. Thirdly, of having insulted the authority of four commissioners sent by the Committee of Public Safety to arrest you. These accusations have been preferred against you before this committee, which feels called upon to investigate them carefully. If they decide that there is sufficient evidence to warrant it, they will bring the case before the Revolutionary Tribunal. Now that you have heard the charges, I ask you: Do you wish to employ counsel?"

" With the permission of the committee I leave my case in the hands of a member of the convention, Citizen Danton," said Tournay.

"Call the first witness," said St. Just.

"Citizen Lebœuf to the stand," cried the clerk.

The bulky form of Lebœuf lumbered forward. His face was red and his eyes heavy. His testimony was given hesitatingly, as if he were endeavoring to conceal some of the facts. He deposed that the accused, Tournay, had assisted in rescuing the Citizeness de Rochefort from the prison boat number four on the River Loire on the fifth Nivose. Cross-examined by Danton, he admitted reluctantly that he could not swear to the identity of the accused, but felt certain it was he. It was a man of just his height and general appearance; he had good reason to know that the citizen colonel was much interested in the fate of the Citizeness de Rochefort.

Danton dismissed him with a contemptuous wave of the hand, and Lebœuf retired, outwardly discomfited and purple of face, yet with a certain inward sense of relief that the examination was over.

"The citizen colonel admits that he escorted a woman to the frontier," Danton went on, "but it was under a passport issued by the Committee of Public Safety. It has not been proven that this woman was the escaped prisoner, Citizeness de Rochefort. He also admits having refused to accompany the commissioners to Paris, and having expelled them from his camp. For this act of discourtesy to the committee he offers an apology, and pleads in extenuation that it was on the eve of a battle in which his presence was necessary to our armies."

Robespierre turned to St. Just and Couthon. They held an animated discussion, during which both the latter were seen to remonstrate. Finally at a signal from the president, the entire committee withdrew for consultation.

Tournay glanced about the room. He knew that he had the interest and sympathy of most who were present, and from the manner in which the inquiry had been conducted, he felt little anxiety as to the result.

He had not long to wait before the members of the committee entered the room and took their places.

The president touched the bell. St. Just rose, and speaking with apparent reluctance said : —

" The committee do not find sufficient evidence to warrant the trial of Colonel Robert Tournay upon the charge of treason to the Republic."

A cheer rang through the room, which was re-echoed in the corridor and out into the street beyond.

The president touched his bell sharply. St. Just continued : —

" The committee relieves Colonel Tournay from his command for the present. He will await here in Paris the orders of the committee in regard to returning to the army. The inquiry is now ended, and the meeting adjourns."

Tournay walked out of the court accompanied by Danton and through the street to his friend's lodgings, followed by an admiring crowd cheering the hero of Landau.

Two incidents took place in quick succession during the short walk to Danton's house.

These incidents had no relation to each other, yet they both gave Tournay the uncomfortable sensation that besets a man when he is contending with unknown or secret forces.

In passing by the Jacobin Club he saw a man enter at the door. He could not see the face, but the figure and movements were so much like those of de Lacheville that had he not felt sure that it would be equivalent to the marquis's death-sentence for him to be found in Paris, he would have been certain it was his enemy. The idea was so unlikely, however, that he dismissed it from his mind.

As they passed down the Rue des Cordelières and reached the door of Danton's house, a man, issuing from the crowd, brushed closely against Tournay's shoulder. In doing so the colonel felt a letter slipped into his hand. "From a friend," sounded in his ear. "Examine it when alone." Tournay mechanically put the paper in his pocket, and followed Danton into the house, upon the giant uttering the laconic invitation : —

"Come in."

"You have not said a word about the prompt dismissal of the charges against me," said Tournay, as they entered the dingy room which served Danton for office as well as salon.

The giant threw off his coat and filled his pipe. Taking a seat he began to smoke rapidly.

"There is more behind it," he said.

" What do you mean ? "

" Did you not notice that no attempt was made
to convict you ? "

" I did, but I attributed it to lack of evidence
on their part."

" Lack of evidence ! " repeated Danton. " They
are capable of manufacturing that when needed."

" I confess I thought it possible that the popularity of the army with the people had something
to do with it."

Danton smiled pityingly.

" I tell you that there is something behind it all.
I cannot account for Robespierre's sudden change.
It was he who directed your acquittal. There is
something behind all this. He works in the dark,
and secretly. Tournay, I mistrust that man as
much as I hate him," and he began to smoke violently.

" Why do you not crush him, Jacques ? " asked
Tournay coolly.

" Ay, that's the question I often ask myself,"
said Danton, lifting up his mighty arm and looking
at it, smiling grimly the while as if he were thinking of Robespierre's sallow face and puny body.

" If you don't crush him, he will sting you to
death," added Tournay impressively, as he rose to
go.

Danton doubled up his arm once more till the
muscles swelled into great knots upon it. " Ha,
ha," he laughed, " I don't fear that, Tournay; he's
too much of a coward to lay hands upon me."

" Do you never fear for your own safety when

you see so many falling beneath the hand of this man who rules France?" asked Tournay.

Danton started at the words "rules France."

"Yes, he does rule France. He rules the tribunal. He rules me, curse him! But as for fearing him, Jacques Danton fears nothing in this world or the next."

"Good-night," said Tournay shortly. "But remember, Jacques, you, of all men, can crush the tyrant if you will."

"Good-night," said Danton, placing his huge hand on Tournay's shoulder. "Be assured that Robespierre is holding something back. There is something behind the mask. Be prepared."

Tournay laughed. "I cannot, perhaps, say unreservedly that I fear nothing in this world or the next, Jacques, but be assured, I do not fear him." And he walked away with head erect and military swing, toward the Rue des Mathurins. Danton resumed his pipe, muttering to himself like some volcano rumbling inwardly,—

"Jacques, you can crush him if you will!"

CHAPTER XV

THE PRESIDENT'S NOTE

As Tournay entered the doorway of 15 Rue des Mathurins an excited little man brushed quickly past him, muttered an apology, and ran hurriedly up the street. Under his arm he carried a handsome coat.

"I'll wager that's some thief who has been plying his trade upstairs," thought Tournay. "It was clumsy on my part to let him get by me. But I'm too tired to run after him. He can wear his stolen finery for all me." And he climbed up the stairs to the fourth landing.

"Welcome, my general!" cried Gaillard, rising up and throwing to one side the theatrical costume into which he was neatly fitting a patch.

"Not general yet, my little Gaillard," was the reply, as the two friends embraced warmly.

"How? Not a general yet?" exclaimed the actor. "Why, all the city is ringing with news of the victory of Wissembourg and the hero of Landau!"

"That may be, my friend, but I have not received my promotion, and, what is more, I am not expecting it. I shall be quite satisfied to have the convention send me to the front again, where there is work to be done."

"Bah! Is the convention mad that it overlooks our bravest and best officer?" exclaimed Gaillard in a tone of disgust.

"Wait until you have heard what I have to tell you, and then say whether I shall not be fortunate if permitted to return to my command, even if it be but one regiment."

"Danton is right," said Gaillard, when the colonel had finished his account of the day's proceedings. "Undoubtedly there is something behind all this; what it is, the future will show."

"In the mean time let us have something to eat," said Tournay; "I am as hungry as a wolf. Is there any food in the house?"

"An unusual supply," was Gaillard's answer. "We will dine in your honor, colonel, and though the convention has not seen fit to adorn your brow with laurels, I will make some amends by pledging your health in a glass of wine as good as any that can be found in Paris to-day."

"I shall be pleased to eat a dinner in any one's honor, for I have eaten nothing since daylight, and it is now four o'clock."

"Sit down for one moment then, while I take a few last stitches in my work here. I had expected to wear a new costume in the piece to-night, 'Le Mariage de Figaro,' but the tailor brought a garment that fitted abominably, and to the insult of a grotesque fit he added the injury of an exorbitant bill, so I refused the coat and dismissed him with an admonition."

"I must have encountered your tailor as I came

up," said Tournay. "He was very pressed for time, and seemed to have taken your admonition much to heart."

"Not exactly to heart," replied Gaillard, his mouth widening with a grin, "for I emphasized my remarks rather forcibly with my shoe. I kicked him down one flight of stairs, and he ran down the others."

"I am afraid your dramatic nature causes you to be rather precipitate at times, Gaillard," remarked Colonel Tournay, smiling.

"On this occasion all the precipitation was on the part of the tailor," replied Gaillard. "Well, this old costume is mended ; it will have to serve me for a few nights. Now for dinner. Take your place at the table. I shall sit at the head, and you, as the guest, shall occupy the place at my right hand. You will excuse me for one moment, will you not, while I serve the repast?" and before Tournay could answer Gaillard had left the room.

Tournay seated himself at the table, and took from his pocket the letter which had been placed in his hands on the street. It was addressed in a large hand to "Citizen Colonel Robert Tournay." The writing was that of a person who evidently wielded the pen but occasionally, and he could not be sure whether it came from a man or woman. He broke the seal and read : —

CITIZEN COLONEL, — Your attitude toward some of the members of the Convention has made you a number of enemies. Do not take the dis-

missal of the charges brought against you before
the committee as an evidence that these enemies
are defeated; they have merely resolved to change
their tactics during your present popularity. Had
you been defeated at Wissembourg and Landau,
you would not now be at liberty. You may be
sure these men have your ultimate downfall in
view. Distrust them all.

Tournay ran his eyes hastily over a list of a
dozen names, among which were Couthon, St. Just,
and Collot-d'Herbois.

"Here it is, hot and succulent from the kitchen
of Citizeness Ribot," called out Gaillard, appearing from an inner room with a steaming dish,
which he placed before him. "What have you
got there?" he asked, blowing on his fingers to
cool them.

Tournay handed him the paper. "All of them
either friends or tools of Robespierre," was Gaillard's comment. "How did this come into your
hands?"

Tournay told him. His friend stepped to the
fireplace.

"What are you going to do?" inquired Tournay.

"I make it a point never to keep anything with
writing on it. It may be a tradition of my profession, for on the stage trouble always lurks in
written documents. We must burn this."

"Do not be so hasty, Gaillard; you may burn it
after I have committed those names to memory."

"Then I will put it here on the chimney-piece for the present. Don't carry it about you. It is a dangerous paper in times like these."

"Very well, I will be guided by your counsels. And just at this moment you advise dining, do you not?" and Tournay turned to the dish on the table. "It has a very agreeable odor. What is it?"

"The menu, to-day, consists of three courses; bread, salt, and," — here the actor removed the cover of the dish with a flourish — "rabbit ragout."

"Will you assure me that the rabbit did not mew at the prospect of being turned into a ragout?" inquired Tournay, holding out his plate while Gaillard heaped it with the stew.

"You will have to ask the cook, my little wargod. When I delivered to her the material in its natural state it consisted of two little gray tailless animals with long ears; but to exonerate her, I call your attention to the house-cat at this moment poking her nose in at the door. And let me say further, that whether it be cat or rabbit you seem to be able to dispose of a goodly quantity of it."

"My dear Gaillard, I am a soldier and can eat anything," was Tournay's rejoinder.

"But cast not your eyes longingly upon the poor animal who has come in attracted by the smell of dinner; she is my especial pet. Let me divert your attention from her by pouring you a glass of wine."

"Gaillard, your dinner is most excellent; your pet shall be safe."

Gaillard filled two glasses with wine.

"Your very good health, Colonel Tournay, of the Army of the Moselle."

"Yours, my dear friend Gaillard."

The two friends rose and touched glasses over the little table.

"That wine is wonderful," said Tournay as he put down the glass. "What do you mean by drinking such nectar? Do you live so near the top of the house in order that you may spend your savings on your wine cellar?"

"That bottle is one of six presented to me by our neighbor, Citizen St. Hilaire. He has been living modestly in the attic overhead, but he evidently had a knowledge of good wine."

"Ah, Citizen St. Hilaire," repeated Tournay. "He is a man who should well know good wine; but you said he has been living overhead. Is he not there now?"

"Three days ago he disappeared. He left a note for the Citizeness Ribot with the money due for rent, and stated that he should not return. His action was explained next morning when a gendarme from the section made his appearance and inquired for Citizen St. Hilaire. Since then his chamber is watched night and day. I doubt if he returns."

"He is quite capable of keeping out of danger or getting into it, as the fancy suits him, if he is the man I once knew," remarked Tournay.

Gaillard filled the glasses again. "Let us not talk about him in too loud a tone," he said, "but quietly pledge him in his own Burgundy."

Tournay took the proffered glass. The gentle
gurgle down two throats told that St. Hilaire's
health was drunk fervently if silently.

"With your permission I will propose a toast,"
said Tournay, as Gaillard emptied the last of the
bottle into their glasses. The actor nodded.

"To the French Republic," exclaimed Tournay.
"May victory still perch upon her banners."

"To the Republic," echoed Gaillard.

Again the glasses clinked over the small wooden
table.

"As long as we have victory," continued Tournay, "what care we whether we be colonels, generals, or soldiers of the line? Our victories are
the nation's. All are sharers in its glory."

"Long live the Republic!" they cried in concert, and set down their empty wineglasses.

"Now I must fly to the theatre," exclaimed
Gaillard; "you have made me late with your re-
publics " —

"And I must to bed," said Tournay. "This
morning's dawn found me in the saddle in order
to reach the convention at an early hour."

"You have made a mistake, citizen sergeant,"
exclaimed Gaillard suddenly, as an officer of gendarmerie appeared at the open door. "The floor
above is where you want to go."

"I want to see the Citizen Colonel Tournay,"
was the reply.

"I am he," said Tournay.

The sergeant awkwardly gave the military salute. "Here is a letter for you, citizen colonel."

Tournay took the paper, and the sergeant turned toward the door.

"Is there any answer required?" asked Tournay, as he broke the seal.

"None through me. Good-night, citizen colonel." And the heavy jack-boots were heard descending the stairs.

Gaillard began hurriedly to make a bundle of his theatrical costume, while Tournay broke the seal and glanced over the contents of the letter.

"Read this," he said, passing the paper to Gaillard, who stood by his side, bundle under arm.

Gaillard read : —

To CITIZEN COLONEL ROBERT TOURNAY, Rue des Mathurins 15.

Will the patriotic citizen colonel call upon the humble and none the less patriotic citizen, Maximilian Robespierre, this evening at seven, to discuss affairs pertaining to the good of the nation? If the Citizen Tournay can come, no answer need be sent.

(Signed) MAXIMILIAN ROBESPIERRE.

17th Pluviose, Year II. of the French
    Republic, one and indivisible.

"He evidently takes it for granted that I will come, for his messenger waited for no answer," added Tournay.

"It's the sequel of this afternoon's inquiry," said Gaillard, as he returned it, "and too exquisitely polite for a plain citizen. What are you going to do?"

"I am going to see him, of course," replied Tournay. "It is the only way to find out what he wants."

Gaillard nodded. "That's true; I almost feel like going with you and remaining outside the door," and Gaillard placed his package on the table.

"That is unnecessary, my friend; I never felt more secure in my life. Go to your performance of Figaro and on your return you will find me here in this easy-chair, smoking one of your pipes."

Gaillard took up his bundle again. "Very well, but mind, if I do not find you seated in that arm-chair smoking a pipe I shall know you are in trouble."

Tournay laughed. "You will find me there, never fear. And now let us go out together."

"I am abominably late!" exclaimed Gaillard, as they parted at the corner. "The director will have the pleasure of collecting a fine from my weekly salary. Good-night — embrace me, my little war god! Au revoir," and the actor hurried down the street, whistling cheerfully.

CHAPTER XVI

BENEATH THE MASK

AN atmosphere of secrecy seemed to pervade Robespierre's house, and Tournay, following the servant along the dimly lighted corridor, passed his hand over his eyes, as one brushes away the fine cobwebs that come across the face in going through the woods.

The rustle of a gown fell upon his ear as he entered the salon, and at the further end of the apartment he saw a woman who had evidently risen at his entrance, and now stood irresolute, with one hand on the latch of a door leading into an adjoining room, as if she had intended making her exit unobserved by him.

She stood in such a manner that the shadow of the half-open door fell across her face, but he could see that she was a young woman of small stature and well proportioned figure. At the sound of his voice she allowed her hand to fall from the latch, then lifting her head erect, walked toward him.

"La Liberté!" ejaculated Tournay. He had not seen her since the day he had left her dancing on the cannon-truck, winecup in hand; but she still kept her girlish look, and except in her dress she had not greatly changed.

She still showed a partiality for bright colors, by her gown of deep crimson. But the material was of velvet instead of the simple woolen stuff she used to wear. Her hair, which had once curled about her forehead and been tossed about by the wind, was now coiled upon her head, from which a few locks, as if rebellious at confinement, had fallen on her neck and shoulders. She wore nothing on her head but a tricolored knot of ribbon, the color of the Republic.

"How does it happen that we meet here?" asked Tournay after a moment, during which he had gazed at her in surprise.

"Never mind about me for the present," she said, looking up in his face, half defiantly, half admiringly; for as he stood before her, framed in the open door, he was a striking picture, with his handsome, bronzed face and brilliant uniform.

"Let us speak of your affairs," she continued. "I am told the committee has ordered you to await its permission before returning to the army."

"How did you know that?" he demanded in surprise.

"Oh, I know many things that are going on in this strange world," and she gave the old toss of her head. "Now do not talk, but listen. You must return to the army. A soldier like you is at a disadvantage among these intriguers. They will suspect you for the simple reason that they suspect every one. You, who are accustomed to fight openly, will fall a victim to their wiles."

"My enemies may find that I can strike back," said Tournay quietly.

La Liberté shrugged her shoulders.

"Did you receive a letter this afternoon?" she asked quickly.

"Did you write that letter?"

"I never write letters," she answered significantly; "but if you received one and read it, you know the names of some of your enemies. What can you do with such an array against you? I repeat, you are no match for them. You must go back to your command."

"That is what I desire above all else," answered Tournay.

"You can go to-morrow, if you wish," said the demoiselle.

"How?"

"By listening to what the president of the committee has to say to you, and agreeing to it. Yield to his demands, whatever they may be, and you will be permitted to set out to-morrow."

"I shall be glad to meet the committee more than halfway. I will agree to everything they wish, if I can do so consistently."

"Consistently!" she repeated. "I see you will be obstinate." Then she stopped and looked full in his face. "I might know that you would after all only act according to your convictions, and that any advice would be thrown away on you. Well, I must say I like you better that way, and were I a man I should do the same."

She placed one hand upon her hip where hung

a small poniard suspended by a silver chain about her waist, and went on earnestly: "But listen to this word of advice. You, who have been so long absent from Paris, do not realize Robespierre's power. It is sometimes the part of a brave man to yield. Give way to him as much as your *consistency* will permit. Now adieu." She turned away; then facing him suddenly with an impulsive gesture she came toward him.

"Compatriot!" she said with an unwonted tremble in her voice, "will you take my hand?" He took the hand extended to him.

"I do not forget, Marianne, that you and I both came from La Thierry. If ever you are in need of a friend, you can rely upon me."

For one moment the brown head was bent over his hand, and La Liberté showed an emotion which none of those who thought they knew her would have believed possible. Then throwing back her head she disappeared through the door beyond, as Robespierre entered from the corridor.

Much absorbed in his meditations, Robespierre did not appear to notice that any one had just quitted the room. He walked very slowly as if to impress Tournay with his greatness, and did not speak for some moments. He no longer affected the great simplicity of dress which had characterized him at the beginning of the Revolution, and the coat of blue velvet, waistcoat of white silk, and buff breeches which he wore were quite in keeping with his fine linen shirt and the laces of his ruffles.

It was Tournay who first broke the silence.

"Citizen president, you see I have been prompt to comply with your request; I am here in answer to your summons."

Robespierre raised his head, and started from his soliloquy.

"Ah yes, you are the citizen colonel who appeared to-day before the committee to answer certain charges."

"I am," replied Tournay.

"Citizen colonel," said Robespierre, "I will be perfectly frank with you. The Committee of Public Safety, whose dearest wish, whose only thought, is the welfare of the Republic," here the president's small eyes blinked in rapid succession, "is not quite satisfied with the condition of affairs in the army."

"I am sorry to hear that, citizen president, and in behalf of the army, I would call the committee's attention to the recent battles in which the soldiers of France have certainly borne themselves with great bravery. I speak now as one of their officers who is justly proud of them."

"It is not the conduct of the soldiers of which the committee finds cause of complaint," replied Robespierre, "but of their generals."

"It is not for me to criticise my superior officers," said Tournay. "I leave that to the nation."

"The committee has good reason to criticise the attitude of certain of its generals, who seem to have forgotten that they are merely citizens. They have been chosen to serve the Republic only for a

time in a more exalted position than their fellow
citizens, yet they have become swollen with pride,
and take to themselves the credit of the victories
won by their armies.   Their dispatches to the convention are couched in arrogant and sometimes
insolent language."

Tournay bowed.   " Again I must refrain from
expressing my opinion on such a matter," he said.

" Ever since the treason of General Dumouriez," Robespierre went on, " the committee has
had its suspicions as to the conduct of several of
its generals.   Hoche is one."

Tournay started.

" What you are pleased to impart to me, citizen
president, sounds strange.   Permit me to state
that I feel sure the committee's suspicions are
unfounded."

Robespierre looked at him closely.   " Does
General Hoche take you into his entire confidence ? " he inquired quickly ; his weak eyes
blinking more rapidly than ever.

" No, I am merely a colonel in his army.
Though I have good reason to believe he places
confidence in me, he naturally does not inform me
of his plans before they are matured."

" Citizen colonel, the committee also places
great confidence in you, and for that reason it
wishes you to return at once to the army."

" I obey its orders with the greatest pleasure in
the world," said Tournay.

" The committee also desires," Robespierre
continued, " that you send to its secretary each

week a minute report of everything that passes under your notice, particularly as regards the actions of Citizen General Hoche. Do not regard anything as too trifling to be included in your report; the committee will pass upon its importance."

Tournay had listened in silence. His teeth ground together in the rage he struggled to suppress. He felt that if he made a movement it would be to strike the president to the floor.

"I must decline the commission with which the committee honors me. I am not fitted for it," he replied.

"The committee has chosen you as eminently fitted for the work. The confidence that General Hoche places in you makes you the best agent the committee could employ."

"Then tell your committee, citizen president, that it must find some less fitting agent to do its dirty work. My business is to fight the enemies of France, not to spy upon its patriots."

Robespierre's sallow face became a shade more yellow. "Have a care how you speak of the committee. In the service of the Republic all employment is sacred and honorable."

"I prefer my own interpretation of the words," answered Tournay, with a look of scorn.

"And yet you yourself have somewhat strange ideas of what is honorable," remarked Robespierre sneeringly.

"I do not understand what you mean," replied Tournay.

Robespierre stepped to the wall and pulled the bell-rope. "Perhaps when it is made clear to you, your mind may change."

The colonel made no reply, but the next moment uttered an exclamation of surprise as the Marquis de Lacheville entered the room. Robespierre turned toward Tournay with the shadow of a smile hovering on his thin lips.

"You know this citizen?" he asked in his harsh voice.

Tournay looked at the marquis curiously, wondering why he had jeopardized his own safety by returning to Paris. The look of hatred which the nobleman shot at him served as an explanation.

"I know him as a former nobleman, an emigré, who is proscribed by the Republic; I wonder that he puts his life in danger by returning to the land he fled from."

The marquis made an uneasy gesture, and was about to speak when Robespierre said: —

"He has taken the oath of allegiance to the Republic."

Tournay laughed outright at this. "And do you trust his oath?" he asked.

"And for the service he now renders the nation, his emigration and the fact of his having been an aristocrat are to be condoned." As he spoke, a grim smile hovered about Robespierre's lips. It faded away instantly, leaving his face as mirthless and forbidding as before.

"Shall we ask the Citizen Lacheville to tell us when he last saw you?" he went on sternly.

"It is unnecessary. We met last at Falzenberg," said Tournay, eyeing him with disdain.

"Where you were on terms of intimacy with Prussian officers," said de Lacheville. "I will not dwell upon the fact of your having assisted an aristocrat to escape from prison; but I will testify to your having come in disguise to the enemies of France and entered into a secret understanding with them. I was serving those same enemies at the time, I will admit," and the marquis shrugged his shoulders, "but as the Citizen Robespierre has said, I have repented of it, and have come here to make atonement by faithful devotion to the nation. One of the greatest of my pleasures is to help unmask a hypocrite."

Tournay addressed Robespierre.

"Do you believe this man's story?"

"You have already admitted having gone over the frontier," was the suave rejoinder.

"I did go, yes."

"Will you deny having been closeted alone with General von Waldenmeer?"

"No, but" —

"Do you suppose any tribunal in the land would hold you guiltless upon such testimony and such admissions?"

"Permit me to ask you two questions," said Tournay.

Robespierre acquiesced.

"Admitting that this — *citizen's* accusation is true, why did I return to Wissembourg and do my best to defeat the enemy with whom I am accused by him of being on friendly terms?"

"There are hundreds of similar precedents — Dumouriez's, for example."

"Admitting, then, that I have already been false to one trust, how is it that you are prepared to trust me now to play the spy for your committee?" continued Tournay, with contempt ringing in his voice.

Again the peculiar smile flitted across Robespierre's pale features.

"All men are to be trusted as far as their self-interest leads them," he answered. "None are to be trusted implicitly. You will be watched closely and will doubtless prove faithful. It will be to your decided advantage to attend to the committee's business efficiently. Your little interview with the Prussian general, from which nothing has resulted, may be forgotten for the time."

Tournay's anger during the interview had several times risen to white heat. Not even his sense of danger enabled him longer to repress it.

"I have already told you that I would have nothing to do with the commission of your committee!" he cried hotly. "And as for this man's accusations, let him make them in court and I will answer him. Let him repeat them in the streets and I will thrust the lies back into his throat and choke him with them." As he spoke he advanced toward de Lacheville who paled and retreated a step or two. "If any man accuses me of disloyalty to the Republic," continued Tournay, turning and addressing Robespierre, "unless he takes revenge behind the bar of a tribunal he shall answer

to me personally.   I will defend my honor with
my own hand."

Robespierre turned pale and took a step or two
in the direction of the bell-rope.

"You may have an opportunity to answer the
charges before the tribunal," he said coldly.

"Why did you not bring them in to-day's inquiry?" demanded Tournay.

"I do not announce my reasons nor divulge my
plans," was the reply.   "It is enough to know
that I had need of you.   Neither am I in the
habit of having my will opposed.   You would do
best to yield before it is too late."

"Robespierre," cried Tournay, the blood mounting to his forehead, "you have played the tyrant
too long!   You are not 'in the habit of having
your will opposed?'   I have not learned to bend
and truckle to your will, doing your bidding like
a dog; and, by Heaven! I will not now.   Bring
your charges against me before your tribunal,
packed as it is with your creatures, and I will answer them, but my answer shall be addressed to
the Nation.   My appeal will be to the People.   I
will denounce you for what you are, a tyrant.
And a coward — too" — he continued, as Robespierre, with ashen lips, rang the bell violently.
"You shall be known for what you are, and when
you are once known the people will cease to fear
you."

He strode toward the committee's president,
who, with trembling knees, stood tugging at the
bell-rope.   De Lacheville had long since fled from

the room; and Robespierre, pulling his courage
together with an effort, lifted his hand and pointed
a trembling finger at Tournay.

"Stop where you are!" he shrieked. "Come
a step nearer me at your peril!"

"I am not going to do you any injury," was
Tournay's reply in a tone of contempt; "I despise
you too much to do you personal violence; I leave
you to your fears, citizen president."

There was a sound of heavy footsteps in the
corridor, and Tournay moved toward the door to
be confronted by a file of soldiers.

"Henriot, you drunken snail," cried Robespierre, "why did you not answer my summons?
Arrest this man."

Tournay turned a look upon Robespierre which
made the latter quail notwithstanding the guard
that surrounded him.

"You had this all arranged," said the colonel
quietly.

"I was prepared," replied Robespierre grimly.

Tournay turned away with contempt. "Dicta-
tor, your time will be short," he murmured.

"Come, citizen colonel," said the Commandant
Henriot, "I must trouble you for your sword."

"Where are you going to take me?" asked
Tournay as he delivered up his weapon.

Henriot glanced at his chief as if for instructions.

"To the Luxembourg," was the order. Then,
without looking at Tournay, Robespierre left the
room.

"May I send word to a friend at my lodgings?" Tournay asked of Henriot.

"No," was the short rejoinder, "you must come with me on the instant."

In the corridor stood de Lacheville. He smiled triumphantly as he saw Tournay pass out between the file of soldiers.

"De Lacheville," said Tournay scornfully, "you have played the part of a fool as well as a coward. A few days and you also will be in prison."

His guards hurried him on, and he could not hear de Lacheville's answer.

At the doorway that led into the street stood La Liberté.

"Out of the way, citizeness!" growled Henriot.

"Out of the way yourself, Citizen Henriot," was the woman's reply, and she pushed through the soldiers until she stood at Tournay's elbow.

"Come, citizeness, none of that; you cannot speak to the prisoner," growled Henriot a second time.

"I was afraid of this," she whispered in Tournay's ear.

"Will you take a message for me?" he asked in a quick whisper.

"Yes."

"Go to Gaillard, 15 Rue des Mathurins, wait until he comes. Tell him I am arrested. That is all."

With a nod of intelligence, La Liberté left his side and disappeared in the darkness.

CHAPTER XVII

PIERRE AND JEAN

As Gaillard stepped out from the theatre into a dark side street a hand fell upon his right shoulder. He looked around and saw a tall gendarme standing by his side. The prospect did not please him, so he turned to the left and saw another gendarme standing there. This one was short, and stout with a smile on his red face. Then Gaillard stopped.

"Well, citizens of the police," he exclaimed, "I don't need any escort. I can find my way home alone."

"Is your name Gaillard?" asked one.

"I have every reason to believe so," was the reply.

"Actor?" demanded the other.

"Ah, there I am not so certain," he answered.

"How? You do not know your own vocation?"

"My friends say I am an actor, and my enemies dispute it. What is your opinion?"

"I can say you are an actor, for I have seen you act," said the stout gendarme. "And a very good actor you were. You made me laugh heartily."

"Then I shall count you among my friends!" exclaimed Gaillard. "And between friends now, what is it that you want of me?"

" We are going to take you to the Luxembourg."

" What for ? "

" I will read you the warrant," said the tall gendarme. " Come under the light of the lantern yonder."

Gaillard accompanied the two police officers to the other side of the street.

One of them took a large paper from his breast-pocket : —

" Warrant of arrest for the Citizen Gaillard, actor of the theatre of the Republic. Cause: Friend of the Suspect Tournay, and, therefore, to be apprehended."

Gaillard repressed the start that the sight of his friend's name gave him. " ' The Suspect Tournay.' My colonel has been arrested," he said to himself. Then heaving a deep sigh he exclaimed aloud in a pathetic tone of voice : —

" It is very sad to think I should be arrested just as I was going to have such a good part in the new piece at the theatre."

" Was it a funny one ? " inquired the short gendarme.

" Funny ! why if you should hear it, you 'd laugh those big brass buttons off your coat."

" It 's a shame you can't play it," was the sympathetic rejoinder.

" I 'll tell you what you can do," said Gaillard. " Go with me to my house, 15 Rue des Mathurins, and let me fetch the part so that I can study it while in prison; then, if I should be released soon I shall be prepared to play the part."

"It's against our orders," said the tall gendarme. "We must take you at once to the Luxembourg."

"It's very near here," persisted Gaillard, "and I will read one or two of the funniest speeches while we are there."

"It will not take us more than fifteen minutes," interposed the stout gendarme, looking at his mate.

"And when I am released," said Gaillard persuasively, "and play the part, I'll send you each an admission."

"Well," said the tall gendarme, "we'll go."

"You see," explained Gaillard as they walked off in the direction of the Rue des Mathurins, "my arrest is a mistake, that's clear. Whoever heard of an actor being mixed up in politics!"

"That's so," remarked the short gendarme.

"Yes," admitted the long one, "I have arrested many a suspect, and you're the first actor. But I have my duty to perform, and if the warrant calls for an actor, an actor has to come."

"Of course," agreed Gaillard, "you are a man of high principle, as any one can see."

Gaillard knew that as soon as he was arrested his rooms would be searched for any evidence of a suspicious nature. In all the house there was only one document which could possibly compromise either himself or Tournay, and that was the letter his friend had received that same afternoon, and which was now lying upon the chimney-piece.

"Here we are at No. 15; I live on the fourth floor," he said, as they came to the door.

"Whew!" exclaimed the stout gendarme. "You'll have to give us half a dozen of the best jokes if we go way up there."

"You shall have as many as you can stand," answered Gaillard. "Now, citizen officers, mind the angle in the wall, that's it. It's not a hard climb when you're used to it."

"Whew!" exclaimed the stout man as they entered Gaillard's apartment, "I could not climb that every day." He sank down in a chair and mopped the perspiration from his brow.

"I wish I was sure of climbing it every day of my life," said Gaillard. "It's thirsty work, however, so let us have something to refresh ourselves with;" and he took out from the closet a bottle of the choice Burgundy and three glasses.

"Here's to the gendarmerie," he said as he filled the glasses.

A moment later two pairs of lips smacked approvingly in concert.

"That's a vintage for you," said the short gendarme approvingly.

"I never drank but one glass of better wine than this in my life," said the tall gendarme meditatively.

"When was that?" asked Gaillard as he filled the glasses again.

"That was when the Count de Beaujeu's house was sacked, and the citizens threw all the contents of his wine cellar into the street."

"You did not drink a glass that time," remarked the stout gendarme, "you had a hogshead."

The tall man scowled.

" Well, there 's plenty of this," said Gaillard ; " have another glass ? "

" We will," said both of the gendarmes. " Let us have a few of the funny lines of your new part, citizen actor," said the stout gendarme swallowing his third glass of Burgundy.

" Willingly ! " exclaimed Gaillard. He turned toward the chimney-piece and took from it the manuscript of his part. Close beside it lay the letter. His fingers itched to take it, but the eyes of the police officers were upon him so closely that he dared not touch it.

" Let us fill our glasses again before I begin," said the actor, producing another bottle from the closet.

" How many bottles of that wine have you ? " inquired the tall gendarme.

" Two more besides this," answered Gaillard, drawing the cork.

" We might as well drink them all, now that we are here," said the officer solemnly.

" It would be a pity to leave any of it," Gaillard acquiesced.

The short gendarme nodded his approval.

" I wish I had a hogshead of it," thought Gaillard. " I 'd put you both in bed and leave you."

After filling the glasses once again, Gaillard took up the lines and began to act out his part. If he had been playing before a large and enthusiastic audience, he could not have done it more effectively.

The stout gendarme was soon in such a state of laughter that the tears ran down his red cheeks. His merriment continued to increase to such an extent as to alarm his companion.

"He'll die of apoplexy some day, if he is so immoderate in his raptures," said the tall man, shaking his head sadly.

The fat gendarme was now coughing violently. Gaillard stopped to slap him on the back. When the paroxysm was over, the actor brought out the two remaining bottles of Burgundy.

"A little of this wine may relieve your throat," he said, and filled the glasses all round.

"Continue, my friend," called out the jolly-faced officer; "don't stop on my account."

Gaillard went on with his rehearsal. The tall gendarme drank twice as much wine as his stout companion, who was now rolling on the floor with shouts of laughter.

Finally, when the merry fellow could laugh no more, and the last drop of wine had disappeared, the tall gendarme stooped, and lifting his fallen companion to his feet leaned him up against the wall. "Jean," he said, "thou art drunk. Shame upon thee." Then he turned toward Gaillard. "Come, citizen actor, we must take you to the Luxembourg."

"Let us at least smoke a pipe of tobacco before we go," said Gaillard, bringing out smoking materials from the closet.

"No time, citizen; as it is we may get in trouble through Jean's indulgence in the bottle." The short gendarme certainly showed the effect of the wine he had taken, though he straightened up and denied it.

"Pierre, thou liest, thou hast taken twice the quantity I have," he rejoined, waving his hand toward the empty bottles.

This also was true; and Gaillard looked with wonder at the solemn countenance of the tall gendarme.

"In any case, let us light our pipes and smoke them as we go along the street," said the actor as he filled the pipes and handed one to each of the police officers.

"I'm quite agreeable to that," said Gendarme Pierre.

Gendarme Jean made no reply, but endeavored to light his pipe over the flame of the candle.

Through a defect in vision occasioned by his potations, he held the bowl several inches away from the flame and puffed vigorously.

At this the tall gendarme laughed audibly for the first time during the evening. Gaillard felt relieved. "He can laugh," he murmured.

"Wait one moment and I will give you a light," he said, and taking a piece of paper from the chimney-piece he carelessly twisted it in his fingers, ignited it in the candle's flames, and held it over Jean's pipe. Then he repeated the service to Gendarme Pierre, and ended by lighting his own pipe, holding the offending list until the flame touched his fingers and it was entirely consumed.

"Forward, my children!" cried the stout gendarme gayly. "We must be off. Shall we place seals upon the doors, comrade?" he said addressing his friend Pierre.

"No, my little idiot Jean, you will remember we are not supposed to have come here at all. The seals will be placed here by men from the section. Hurry forward now."

They descended the stairs in single file. The tall gendarme leading, and stout Jean bringing up the rear. He would stumble from time to time and strike his head into Gaillard's shoulders. "Very awkward stairs," he would murmur in apology, "very awkward."

Once in the street he got along better, although his knees were a little weak, and he showed an inclination to sing.

"Be quiet, Jean," expostulated his companion in arms; "you will get both of us in trouble."

"As mute as a mouse, my clothespin," was the obedient reply.

"You would better take his arm, citizen actor. We shall get along faster." Gaillard complied, and arm in arm they walked off in the direction of the Luxembourg.

"What's this?" demanded the warden in the prison lodge, rubbing his sleepy eyes as three men appeared before him in the gray light of early morning.

"Hector Gaillard, actor; domicile Rue des Mathurins 15; suspect. Warrant executed by Officers Pierre Echelle and Jean Rondeau," said the tall gendarme.

The sleepy guardian turned over the pages of his book.

"Ah yes, here it is. Bring your prisoner this way, citizen gendarme."

Whereupon the stout gendarme, who had been quiet for some time, burst into tears.

"In God's name, what's the matter with him?" asked the astonished warden.

"He always does that way," said the gendarme Pierre. "'Tis his sympathetic nature. He gets very much attached to his prisoners. Cease thy tears, Jean, thou imbecile," and he cursed his brother gendarme under his breath.

Jean drew a long sob. "Adieu, my friend," he said, throwing his arms about Gaillard's neck.

"Why weepest thou?" inquired the actor pretending to be much affected.

"I am afraid they will guillotine thee, my beautiful actor, before I have laughed all the brass buttons off my coat at the play."

"Courage, my friend," replied Gaillard; "I trust for thy sake that I may live to act in many plays. Adieu, my gendarme," and he was led away to a cell.

CHAPTER XVIII

THE LUXEMBOURG

ROBERT TOURNAY breathed easier after having sent the message to Gaillard by La Liberté. Gaillard at least was not likely to become implicated; and the anonymous communication once destroyed, nothing of an incriminating nature would be found, should their lodging be visited. Nevertheless, he could not repress a feeling of disquiet as the iron door of the Luxembourg clanked behind him and he found himself a prisoner.

The cell into which he was conducted was absolutely dark.

"It will not be so bad during the day," volunteered the jailer. "There is a small window that looks out on the courtyard." Tournay drew a sigh of thankfulness on hearing this.

"Your bed is near the door. Can you see it?" asked the jailer.

"I can feel for it," replied Tournay. "Yes, here it is."

"Very well, I will now lock you up safely. Pleasant dreams in your new quarters, citizen colonel." And with this parting salute the cheerful jailer went jingling down the corridor, leaving Tournay in the darkness, seated on the edge of his

· narrow bed, with elbows on knees and his chin resting in the palms of his hands.

Suddenly he sat up straight and listened attentively. The sound of regular breathing told him that he was not the sole occupant of the cell. "Whoever he may be, he sleeps contentedly," thought Tournay; "I may as well follow his good example." In a very few minutes a quiet concert of long-drawn breaths told of two men sleeping peacefully in the cell on the upper tier of the Luxembourg prison.

The little daylight that could struggle through the bars of the tiny window near the ceiling had long since made its appearance, when Robert Tournay opened his eyes next morning.

His fellow prisoner was already astir; and without moving, Tournay lay and watched him at his toilet. He was most particular in this regard. Despite the diminutive ewer and hand basin, his ablutions were the occasion of a great amount of energetic scrubbing and rubbing, accompanied by a gentle puffing as if he were enjoying the luxury of a refreshing bath. After washing, he wiped his face and hands carefully on a napkin correspondingly small. He proceeded with the rest of his toilet in the same thorough manner, as leisurely as if he had been in the most luxurious dressing-room. A wound in his neck, that was not entirely healed, gave him some trouble; but he dressed it carefully, and finally hid it entirely from sight by a clean white neckerchief which he took from a little packet in a corner of the room near the head of his bed. Having adjusted the neckcloth to his satisfaction, he put on a well-brushed coat, and, sitting carelessly upon the edge of the table, — the room contained no chair, — he began to polish his nails with a little set of manicure articles which were also drawn forth from his small treasury of personal effects.

The light from the slit of a window above his head fell on his face. It was thin and haggard, like that of a man who had undergone a severe illness, but, despite this fact, it was an attractive face, and the longer Tournay looked at it, the more it seemed to be familiar to him, recalling to his mind some one he had once known.

Suddenly the colonel sprung to his feet.

"St. Hilaire!" he exclaimed aloud, answering his own mental inquiry.

St. Hilaire rose from his seat on the table and saluted Tournay graciously.

"I am what is left of St. Hilaire," he replied lightly. "And you are — For the life of me I cannot recall your name at the moment. Though I am fully aware that I have seen you more than once before this."

"My name is Robert Tournay."

"Of course. I should have remembered it. You must pardon my poor memory." Then, looking at him closely, he continued: "You wear the uniform of a colonel. You have won distinction, and yet I see you here in prison."

"It matters not how loyal a soldier or citizen one may be if one incurs the enmity or suspicion of Robespierre," was the answer.

"What you say is true, Colonel Tournay," said St. Hilaire.

"Do you also owe your arrest to him?" asked the colonel.

"No," replied St. Hilaire, resuming his former seat. "I became involved in a slight dispute with some of the gendarmerie about a certain question of — of etiquette. The altercation became somewhat spirited. They lost their tempers. I nearly lost my life. When I regained consciousness I discovered what remained of myself here, and I am recovering as fast as could be expected, in view of the rather limited amount of fresh air and sunlight in my chamber."

Tournay thought of the brilliant and dashing Marquis Raphael de St. Hilaire as he had seen him in his boyhood, and looked with deep interest at the figure sitting easily on the edge of the table in apparent contentment, cheerfully accepting misfortune with a smile, and parrying the arrows of adversity with the best of his wit, like the brave and sprightly gentleman he was.

"The resources here are somewhat limited," St. Hilaire continued. "But by placing the table against the wall and mounting upon it one can squeeze his nose between the bars of the window and get a glimpse of the courtyard beneath. Occasionally the jailer has taken me for a promenade there. It seems that we prisoners on the second tier are considered of more importance, or else it is feared that we are more likely to attempt to escape, for we are kept in closer confinement

than those who are on the main floor. Although
this may be construed as a compliment, it is nevertheless very tedious. But I am keeping you from
your toilet by my gossip. I have left you half of
the water in the pitcher. Pardon the small quantity. We will try to prevail upon our jailer to
bring us a double supply in future. He is an
obliging fellow, particularly if you grease his palm
with a little silver."

Tournay accepted his share of the water with
alacrity grateful for the courtesy that divides with
another even a few litres of indifferently clean
water in a prison cell.

After this toilet, and a breakfast of rolls and
coffee, partaken together from the rough deal
table, the two prisoners felt as if they had known
each other for years.

The lines of their lives had frequently run near
together during the years of the Revolution, yet in
all that whirl of events had never crossed till now,
since the summer day in the woods of La Thierry,
when the Marquis de St. Hilaire had placed his
hand upon the boy's shoulder and bade him save
his life by flight.

By some common understanding, subtler than
words, no reference to past events was made by
either of them. They began their acquaintance
then and there; the officer in the republican army,
and the Citizen St. Hilaire; fellow prisoners, who
in spite of any misfortune that might overtake
them would never falter in their devotion and loyalty to their beloved country, France, and who

recognized each in the other a man of courage
and a gentleman.

So the day passed in discussing the victories
of the armies, the oppression and tyranny prac-
ticed by the committee, and the prospects of the
future.

A few days after Tournay's incarceration the
turnkey came toward nightfall to give them a
short time for recreation in the courtyard. This,
though far from satisfying, was hailed with pleasure by the prisoners, and especially by Tournay,
who, accustomed to the violent exertion of the
camp and field, chafed for want of exercise.

They were escorted along the upper corridor,
whence they could look down into the main hall
on the first floor of the Luxembourg. Here, those
prisoners who were happy enough not to be confined under special orders, had the privilege of
congregating during the hours of the day and early
evening. Looking down upon this scene shortly
after the supper hour, Tournay drew a breath of
surprise. He felt for a moment as if he were
transported back to the days before the Revolution
and was looking upon a reception in the crowded
salons of the château de Rochefort where the baron
entertained as became a grand seigneur. The republican colonel turned a look of inquiry toward
St. Hilaire. The latter gave a slight shrug as he
answered : —

" The ladies dress three times a day and appear
in the evening in full toilet. As for the men,
they also wear the best they have. You will see

that many wear suits which in better days would
have been thrown to their lackeys. Now they are
mended and remended during the day, that they
may make their appearance at night, and defy the
shadows of the gray stone walls and the imperfect
candlelight quite bravely." And St. Hilaire himself pulled a spotless ruffle below the sleeves of
his well-worn coat.

"And so," mused Tournay, "they can find the
heart to wear a gay exterior in such a place as
this?"

"No revolution is great enough to change the
feelings and passions of human nature," replied
St. Hilaire. "They only adapt themselves to new
conditions. Here, within these walls, under the
shadow of the guillotine, Generosity, Envy, Love,
and Vanity play the same parts they do in the
outer world. Affairs of the heart refuse to be
locked out by a jailer's key, and these darkened
recesses nightly resound with tender accents and
the sighs of lovers. Bright eyes kindle sparks
that only death can quench. Jealousy, also, is
sometimes aroused, and I am told that even affairs
of honor have taken place here."

"I should never have dreamed it possible," said
the soldier, looking with renewed interest upon the
moving picture at his feet; from which a sound of
vivacious conversation arose like the multiplied
hum of many swarms of bees.

St. Hilaire leaned idly with one arm on the
gallery rail, while he flecked from his coat a few
grains of dust with a cambric handkerchief. Sud-

denly he straightened himself and grasped the railing tightly with both hands.

" Good God! can it be possible? " he exclaimed to himself.

Tournay looked at him, surprised by his sudden change of manner. St. Hilaire did not notice him, but looked intently at some one in the hall below.

Tournay followed the direction of his companion's eyes and saw a young woman, with childish countenance, standing by the elbow of a woman who was seated in a chair occupied with some needlework.

" Countess d'Arlincourt," St. Hilaire continued sadly, speaking to himself. " I hoped that I had saved her."

The woman glanced upward, and her large blue eyes met St. Hilaire's gaze. After the first start of surprise her look expressed the deepest gratitude, while his denoted interest and pity.

Then he turned away. " Come citizen jailer," he said, addressing the attendant, " lead us back to our cell."

As Tournay was about to follow St. Hilaire, he saw, to his amazement, the figure of de Lacheville standing apart from the rest, in the shadow of the wall, as if he preferred the gloomy companionship of his own thoughts to the society of his fellow beings in adversity.

" Do you see that man skulking in the shadow by the wall? " asked Tournay, pointing de Lacheville out to the jailer. " When did he come here? "

" A few days ago. Either the same evening

you were brought in, or the day following," was
the reply.

"The same evening!" exclaimed Tournay to
himself as he followed St. Hilaire to their cell.
"Robespierre has indeed been consistent in that
poor devil's case."

The Countess d'Arlincourt drew up a little
stool and placed herself at the feet of her friend,
Madame de Rémur. The latter was still a woman in the full flush of beauty. She was dressed
in black velvet which seemed but little worn, and
which set off a complexion so brilliant that it
needed no rouge even to counteract the pallor of
a prison.

The countess leaned her head against the knees
of her friend, allowing the velvet of the dress to
touch her own soft cheek caressingly.

"Do not grieve, my child," said Madame de
Rémur, laying down her embroidery and placing
one hand upon the blonde head in her lap.
"Grieve not too much for your husband; there is
not one person in this room who has not to mourn
the loss of some near friend or relative, and yet
for the sake of those who are living they continue
to wear cheerful faces. I only regret that you,
who were at that time safe, should have surrendered yourself after the count was taken. It
has availed nothing, and has sacrificed two lives
instead of one."

"Hush, Diane; a wife should not measure her
duty by the result. He was a prisoner. He was
ill. It was my duty to come to his side."

"Your pardon, dear child. You, with your baby face and gentle manner, have more real courage than I. I hardly think I could do that for any man in the world."

"You always underrate yourself, dear Diane, you who are the noblest and most generous of women!" exclaimed the countess, rising. "Now I am going to speak to that poor little Mademoiselle de Choiseul. It was only yesterday that they took her father." And Madame d'Arlincourt moved quietly across the room.

"I cannot understand the courage and devotion of that child," said Madame de Rémur, addressing the old Chevalier de Creux who stood behind her chair. "I might possibly be willing to share any fate, even the guillotine, with a man if I loved him madly; but " — and Madame de Rémur finished the sentence with a shrug of her shoulders.

"Perhaps the countess loved her husband," suggested the young Mademoiselle de Bellœil who sat near the table, bending over some crochet work, but at the same time lending an ear to the conversation.

"How could she?" said Diane, "he was so cold, so austere, and so dreadfully uninteresting, and then I happen to know she did not, because " —

"Because she loved another gentleman," said the chevalier, completing the sentence with a laugh. "Under the circumstances I do not know whether I admire the countess's loyalty in following her husband to prison, or condemn her cruelty in leaving a lover to pine outside its walls."

"She was always a faithful wife, I would have you understand, you wicked old Chevalier de Creux!" exclaimed Madame de Rémur, looking up at him as he leaned over the back of her chair.

"Perhaps the lover may be confined in the prison also," suggested the philosopher, who had also been a silent listener to the dialogue.

"More than likely," assented the chevalier dryly.

"Whether he were here or not," said madame decidedly, "she would have done the same."

"Here is the Count de Blois," said the chevalier ; "let us put the case before him."

"Oh, you men," laughed Madame de Rémur. "I will not accept the verdict of the best of you. But the count is accompanied by the poet ; let us get him to recite us some verses." And she tossed her fancywork upon the table at her side.

Monsieur de Blois, with his arm through the poet's, bowed low before them. The count had been in the prison for over a year, and the poor gentleman's wardrobe had begun to show the effect of long service.

"They have evidently forgotten my existence entirely," he had said pathetically one morning to a friend who found him washing his only fine shirt in the prison-yard fountain. "When this shirt is worn out, I shall make a demand to be sent to the guillotine from very modesty."

A few days later he had received a couple of shirts and a note by the hand of the jailer.

"Dear de Blois," the letter had read. "I am

called, and shall not need these. If they prevent
you from carrying out your threat of the other
morning, I shall go with a lighter heart.

Yours, V. de K."

"De Blois!" said the chevalier, drawing the
count away from the table of Mademoiselle de
Bellœil, "you are called to decide a point of the
greatest delicacy."

The count put his glass to his eye as if to look
at the chevalier and the philosopher, but in reality
he only saw Mademoiselle de Bellœil bending over
her embroidery.

"If a lady," continued the chevalier, his bright
eyes twinkling, "voluntarily puts herself into a
prison where are confined both her husband and
her lover, what credit does she deserve for her
action? Can it be called self-sacrifice?"

Before replying, the count looked attentively at
the group before him: at the philosopher's impen-
etrable countenance; at the chevalier's quizzical
and wrinkled brown physiognomy; then at Madame de Rémur's handsome face, and lastly and
most tenderly at the drooping eyelids of the deli-
cate Mademoiselle de Bellœil.

"She would be twice revered," replied de Blois.

Mademoiselle de Bellœil's needle stopped in its
click-click.

"Why so, monsieur le comte?" inquired the
philosopher. "If she has a double motive for the
sacrifice, should not the honor of it be only half as
great?"

"She should receive credit for her loyalty to

the husband whom she had sworn to obey, and homage for her devotion to the lover on whom by nature she has placed her affections," replied the count, bowing to Madame de Rémur, while he noted with a certain satisfaction the smile of approval on the lips of Mademoiselle de Bellœil.

"And no one has said that she has a lover," declared Madame de Rémur warmly.

"Did you not imply as much, dear madame?" asked the old chevalier slyly.

"I intimated that she might have had one — if — let us change the subject. I move that the poet read us his latest verses. I am dying for some amusement."

"Ladies and gentlemen," cried the old chevalier, clapping his hands together to attract the attention of all those in the room, "this brilliant young author and poet, who needs no introduction to you, has consented to read his latest production. Will you kindly take places?"

There was some polite applause. "The poem! let us hear the poem," buzzed upon all sides, and the throng began to settle down around the poet, the ladies occupying the chairs, and the gentlemen either leaning against the walls or seated upon stools by the side of those ladies in whose eyes they found particular favor.

In a few moments a hush of expectancy fell upon an audience delighted at the prospect of being entertained.

"This is a play in verse," began the poet, taking a roll of manuscript from his pocket.

"A play! how charming," said Mademoiselle de Bellœil.

"It is in three acts," continued the author. "Act first, in the prison of the Luxembourg, where the young people first meet and fall deeply in love."

A rustle of approval ran through his audience.

"Act second is in the prison yard where they are separated, she being set at liberty and he conducted to the guillotine."

"Oh, how terrible!" murmured the young damsel.

"One moment, monsieur le poëte," said Madame de Rémur. "How does it end? I warn you that I shall not like your play if it ends unhappily."

"You shall judge of that in a moment, madame," replied the poet, bowing to her graciously.

"In the third act," he continued, "the lovers are brought together under the shadow of the guillotine, whither she has followed him. The knife falls upon both of them in quick succession, and their souls are united in the next world, never to be separated more."

"What a beautiful ending," cried Mademoiselle de Bellœil, and the exclamation on the part of the audience showed that her sentiment was echoed generally.

"Continue," said Madame de Rémur. "I was afraid it was going to end unhappily."

The chevalier took a pinch of snuff and settled himself back in the arm-chair which was accorded to him as a tribute to his advanced age ; and the poet unfolded his manuscript and began to read.

It was an intensely appreciative audience that listened to the dramatic work of the poet. They followed with breathless interest the meeting of the young lovers in the hall of the Luxembourg; assisted smilingly at their rendezvous in the corridors and shadowy corners of the old prison; and sighed gently during the most tender passages. At the scene of separation, tears of regret flowed freely, and in the meeting in the last act, tears of joy and sorrow mingled together in sympathetic unison.

As the young poet ended he folded up his manuscript and bowed his blushing acknowledgments to the storm of applause that greeted him.

The wave of approbation had not ceased to resound through the room when the outer door opened, and the jailer and some half a dozen gendarmes entered abruptly.

Instantly the hum of conversation stopped, and an icy chill fell upon the assemblage. Faces that the moment before were wreathed in smiles now became pale and marked with fear.

"The call of to-morrow's list to the guillotine," rang out through the room in harsh notes.

Amid the silence of death, a captain of gendarmerie took a slip of paper from his pocket, while a comrade held a lantern under his nose. Some of those who listened wiped the clammy perspiration from their foreheads, others trembled and sat down. Some affected an air of indifference, and began a forced conversation with their neighbors; but all ears were strained. Each dreaded lest his own name or that of some loved one should be called out by that monotonous, relentless voice.

"Bertrand de Chalons."

An old man stepped forward.

"Annette Duclos."

There was a pause after each name, during which the suspense was intensified.

"Diane de Rémur."

Madame de Rémur laid aside her work and rose.

"Diane! Diane! I cannot bear it!" cried the Countess d'Arlincourt, throwing her arms about her friend's neck. "Oh, sirs, have pity!"

"Hush, my dear," replied Madame de Rémur soothingly. "Chevalier, look to the poor child; she is hysterical." The chevalier gently drew the countess aside, then took Madame de Rémur's hand and silently bending over it, put it to his lips.

"Take your place in the line, citizeness," called out a gendarme, and Madame de Rémur stood with the others.

"André de Blois!"

As de Blois' name was called, a shrill cry echoed through the room, and Mademoiselle de Bellœil fell back into the chair from which she had just risen. She did not swoon, but sat like one in a dream, staring with wide-open eyes.

The count stepped to her side.

"Adèle," he said, bending down and speaking in a low voice, "give me one of those roses you are wearing on your breast." Mechanically she took the flower from her bosom and put it in his hand. He placed it over his heart. "It shall be

here to the last," he said softly; "now farewell;"
and he pressed a kiss upon her cold lips.

"Maurice de Lacheville."

A man crouched down behind a group of prisoners, and all heads were turned in his direction.

"Maurice de Lacheville, you are called," said
a gendarme, going up to him and seizing him by
the arm with no gentle grasp.

"There is some mistake," cried de Lacheville
pitiably.

"There is no mistake, your name is here."

"I say, there must be some mistake. My arrest
was a mistake. I was promised " —

"Into the line with you," was the gruff inter-
ruption. "Many would claim there was a mistake
if it would avail them to say so."

"But in my case it is true," pleaded de Lacheville. "Send word to Robespierre; he promised " —

"Into the line, I tell you!" cried the exasper-
ated gendarme. "There is no mistake; your name
is written here. You go with the rest."

"One moment, one little moment," implored the
wretched marquis in an agony of fear. "Oh,
messieurs the gendarmes, if you will but hear me,
I have an important communication to make."
All this time he was fighting desperately as the
two officers of the law dragged him toward the
door.

"Silence, idiot!" yelled the angry captain, "or
I will have you bound and gagged. Take example
from these women who put you to shame."

"Idiot that I was," cried de Lacheville, "why did I ever return from a place of safety? None but a fool would have trusted the word of Robespierre."

"Bind him," ordered the captain.

With a strength no one would have believed that he possessed, de Lacheville threw off those who held him.

"Stand back!" he shouted wildly, as the officers endeavored to seize him. He drew an object quickly from his pocket.

"Take care, Jean. He has a weapon," cried one.

There was a report of a pistol, and the marquis fell forward to the floor.

A murmur of horror filled the prison hall. Women fainted, and men turned away their heads. The gendarmes hastened to bend over him.

"I believe he is dead, captain," said one after a brief examination.

"Carry him out with the others just the same," ordered the captain. "Pierre, continue with the list."

"Bertrand de Tourin."

"Here."

"Adèle de Bellœil."

There was a cry of joy in the answer: —

"I am here. The Blessed Virgin has heard my prayer;" and Mademoiselle de Bellœil stepped forward. "André, I come with you; we shall go together where they can never separate us." And she threw herself into the arms of her lover.

"About face — fall in — forward ! march." The heavy door closed, and those who had been called were led away, while those remaining in the prison went quietly to their cells, to recommence the same life on the morrow until the next roll-call.

"The nobility of France," said the chevalier to the philosopher, "may not have known how to live, but it knows how to die."

"Except the Marquis de Lacheville," was the reply.

"Bah. He was always one of the canaille at heart; he only proves my assertion," and the chevalier took an extra large pinch of snuff and limped off to his mattress of straw.

CHAPTER XIX

"WHAT are you bringing us now?" growled a voice from a corner of the cell. Gaillard heard the rustling of straw, but his eyes were not enough accustomed to the gloom to enable him to see what sort of being it was who gave utterance to this harsh welcome.

"Are not two enough in a trap like this?" the speaker went on, rising and coming forward. "There's hardly enough air for us as it is, without your putting in another one."

"So it's you, Tappeur, complaining again," remarked the jailer. "You had better be thankful you're not four in a cell as they are in most of them. The prison is full to overflowing. No matter how many they take out, there's always more to fill their places. You'll have to make the best of it." And he closed the door with an unfeeling slam.

Tappeur brushed some of the straw from his hair and beard. "A plague upon these suspects that fill up our prisons!" he exclaimed with an oath; "we honest criminals have to put up with the vilest accommodations because you crowd us to the wall by force of numbers. You *are* a suspect, are n't you?" he demanded, coming nearer and putting a dirty face close to Gaillard's.

The cell which they occupied was below the level of the ground. Overhead at the juncture of the ceiling and wall was a grating through which came all the light and air they received.

"You are a suspect, is it not so?" repeated Tappeur as Gaillard made no answer.

"I have not the honor of being an 'honest criminal,'" replied the actor, drawing away with a movement of disgust from the seamed and distorted visage thrust close to his.

"Bah, I thought not," said Tappeur with another oath. "Well, suspect, come over here under the grating and let me take a good look at your face," and he seized Gaillard roughly by the arm.

Tappeur received a violent blow on the chest which sent him reeling into a dark corner of the cell, clutching at the empty air as if to sustain himself by catching hold of the shadows. His fall to the ground was followed by an explosion of oaths in a new voice, in which explosion Tappeur himself joined vigorously.

"I 've stirred up a nest of them," said Gaillard to himself, and then stood awaiting developments.

The torrent of profanity having exhausted itself, Tappeur emerged from the shadowy recess of the wall followed by a smaller man.

"How do you like my looks?" inquired Gaillard cheerfully.

"I 'm satisfied for the present," replied Tappeur.

" Your fist is hard enough ; what may your trade be ? "

" I have no regular profession, I 'm a little of everything. What 's yours ? "

" I belong to the ' Brotherhood of the Ready Hand.' Our motto is ' Steal and Kill ; ' our watchward ' Blood and Death ; ' and our coat of arms ' A Cord and Gallows.' " And Tappeur chuckled gleefully.

" You are evidently a rare accumulation of talent and virtue. I should enjoy knowing more of you. Is this a member of your band ? " and Gaillard pointed to the man who had just been awakened, and who was yawning and stretching his arms.

" Our band, oh no, this is the great Petitsou."

" And who is Petitsou ? "

" What ! you don't know Petitsou ? " demanded Tappeur pityingly.

" Never heard of him."

" He never even heard of you, Petitsou ! " exclaimed Tappeur, turning to his companion with a gesture of disgust.

Petitsou shrugged his shoulders in reply, as if to say, " He has been the only loser."

" Pray let me be compensated for my ill fortune, by learning all about you now, Citizen Petitsou."

" I have made more counterfeit money than any man in France now living, I might say more than any man who ever has lived, but I believe some one or two of the old kings have surpassed me," said Petitsou.

"He is an artist," whispered Tappeur; "he does not make you a clumsy, bungling coin only to be palmed off upon women and blind men. He creates an article finer to look at than the government mint can produce. *Pardieu*, I'd rather have a pocket full of his silver than that bearing either the face of Louis Capet or of this new Republic." And Tappeur looked at his friend the artist admiringly.

"It was when the government issued these assignats that my great fortune was made," continued Petitsou. "In fact, it was too much success that brought me here. I found them so easy to make that I manufactured them by the wholesale. I stored my cellar with them. I even had the audacity to make the government a small loan in assignats on which I did the entire work myself, reproducing the very signatures of the officials who received the funds. Oh, it was a rare sport."

"But your forgeries were finally detected?" said Gaillard inquiringly.

"The workmanship and the signatures never. I could have gone on making enough to buy up the whole government, but for a mishap. I made a glaring error in the date of a certain issue of assignats. I never liked the new calendar, and always had to take particular care to get it right, but one day my memory slipped up, and I dated a batch of one hundred thousand francs, November 14, 1793, instead of 25th Brumaire, year II. Oh, that was an unpardonable slip, and I deserved to pay the penalty."

"It seems cruel," remarked Gaillard, "to keep a useful member of society, like you, in this filthy dungeon."

"The greatest cruelty is in keeping the materials of my trade away from me. They know my love for my art, and take delight in torturing me. Although I promise not to try any dodge, they won't trust me. If they would only let me have a little pen, ink, and paper, I should be happy."

"Pen, ink, and paper?" repeated Gaillard. "That's a modest desire."

"They won't let him have them," put in Tappeur. "He'd play them all sorts of tricks. He'd forge all sorts of documents, and worry the life out of the jailers."

The door opened a few inches, and a jug of water and a large square loaf made their appearance, pushed in by an invisible hand.

"Let's divide our rations for the day," suggested Petitsou. "Have they given us a larger loaf, Tappeur, on account of our increased number?"

"But very little larger," replied Tappeur, picking up the loaf of black bread and surveying it hungrily.

"Is that all we receive in the way of food?" asked Gaillard ruefully. He had missed his usual supper after the theatre the night before, and was quite ready for breakfast.

"That's all, unless you've got money. You can buy what you like with that." And Tappeur eyed him slyly out of his deep-set eyes.

"What do you say to some wine in place of this cold water, and some white bread, with perhaps a little sausage added by the way of relish?" suggested Gaillard mildly.

"Hey, you jailer!" called out Tappeur, frantically rushing toward the door, fearful lest the man might be out of hearing. The jailer retraced his steps reluctantly.

"A commission from the new lodger. A bottle of wine. A white loaf in place of this vile, sour stuff, and some sweet little sausage. A little tobacco also. Am I not right, my comrade?" asked Tappeur, looking at Gaillard inquiringly.

"Some tobacco, of course," nodded Gaillard, producing a coin.

"Have it strong; I have tasted none for so long that it must bite my tongue to make up for lost time. Hurry with thy commissions my good little citizen jailer; the new lodger is hungry, and we, too, have no small appetites."

"Tobacco," said Petitsou, "next to ink and paper, I have longed for that. And I have money, too!" and he produced a five-franc piece. "As good a piece of silver as ever rang from the government mint, and yet that cursed jailer refuses to take it, or bring me the smallest portion of tobacco for it. The donkey fears I have manufactured it here on the premises, or that I extracted it from thin air like a magician."

The breakfast being brought, Tappeur rolled a couple of large stones toward the lightest portion of the cell, and placed a board across them for a table. They had nothing to sit upon but their heels. The two criminals had accustomed themselves to this method of sitting at meals, but Gaillard found it more comfortable to partake of his food standing with his shoulders to the wall.

" Fall to, comrades!" cried Tappeur, breaking off an end of the loaf and taking a sausage in his other hand. " There's no cup, so we must drink from the bottle." And he handed the wine to Gaillard first, by way of attention.

Gaillard put the bottle to his lips and took a long draught of the contents while Tappeur watched him anxiously. He then passed it over to Petitsou, who treated it in a like manner. Tappeur received it in his turn in thankful silence, and after having punished it severely, put it down by his side. Gaillard helped himself to a piece of bread and a sausage, and ate with good appetite, leaving his new companions to finish the wine, to the evident satisfaction of those two worthies.

" You have a hard fist, my brave comrade!" exclaimed Tappeur, filling a pipe as short and grimy as the thumb that pushed the tobacco down into the bowl. "A hard fist and a free purse and Tappeur is your friend for life." To give emphasis to his words he puffed a cloud of blue smoke up into Gaillard's face, and drained the last few drops of wine in the flagon.

" That's very good stuff," he continued, balancing the empty bottle upon its nose, " but brandy would be more satisfying."

Gaillard refused to take the hint, and turned

away to spread his cloak in a corner of the cell, where he lay down upon it and was soon in a deep sleep.

Week followed week, and Gaillard continued to live below the ground far from the sunlight which he loved so dearly, while Tournay, confined in the cell upon the second floor, wondered why he received no word from the friend in the outside world.

Thus they lived within one hundred yards of each other, thinking of each other daily, and with no means of communication. One thing Gaillard had to be thankful for, and that was the sum of money the theatre manager had paid him on the very night of his arrest. With it he had purchased many comforts to make his life more bearable. He had procured a fresh supply of straw and a warm blanket for his bed; some candles and a rough chair upon which he took turns in sitting with the two jail-birds, his companions, although at meals he always occupied it by tacit consent.

Under the influence of the additional food which Gaillard's purse supplied, Tappeur grew fat and better natured, though he swore none the less, and drank and smoked all that Gaillard would provide for him. Indeed, he thought the actor a little niggardly in furnishing the brandy, and one day, after a good meal, was inclined to be swaggering, intimating that, with respect to drink, the rations should be increased. Whereupon Gaillard cut off his potations entirely for twenty-four hours, and he became as meek as a lamb and remained so ever after.

Both the bully and Petitsou would frequently regale Gaillard with long accounts of their past crimes. During the recitals, Tappeur, although always boastful on his own account, showed a certain deference to the forger.

" I can cut a throat or rob a purse with the best blackguard in France," he would say to the actor, " but that little Petitsou is the true artist."

Notwithstanding these diversions, the time dragged wearily, and Gaillard's face began to lose its roundness, while the smile did not broaden his wide mouth so frequently as of old. His money began to get low, and he looked forward with dread to the time when it would be entirely gone and he would have to divide the musty black loaf and the pitcher of fetid water with the two criminals, without the wherewithal to buy even such good nature and entertainment as they could furnish. He longed for the time of his trial to come. He knew from what he had heard of the experiences of others, that he might be called for trial any day, or that he might languish in jail for months, forgotten and neglected. Every day when he asked the jailer who brought their food, " Have I not been called for trial? " and received the response, " Not to-day," his heart sank lower.

One day when he had only five francs left in his purse, and had refrained from ordering any wine, much to Tappeur's disgust, the jailer came to inform him that he was to come forth for trial.

" Good luck attend you, citizen actor," said

Petitsou, with some show of friendship, as Gaillard prepared to leave them, smiling.

"As we must lose you in one way or another," called out Tappeur after him as he disappeared down the corridor, "let us hope that the national razor will not bungle when it shaves you, my brave."

Gaillard's spirits rose as he came up to the light of day. In a few hours he would know what his destiny would be, and the fresh air gave him renewed courage to meet it. His wish to learn just what fate had overtaken Tournay gave him an additional interest in life.

Passing through the main corridor he heard his name called, and looking toward the corridor of the upper tier he saw the face of his friend.

It was only an instant, and then Gaillard passed out with others to the street. At first Tournay's heart throbbed with apprehension at the sight of his friend. He had feared all along that had Gaillard been at liberty he would have received some message from him, or other evidence of his existence, and now his fears were confirmed. Yet somehow the very sight of Gaillard's cheerful face, smiling up at him, reassured him.

"Am called for trial," the actor's lips framed. "And you?" Tournay made a negative gesture.

"Paper destroyed," Gaillard next signaled with his lips, but he dared not make the words too plain for fear of detection, and the message was lost on Tournay. Then they saw each other no longer.

It was into a small court room that Gaillard saw
himself conducted.   He looked round with surprise.   The trials were usually attended by large
and interested crowds of people.

"I am evidently considered of small importance, and so am disposed of by an inferior court,"
thought he.   "So much the better."

The case being tried at the moment was one of
petty larceny.   "The other courts must be doing
an enormous business, to oblige them to turn some
of us over to these little criminal courts," continued Gaillard musingly as the affair in question
was disposed of and he was called.

"Read the act of accusation," said the judge,
"and hurry the affair.   I wish to go to dinner."

"Don't let me detain you," thought Gaillard.
Then he put his hands to his head to ascertain if
his ears were in their proper place, for he could
not understand a word of the accusation as read
by the clerk.   He heard a jumble about "coat,"
"personal assault," "refused payment," then looked
in bewilderment at the judge and prosecuting at-
torney, till from them his eyes wandered about the
dingy court room.   All at once the sight of a face
in the witness box caused a light to flash through
his brain, and elucidate the whole matter.   He
recognized his tailor, who sat with vindictive eyes,
holding over his arm the identical coat that had
been the cause of the dispute on the very day of
his arrest.

Gaillard could barely repress his merriment.

The rancor of the little tailor had followed him to prison, and dragged him out to answer a complaint of assault and intent to defraud.

" I wonder," thought Gaillard, " if I am convicted and sentenced for this crime, and subsequently condemned to the guillotine, which penalty I shall have to pay first? "

" Have you any counsel, prisoner? " demanded the judge.

" I will plead my own case," replied Gaillard cheerfully.

" Call the complainant and witness."

After a long recital on the part of the tailor of the history of the coat, and the treatment he had received at the hands of the brutal prisoner, during which the judge yawned, indicating his desire to get out to dinner, Gaillard took the stand.

" My sole defense," said he smilingly, " is that the tailor wittingly, maliciously, and falsely, endeavored to palm off upon me, a poor actor, a garment never made for me."

" How will you prove it? " demanded the judge.

" By simply trying on the coat," answered Gaillard. " If you decide it was made for me, I will abandon my defense."

" Let the prisoner have the garment," ordered the judge.

Gaillard slowly proceeded to divest himself of his own coat and don the offending garment which the tailor now presented to him reluctantly.

It had fitted him badly on the first occasion he had tried it on, and now, by a slight contortion of his supple body, the actor made the misfit ridiculously apparent.

The court officers grinned, even the judge could not repress a smile, and the tailor looked foolish.

" That is quite sufficient," said the justice. " How much did the tailor want you to pay for this grotesque garment? "

" Two hundred francs the bill calls for."

" Two hundred francs? " ejaculated the judge.

" In gold coin," emphasized Gaillard.

" It is very expensive material," explained the tailor ruefully.

" Down how many flights of stairs does the complaint state the prisoner kicked the tailor? " asked the judge.

" Only one short one," volunteered Gaillard, grinning at the discomfited tailor.

" Only one short one? " repeated the judge. " You were very moderate; such an absurd garment would have justified three flights."

There was a laugh in the court room. The judge tapped for order.

" The prisoner is discharged," he said.

Gaillard rose and looked for the guards who had escorted him from the Luxembourg, thankful for the brief respite he had had from the tedium of confinement.

" You are a free man, Citizen Gaillard," said the judge, waving his hand toward the open door.

" Do you mean I can leave the court room by that door? " asked Gaillard, his heart rising up in his throat.

"Certainly; I dismiss the complaint."

"Thank you, your honor," said Gaillard, stepping quickly through the doorway into the street.

"Your honor!" gasped a court attendant hurriedly appearing at the judge's desk.

"I have no time to listen to anything further now. I am off to dinner," said the judge snappishly.

"But does your honor know? Is your honor aware that the prisoner was a suspect from the Luxembourg, brought here by me for trial on this charge of assault, to be returned after" —

"Bring him back at once!" yelled the judge. "You idiot, why did n't you say so before?"

"But, your honor, I" —

"After him, constables; be quick, he cannot have gone fifty yards."

Half a dozen men rushed into the street and looked in all directions. But Gaillard was not to be seen.

CHAPTER XX

UNCLE MICHELET

ONE April day a wave of excitement swept through the entire prison. It was repeated in every cell and whispered in every ear.

"The lion has been taken in the mesh! The great Danton is a prisoner in the Luxembourg!"

At first Tournay could not believe the report. It seemed as if those giant arms need but to be extended to break the bonds that held them, and allow their owner to walk out into the air a free man.

Yet it was indeed true, and one day, for a few moments only, Tournay had an opportunity to see and converse with the fallen chieftain as he stood in the door of his cell, talking in a loud voice to all who were near enough to hear him.

As Danton saw Colonel Tournay he ceased speaking and held out his hand. In his eyes there was a peculiar look which the latter understood.

"You see, it has come at last even to me," said Danton quietly.

"Ah, why did you not crush the snake before it entwined you with its coils?" asked Tournay sadly.

"I did not think he would dare do it," replied

Danton. "Robespierre is rushing to his ruin. What will they do without me? They are all mad."

"You should have distrusted their madness, even if you did not fear it," was the rejoinder.

"The end is near," answered Danton. "It is fate. Yet if I could leave my brains to Robespierre and my legs to Couthon, the Revolution might still limp along for a short time," and he laughed roughly. "Good-by, Tournay," he said in a tone of kindliness. "You are a brave man and a true Republican; such men as you might have saved the Republic, but it was not to be." He entered his cell, and Tournay never saw him again.

The next day Danton was taken to the conciergerie and to his trial, and the day following to the guillotine. The lion head was parted from the giant trunk, and the Revolution swept on.

The weeks dragged on monotonously to Colonel Tournay and St. Hilaire in the Luxembourg. The trees in the gardens beyond their prison walls had put forth their leaves, and the song of birds was borne sometimes even into the recesses of their cell.

"Why are we left to rot here in this stifling place?" exclaimed Colonel Tournay for the thousandth time. "Why are we not even called for trial? Has Robespierre forgotten our existence?"

"Let us hope that he has," rejoined St. Hilaire. "As long as we are overlooked we shall get into no worse trouble. We are not so very uncomfort-

able here," and St. Hilaire sprang upon the table
to put his nose out between the window bars, like
a fox in a cage, to get what air there was stirring
and to look at the little patch of blue sky.

Tournay smiled sadly. He envied St. Hilaire
his cheerfulness and adaptability, while he felt his
own spirit breaking under the long confinement.

He sat down upon the edge of the bed and wondered what had happened in the world since he had
been cut off from it. His thoughts were frequently of Gaillard, and he wished he could learn
something about his friend. As he was sitting
thus, oppressed by the warmth of a June afternoon, the turnkey entered the cell.

"There is an old man come to see you," he said,
addressing Tournay. "Your uncle from the pro-
vinces, I believe. You may see him outside here
in the corridor."

"I wonder who this visitor may be," thought
Tournay as he followed the turnkey. "Had I
not received word of my poor father's death two
months ago I should expect to find him."

An old man stood leaning on his cane at the
end of the corridor. He seemed quite feeble, and
the jailer, moved to compassion by his infirmity,
placed a stool for him to sit upon.

"My nephew!" exclaimed the old man in trem-
ulous accents as Tournay made his appearance.

Apparently the old man had made some mistake. To Colonel Tournay's eyes he was an entire
stranger; but being aware that the slightest suspicion aroused in the mind of the prison authori-

ties sometimes led to very serious consequences, he determined to wait until the turnkey was out of hearing before undeceiving the mild-eyed old gentleman.

"My uncle," he answered, taking the venerable citizen by the outstretched hand, "how did your old legs manage to " —

The septuagenarian squeezed the colonel's hand until the fingers cracked.

"My old legs would have brought me here long before," said the voice of Gaillard in guarded tones, "but it took me two weeks to get this disguise!"

"Gaillard! In heaven's name can it be you?"

"'T is I! I may have aged since we last met, my colonel, but my heart is as young as ever."

"My dear Gaillard, how did you manage to . leave this prison? What are you doing? Is this not dangerous?" asked Tournay, putting the questions in rapid succession.

"Gaillard's liberty would not be worth a brass button if he should come here," replied the actor, "but old Michelet has nothing to fear. I have been playing hide and seek with the police for the past fortnight. I am now living at 15 Rue des Mathurins."

Even Tournay, who knew his friend so well, started.

"It is a very long story, and I can only give you an outline of it," said Gaillard, seating himself on the stool and leaning heavily on his cane, while he turned his face so that he could see from

one corner of his eye every motion the turnkey
might make.

"I escaped from my dungeon below the ground;
I will tell you how when we have more leisure.
The first thing I thought of, when I was once out
in the free air, was a bath. I wanted to drown
out the recollection of assassins and dirty straw,
vile air and counterfeiters with whom I had been
on such intimate terms for so many weeks.

"I was afraid to go to any bath houses lest I
should be seen and recognized; besides, I had no
money, so I finally concluded to try the river. I
therefore skulked in unfrequented byways until
nightfall, when I went swimming in the Seine
by starlight, and I can assure you I never before
appreciated the kindly properties of water to such
an extent. My next desire, after I had slept in
the arches of the bridge St. Michel and broken
my fast with a crisp roll, was to see you."

"My dear old uncle!" exclaimed Tournay
aloud, placing his hand affectionately on Gaillard's shoulder.

"I knew that I should be safe if I could procure
a good disguise, but that it would be folly to attempt it without one," continued Gaillard. "The
want of money was still an obstacle. 'Among the
costumes in my chest at home,' thought I, 'is material to disguise a whole race of Gaillards.' Ah,
but how to reach them? That was the matter
that required careful study. Those annoying little
red seals that the government places on the doors
of all arrested persons are terribly dangerous to

meddle with. Yet within were clothing and disguises, and a very little sum of money stowed away for an emergency. Meanwhile, in the evening, I promenaded down the Rue des Mathurins to look the ground over. There, planted in front of the house, staring up at the windows of our apartment, was a great hulking gendarme.

"That night I slept again under the St. Michel bridge, — commodious and airy enough, but a little damp in the morning hours. Before daylight I was up and off to the Rue des Mathurins, drawn like a criminal to the scene of his misdeeds, to inspect the enemy unseen by him.

"There is a certain mouselike gratification in watching from afar the cat, which, with claws extended, is lying in wait, ready to pounce upon you as soon as you show your nose." And Gaillard stopped to take a pinch of snuff and blink at the light with a pair of mild blue eyes. Then, after applying a colored handkerchief to his nose, he resumed his narrative.

"At all hours of the day, late at night, or early in the morning, there was always some officer of police staring persistently at my windows as if he expected me, furnished with a pair of wings, to come flying in or out of a fourth story. 'Not yet, my fine fellow,' said I, and vanished around the corner.

"One night it rained dismally; a cold mist was rising from the river. The St. Michel bridge had little attraction as a bedroom for me at that moment, I can assure you. Muffling myself in my cloak, I directed my steps toward my old abode, hoping that owing to the inclemency of the weather the officers of the law might be less vigilant. For I had resolved, the opportunity offering, to make an attempt to enter my own domicile that very night. Imagine my disgust when, upon arriving, I saw two gendarmes sheltered in the entrance of the house opposite. Both of them were obtrusively wide-awake and alert.

" I do not know whether one of them noticed me, lurking by the corner, but he immediately started to walk in my direction, and not wishing to run any chances I darted into an alley blacker than a whole calendar of nights, scaled a wall, and found myself in the narrow court which flanks our own building. Here I resolved to wait until I could safely venture out upon the street once more.

" The rain had almost ceased, but I could still hear the gurgle of the water coming down the spout from the roof. You know that water spout, my little colonel? It is made to carry off the water from three houses, is unusually large, and is held firmly in place a few inches from the house wall by iron braces at intervals of five to six feet. I placed my hand on one of these braces, and instantly the thought flashed through my brain, ' It can be done.' "

" You are not going to tell me that you at· tempted to climb up by the water pipe?" de manded Tournay incredulously.

" I divested myself of my cloak, coat, and waist-coat, removed my heavy, rain-soaked shoes, and

began the ascent as bravely as any seaman ordered
to the foretop," replied Gaillard.

"I could reach the brace above while standing
on the one beneath, and partly using my knees
and partly drawing myself up by the arms, I made
quicker progress than I had deemed possible. In
fact, I went up so vigorously that on reaching the
third story I struck my knee against a piece of
loose stucco which was clinging to the wall, waiting for the first strong wind to blow it to the
ground.

"Crash! the plaster fell to the courtyard pavement, where it was shivered into a thousand frag-
ments.

"The blow on my kneecap made me shiver with
pain, and I rested on the brace just outside the
window of the little soubrette, clinging tightly with
both hands to the spout.

"'Thank heaven that it was the stucco that fell,
not I,' I whispered devoutly, just as a window
opened on the floor above, and our old neighbor
Avarie appeared. He is always on the lookout
for robbers, and keeps at his bedside a big blunderbuss, with a muzzle like a speaking-trumpet.

"'Thieves,' I heard him mutter. I kept perfectly quiet, not giving vent even to a breath.

"'Who 's there?'

"I clung close to the shelter of my friendly
water pipe.

"'Speak, or I 'll fire!'

"I knew he could not see me, and if he did fire
his old cannon, I felt sure that it would explode and

blow him into atoms; but the noise would alarm the neighborhood, and I had a vision of a score of lights flashing; night-capped heads appearing in all the surrounding windows; gendarmes running up with their lanterns, and poor Gaillard, clinging like a frightened cat to the water spout.

"That gave me an idea.

"'Miauw!' answered I plaintively.

"'It's a cat!' exclaimed old Avarie in a tone of disgust.

"'Mew — mew — mew,' cried I.

"'What is it?' said a woman's voice, evidently his wife's.

"'Nothing but a cat,' growled Avarie. 'But I think I will let drive at her just because she disturbed my sleep.'

"I stopped my mewing on the instant.

"'Don't,' pleaded the woman, 'the gun may kick.'

"'Bah, do you think I can't handle a gun?' And I heard a click.

"'Good-by to thee, old Avarie,' I said under my breath.

"'Don't be a fool, husband, and awake the whole neighborhood just for a cat!' exclaimed his wife.

"Almost at my window another window was thrown open and the little soubrette's head appeared. She is very fond of cats.

"'Here puss, puss, puss,' she cried.

"'Is that your cat, citizeness?' asked old Avarie.

"'It must be; he has stayed out all night, the

naughty fellow. Kitty, kitty, poor kitty, come in out of the wet.'

" My teeth were chattering with cold and fatigue and that was just what I most desired, but I did not dare to risk it.

" ' You ought to keep the animal at home, and not let him out to disturb everybody's sleep,' called out the testy old man as he closed his window with a bang.

" Luckily for me the little soubrette's attention was all directed toward the roof of the lower extension on the left where her pet evidently had a habit of straying. She did not see me, crouched behind the pipe so near as to almost be able to touch her by putting out one hand. By the way, she looked very pretty in her little white nightcap edged with lace. I was not very sorry, however, to see her close the window and to be left alone with my water spout. A few minutes later I had pushed open the window of my kitchen and wriggled into the room.

" I dared not strike a light for fear of its reflection on the wall opposite, and groped my way about the room in the dark. My heart leaped with joy when I had assured myself that no seal had been placed on the windows nor upon any of the inside doors; the one seal on the outer door evidently having been deemed sufficient. The dust was an inch thick over everything, and I moved about in ghostly stillness, struggling to repress a sneeze. Nothing appeared to have been touched since the night of my enforced departure.

"I hugged myself with a childish glee at being alone in my little home in the dead of night. The thought of the gendarmes outside in the rain made my sides ache with suppressed laughter.

"First, I unearthed my little economies of last winter. Thirteen francs, five sous. 'Gaillard you're a prodigal fellow,' I said to myself as I dropped them into my pouch, 'but it is better than nothing.' Then I collected a few necessities. My beautiful wig of silver hair, and a suitable dress to go with it. I handled lovingly a few other costumes, but had the strength of mind to return them to the chest. I should like to have appeared before you as the 'Spanish outlaw' but it would have been too dangerous. The character of the English 'milord' would have been congenial but equally hazardous. So I sensibly adhered to my sober selection, and tied up all my effects in a neat bundle.

"When all was completed I took one last, longing survey of my rooms, went to the casement, and, dropping the bundle, held my breath. Thud! it reached the bottom and lay there innocently in the court. Not a sound was heard. Old Citizen Avarie, in the adjoining apartment, was snoring in a way that would put his blunderbuss to shame, and the little citizeness below had evidently retired into the recess of her lace-trimmed nightcap to dream of her missing pet.

"Sliding silently from the window I found the iron brace with my toes, and grasped the clammy water pipe with both hands. I could not close the casement. 'Never mind, they will think it was the wind that opened it,' I said, and I descended to the ground with an agility born of practice.

"In the early morning hours I retired to my bridge, put on my silver wig and old man's dress, sunk my other clothes to the river bottom, and appeared in the light of day as an old man.

"I now walk the streets in safety under the very noses of my old enemies, the police; I come to you and I ask, 'How do you like your old uncle?'"

"You deceived me completely, my Gaillard," Tournay confessed; "but tell me this. You said you were still residing at 15 Rue des Mathurins. May I ask in what capacity? As cat?"

"Having little money, I must earn some more in order to live. I went to my dear friend, the theatre director, just as I am, and asked him to employ me about the theatre in any capacity. He did not recognize me, and putting his hand in his pocket, brought out a piece of forty sous."

"'Sorry, my poor fellow, but I have no place for you. Take this.'"

"I would trust my manager with my life, so I leaned forward to his ear. 'I am Gaillard, hunted, proscribed, but always your old friend Gaillard. Call me Citizen Michelet.' He gave me a look for which I could have taken him to my heart, there in his bureau, and hugged him.

"'Citizen Michelet,' he said, 'there is a place of a doorkeeper which you can have. The pay is small, fifteen francs the week, but it may suffice your needs.' I knew it was five francs more than old Gaspard received, — the doorkeeper who drank himself to death, — and I took the place gladly. When one is old, my nephew, one does not despise even fifteen francs," and Gaillard looked pathetically into Tournay's face. " Now I sit every evening at the stage door of the theatre and see the familiar faces pass in and out. They do not recognize me ; but they are beginning to address kindly nods and occasional words to old 'Michelet.

"I found a vacant room to let on the ground floor of No. 15 Rue des Mathurins, so I took the lodging and live there quietly. I am on the best of terms with the gendarmes, and I talk with them out of my window, where we exchange pinches of snuff and other like civilities."

" My dear friend " — began Tournay.

" You might as well call me uncle," interrupted Gaillard, " to accustom yourself to it, for under this guise I shall visit you again."

" My dear *uncle*, it is like a draught of wine to a thirsty man to hear you talk. It is like a ray of sunshine to see your wrinkled old face."

" I hope to be the ray of sunshine to light you out of this prison," said Gaillard.

" I'm afraid that will be a difficult matter," replied Tournay. " I am not so clever as you in wearing disguises."

" You will wear no disguise," answered Gaillard. " Are you in a cell by yourself ? " he asked in the next breath.

" No, strange to say I have a companion, Citizen St. Hilaire."

"That is not so bad; only we shall have to include him in our plans," replied Gaillard. "You can trust him?"

"Implicitly."

"When I lean forward over my stick," said Gaillard, "run your hand stealthily up the back of my head under my long hair. Now."

Tournay did as he was bid.

"Do you feel it?"

"I feel something hard, like a little file."

"Good! You could not expect a chest of tools; the jailer searched me thoroughly. Untie that little file from the hair. Can you do it?"

"I think so."

"I tied it quite firmly for fear it would fall out. Do not be afraid of pulling my hair, but do not pull the wig off. You may take both hands, — the turnkey is not paying any attention, — as if you were arranging your old uncle's coat collar."

"I'll have it in a moment. There!"

"Slip this up your sleeve, my colonel. Now a few questions and remarks. How many bars has your window?"

"Four."

"How long will it take you to file them all?"

Tournay considered. "We could only work in any safety in the middle of the night, perhaps four hours in the twenty-four."

"How long do you think it will take you to cut through the four bars?"

Tournay thought for a moment. "We can

work only at intervals in the dead of night," he replied, " so it may take several days."

" Good! In four days I will bring you a rope."

" In God's name, Gaillard, how can you manage to bring a rope into this place ? "

" I am not certain of that point yet, but I shall manage it," was the cool rejoinder.

" My dear Gaillard, I believe you. If you were to promise me to bring a spire of Notre Dame wrapped up in gold paper I should expect to see it at the appointed hour. With a rope in our possession and the bars cut, we can get down the forty feet to the yard beneath. But there is the sentry, and the difficulty of escape from the yard ! "

" I will take care of the sentry and the escape," replied Gaillard, " and in four days I shall be here again. Meanwhile cut through the bars so that you can push them out of place at any moment. Attention ; here comes the turnkey.

" Good-by, my nephew. Be of good cheer. A good patriot need have no fear," said Gaillard in a quavering voice.

" Good-by, my uncle," rejoined Tournay as he went back to his cell. " I shall see you then next week at the same hour," he called out through the bars of the door.

" Yes."

" Well, then, good-by again. Mind the step. Be careful lest my uncle trip, citizen turnkey ; he is old and rather venturesome for one of his years."

CHAPTER XXI

"AGATHA," said Mademoiselle de Rochefort, "I am going back to Paris."

Agatha turned and looked at her mistress in the greatest surprise.

"Do I understand you, mademoiselle, or am I dreaming? It is impossible that you could have said " —

"I am going back to Paris."

Edmé repeated the words quietly, but there was a decision in her manner which Agatha understood full well. She gave a gasp of consternation and sank into a chair, fixing her wide-open eyes upon Edmé's face, while she waited to hear more.

Edmé was seated in her bedroom in the Castle of Hagenhof. It was evening, and two candles, one upon the dressing-table, the other upon a stand at Agatha's side, gave to the room a mild half-light. The curtains were not yet drawn, and through the large casement the stars gleamed softly.

"During the five months we have lived in absolute quiet and security here at Hagenhof," Edmé continued, looking out of the window at the forest of pine trees that stretched away from the castle like a sea of ink, " we have been completely shut

off from the world outside, hearing almost nothing
of the events taking place there."

"That was your wish, was it not?" asked Agatha as Edmé paused.

Mademoiselle de Rochefort did not make any
direct reply, but continued speaking as if she was
answering her own thoughts, rather than conversing with her maid.

"There was a great battle fought.   It was a
full month afterward that I heard of it and of the
glory won by Colonel Tournay.   The Republicans
were victorious.   Had they been defeated, the
restoration of the Monarchy would have been one
step nearer.   But the allies were defeated, their
finest troops were sent flying back before the raw
recruits.   And I!   Did I mourn the defeat of our
allies as much as I rejoiced in Colonel Tournay's
triumph?   *The hero of Landau!*   That is what
he was called."

Then, turning toward Agatha, she exclaimed:
"How do you think they have rewarded him in
France?   They have thrown this hero into prison.
They have kept him there for months.   And I
heard of it only to-night from the officers who
returned with Colonel von Waldenmeer yesterday.
They spoke of affairs in France.   They said that
the Republic is approaching its final doom.   The
leaders are now at discord.   The terrible Danton
has been sent to the guillotine.   They said that
the officers of the army are being suspected; mentioned Colonel Tournay's arrest, and then casually
passed on to other topics.   I heard no more.   I

. could not listen after that, and came up here as
soon as I could withdraw from the table. Agatha,
I am going back to France."

" Why are you going ? " asked Agatha gently,
fearing to antagonize her mistress in her present
mood.

Again Edmé looked out of the window at the
swaying tops of the mournful pines. " I cannot
stay here," she answered fiercely. " The melan-
choly of the place is killing me."

" Do not be a child, mademoiselle," said Agatha
in the tone of authority she sometimes employed
in reasoning with her beloved mistress. " If you
are not happy here, we will leave. Perhaps we
can go to Berlin, or to London. But never to
France ! "

" Twice has he risked his life for me," said
Edmé, again speaking to herself. " I owe so much
to him, and have repaid him nothing."

" All that is true," persisted the cool-headed
Agatha. " He aided you because he had the
power ; if you could serve him, it would be different. But you can do nothing. If you go to
Paris, you will be arrested and guillotined. That
is all. No, my dear mistress, you must not go."

" I shall go," answered Edmé firmly. " If I
am apprehended, so much the worse."

" You will only place yourself in peril," cried
Agatha. " You must not go ! "

" When Colonel Tournay parted from me,"
said Edmé impressively, " he swore that we should
some day meet again. He would keep his word if

it were possible. Fate has decreed that he shall
not come to me; she decrees, instead, that I shall
go to him."

"Mademoiselle," cried Agatha in a horrified
tone, "what are you saying? Think of your rank,
think of your family, your pride of birth!'"

"My rank!'" laughed Edmé scornfully. "Did
that avail me when I crossed the river Loire? My
pride of birth! Did that protect and bring me
safely out of France? A brave and loyal man
was my sole protection. He is now in the greatest
danger. I am going to him."

There was a ring in her voice as she spoke that
seemed to bid defiance to the long line of ancestry
behind her.

"Now that you know that I am not to be swayed
from my determination, will you go with me or
remain here?"

"I shall go with you, mademoiselle."

"We must leave here clandestinely, Agatha. I
little thought, when the kindly Grafin von Waldenmeer took me under her roof, I should leave it
like this."

"We shall have to travel through France in the
disguise of peasants, mademoiselle," said Agatha.

"We have had some experience in that disguise,
Agatha. You know how well I shall be able to
play my part."

From Hagenhof, starting at dead of night, the
two women traveled to Paris. It took them three
weeks to make the journey that they had once
made in five days. But they were obliged to

travel slowly, as became two women of their class.

On the morning of the twentieth day they found themselves in the Rue Vaugirard in Paris, almost under the very shadow of the Luxembourg. Agatha stopped before the doorway of a small house in the window of which a placard announced that lodgings were to let within.

"This is what we want, mademoiselle," said the girl. "I will knock here."

A woman answered the summons. She was about forty years old, with stooping shoulders, and hands gnarled and twisted by hard work. Her skin was dark, but an unhealthy pallor was upon her face, which, thin and worn, was lightened by a pair of brilliant eyes.

"Can we obtain lodging here, good citizeness?" inquired Agatha. The woman did not reply at once, being busy looking at them closely with her bright eyes.

"Have you any lodgings to let?" said Agatha once more.

"Perhaps," was the reply.

"Perhaps," repeated Edmé somewhat impatiently. "Do you not know?"

"I am Citizeness Privat," the woman answered. "There are lodgings to let in this house, most assuredly, and I have charge of the renting of them; but I act for another, and he," with emphasis on the pronoun, "insists that I shall only take those who can furnish references. Can you do so?"

"Let us come inside and we will see what can

be done," said Agatha, pushing forward. The woman stepped back, and Edmé followed Agatha into the house. Agatha closed the door before speaking.

" Citizeness Privat," she said, " we are two women from the country, who have come to Paris for the first time. We know no one here, and can give you no references except money. Will that not satisfy you ? " And Agatha drew a purse from her pocket.

" It will satisfy me, but not him who employs me. If I disobey him I may lose this place which is my only shelter." Edmé caught a glimpse of a neat sitting-room through a half-open door. The cool and quiet of the house were doubly attractive after the noise and heat of the city streets.

" We must stay here," she whispered to Agatha. The latter opened her purse.

" We will pay you well," she said persuasively. The citizeness shook her head mournfully, and put one hand upon the handle of the door.

" Stay one moment, I implore you ! " exclaimed Edmé impulsively. " Listen to what I have to say."

The citizeness turned her strange eyes upon Edmé. The latter started as she beheld the expression on the pale face.

" Agatha ! look ! " Edmé cried out in alarm, and the next instant the Citizeness Privat had fallen to the floor. Quickly Edmé bent over her. " She has fainted. How cold her hands are ! Look at her face. It is ghastly. It cannot be that she is dead, Agatha?" Edmé continued in a tone of awe.

Agatha took one hand and began to chafe it to restore the circulation while Edmé rubbed the other. "She is breathing," said Agatha. "Perhaps with your assistance, mademoiselle, we can lift and carry her into one of the rooms."

Between them the Citizeness Privat was carried gently into her room and placed upon a bed. To their intense relief, the woman gave a sigh, and opened her eyes as she sank back on the pillows.

"Are you in great suffering, poor creature?" asked Edmé, compassionately surveying the pale features. Citizeness Privat signed that she was not in any pain, and after a few moments, during which her breath came regularly, she said faintly:—

"I shall be better soon; I am used to these attacks of sudden giddiness. My greatest fear is that they may seize me some day while I am in the streets. For that reason I dread to go out alone."

"Let us remove her clothing and put her in the bed where she will be more comfortable," suggested Mademoiselle de Rochefort, and in spite of the feeble remonstrances of the sick woman they soon had her comfortably installed between the sheets.

"You are very good," she murmured.

As Agatha removed the gown a card fell from the pocket to the floor.

"I shall be unable to attend to my task this evening," sighed the woman Privat, as if the flut-

tering pasteboard recalled to mind some urgent
duty. " I can ill afford to let the work go either.
It helps so much towards my support, but to-day
it will be impossible."

Edmé picked up the card, and in doing so
glanced at it casually, then read it with a start : —

FRENCH REVOLUTIONARY TRIBUNAL.

Permit the Citizeness Jeanne Privat to enter
the various rooms of the tribunal when engaged
upon her routine duties.

The Citizeness Privat smiled faintly. " I see
you wonder what I have to do with the tribunal,"
she said ; " I merely go there in the afternoon at
dark and clean up the rooms. There are many of
them, and as I am the only person employed to
look after them, they get into a dreadful state of
disorder and dirt." Here the citizeness was taken
with a fit of coughing.

Edmé thrust the card mechanically into her
pocket, and ran to fetch a glass of water.

" You are very good to me," said she faintly as
soon as she could speak. " I turned you away," a
slight flush coming to her cheek. " Believe me, it
was not my heart that spoke when I told you that
I could not let you have the lodging ; I was merely
obeying the commands of the owner, who allows
me my bare rent for my services. He is very
strict, but at the risk of incurring his displeasure,
I shall refuse to let you go after this kindness."

" Do not fear ; do not trouble about that," re-

plied Mademoiselle de Rochefort quietly, "but tell
me more about your work in the tribunal. Is it
that which has worn you so?"

"No, it is not so wearing, only I am far from
strong, and sometimes I get so fatigued. My
brother, who is a turnkey in the conciergerie, obtained this employment for me, as it was thought
I could do it; but I fear I shall have to give it
up."

Edmé smoothed the counterpane. "Do not
worry," she said gently, "but go to sleep now.
We will remain here until you are better."

The citizeness smiled faintly, her lips moved as
if in apology; then she fell into a quiet sleep.

Agatha turned to her mistress.

"Go into the next room, mademoiselle, and rest
there. I will watch over this sick woman."

"I cannot rest, dear Agatha; I have something
else to do, but you must stay here until I return."

"Where are you going?"

"To the Luxembourg."

"Not now, mademoiselle; wait — I will accompany you."

"No, Agatha, I prefer to go alone; you must
remain here until I come back," commanded
Edmé.

Agatha knew it would be useless for her to remonstrate further, so she resumed her place by the
bedside, and with the greatest anxiety saw her
mistress leave the house, and, passing by the window, disappear up the street.

CHAPTER XXII

CITIZENESS PRIVAT'S CARD

"How does one obtain admission to visit a prisoner, citizen doorkeeper?"

"How does one obtain permission?" repeated the keeper without looking up from the work with which he was occupied. "One waits in that room," and he gave a wave of the pen, "until the proper hour, then if one passes satisfactorily under the inspection of the chief prison-keeper and everything appears to be quite regular, one is allowed to see and converse with the prisoner for a short time."

"I wish to see some one here. Pray tell me where I shall find the chief keeper?"

"I am he," replied the keeper, pausing as he dipped his pen in the ink, and looking over the top of his desk saw a woman neatly but simply dressed, as became a citizeness of the Republic. The outlines of her features were partly hidden by the hood of a gray cloak drawn up about her head, but the shadows cast by this garment were not deep enough to hide altogether the beauty of the oval face beneath it.

"Whom do you wish to see?" he asked, evidently satisfied with his inspection, for he dipped his pen in the ink-bottle and resumed his work of ruling perpendicular lines in a ledger.

" I wish to see the prisoner, Robert Tournay."

The jailer put down his ruler. " That is impossible ; the prisoner Tournay is not here."

" Not here ! Then he has been set at liberty ! " The cry of joy that sprang to her lips checked itself, frozen by the quick negative gesture on the keeper's part. She placed one hand upon the iron rail before her and closed her fingers tightly around it. " He is not — Do not tell me he is dead ! " she whispered, looking up at the inexpressive face with a pleading expression in her eyes, as if the jailer were the arbiter of Tournay's fate.

" Transferred to the conciergerie. You may see for yourself, citizeness," and he held up the book and pointed with his forefinger to the notation upon the neatly ruled page, " ' Trans. to C.' That means that Robert Tournay, former colonel in the army of the Republic, was yesterday transferred to the prison of the conciergerie."

Edmé's heart grew cold. She had no means of knowing the full purport of the change, but she felt that it boded nothing but ill to Robert Tournay.

" Can you tell me why this removal was made ? " she asked, although fearing to hear the answer.

" To facilitate his trial. As every one knows the Revolutionary Tribunal is in the same building with the conciergerie. A prisoner may be brought from his cell in the prison into the tribunal chamber, be tried, sentenced, and returned to his dungeon without once being obliged to go outside.

He only passes out into the streets on his way to the guillotine."

"Has the trial already taken place? Can I see him if I go there at once?" she demanded hurriedly.

As the jailer saw the young woman's evident distress his voice softened a little as he made reply: "That you may be prepared for another disappointment, I tell you now, that in order to visit him in the conciergerie, you will have to be furnished with a written permit from some member of the committee. Robert Tournay is confined 'in secret.'"

"Thank you, citizen jailer," was the faint reply. As Edmé turned and left the prison lodge, the custodian of the Luxembourg bent over his work again. The book was already filled with lists of names, written evenly in long columns. This book was the record of all the prisoners of the Luxembourg. When one left the prison his departure was duly noted in the space opposite his name. His transfer to another jail was indicated by the abbreviation "trans." If he was summoned before the tribunal and acquitted, this fact was chronicled by the letters " acq." If he was sentenced to death by the guillotine, the jailer marked him with a little black cross " X." He had once been a schoolmaster, and it was his pride to keep his prison records with neatness and accuracy.

"Nevertheless, I am going to the conciergerie," said Edmé to herself as she passed along the Rue

Vaugirard; "to the conciergerie," she repeated.
She stopped abruptly in the street as the remembrance of the Citizeness Privat came to her mind.
Putting her hand into her pocket, she drew out
the card. "'Permit the Citizeness Privat to enter
the rooms of the tribunal.' I will be Madame
Privat to-night" was Edmé's resolution. "Once
in the tribunal chamber, I shall at least be very
near the prison."

It was late in the afternoon when she reached
the Quai de l'Horloge that skirted the frowning
walls of the formidable prison. She passed the
iron grating of the yard, and looking in, wondered
why some sparrows which were twittering and
fighting on the pavement beneath an unhealthy
looking tree should remain for a moment in a
prison yard when they had the whole outside world
to fly in. Her pace, which had been a rapid one
all the way from the Luxembourg, slackened as
she approached the main entrance, and her fingers
closed tightly on the card in her pocket, while the
heart beneath the gray cloak beat rapidly.

She did not know where to find the tribunal
chamber. She had never been in that part of
Paris before. She only knew that somewhere in
that pile of gray stone were the old Parliament
rooms, at present converted into the tribunal chambers of the Republic. Once in those rooms she
would be under the same roof with Robert Tournay. Passing along the prison wall, she turned
up the Rue Barillerie, and there saw the words
"Revolutionary Tribunal," in large letters over a

doorway. Here was the place to begin the rôle of the Citizeness Privat.

The June evening was warm, and the air in the street fetid, as if it were poisoned by the prison atmosphere; yet with a quick movement of the hand she pulled the hood closer about her face, and rapidly ascended the stone staircase.

A porter sitting by the doorway looked at her with indifferent gaze, but said nothing as she showed him the permit. She passed into the large hall with a strange feeling, as if she were no longer Edmé de Rochefort.

From the information she had received Edmé knew that there was some means of communication between this hall and the prison. This communication she must discover, but she resolved to set about the task coolly and carefully in order that she might not arouse suspicion in the minds of any chance observer.

She imagined that she heard footsteps in a corridor on the other side of the chamber, and this reminded her forcibly that she must play the part of the Citizeness Privat. She gave a glance around the room, wondering how the worthy citizeness did her work. The room certainly was dirty and needed a good deal of cleaning. Bits of paper littered the floor and were scattered about upon the desks. Upon a set of shelves, some books and pamphlets were buried so deeply in dust that Edmé began to think the Citizeness Privat had been somewhat lax in the performance of her duty. After a short investigation she dis-

covered a broom in an anteroom ; and armed with
this she returned to the hall and began to sweep
into a heap the scraps of paper that littered the
floor. This work soon began to fatigue her, and
it also rolled up billows of dust which settled down
over chairs and tables. She placed the broom in
a corner, and looked about for some easier work
which would serve her turn as well.

She espied a green cloth protruding from the
edge of a table drawer. Opening the drawer she
put in her hand and was surprised to find that the
innocent cloth encased a large pistol. She removed the weapon and returned it to the drawer,
while with the green case as a dust-cloth she made
an attack upon the shelves of books with such violence and success as to cause her to draw back
quickly with a sneeze. She stopped, and, with the
green dust-cloth poised in air, listened attentively.
No sound was heard. Cautiously approaching
the door she looked up and down the passageway.

At the further end of this corridor she could see
a small iron-barred door. This, she rightly con-
jectured, led to the conciergerie, and through it
passed the prisoners when they were brought in
for trial. She determined to pass into the prison
through this door, and went toward it with a firm
step. Taking hold of the bars with both hands,
she pressed her face against the ironwork.

"What do you want here?" demanded a voice,
and Edmé saw in the sombre half light the figure
of a sentry. He stood so near the door upon the

other side that by stretching her hand through the
bars she could have touched him.

"I wish to enter here," Edmé replied.

"One does not enter here, citizeness. Go
around to the main entrance on the Quai."

"It is so far," she demurred pleadingly. "I
have been doing my work here in the tribunal
chambers, and now wish to have a few words of
conversation with the turnkey Privat."

"Who are you?"

"I — I am Jeanne Privat, his sister."

"Well — such being the case, I will let you
come through, but you must be sure to come out
this way, citizeness. If you were seen going out
of the lower entrance, not having entered there, it
might get both of us in trouble. And you might
lose your place as well as I."

As he spoke he opened the lower half of an iron
wicket. "Duck your head a little, citizeness, and
enter quickly."

Edmé did not need a second bidding; the gate
closed with a snap, and she was inside the conciergerie.

"Privat is in the second corridor. Go to the
right and then turn to the left," said the warder.
"There he is now, just at the corner," he added
hastily. "Hey, Privat," and he gave a prolonged,
low whistle, "here is your sister, come to see you."

François Privat was slow of speech as well as of
brain, so he merely stood gaping with amazement
at sight of the young woman who claimed him as
a brother, and who bore not the slightest resem-

blance to his sister Jeanne. Edmé stepped quickly forward toward the turnkey, saying in a low voice as she approached him : —

"I bring *a message* from your sister ; the good sentry should have told you." Then in the same breath, she went on hurriedly to say : "The poor woman was taken quite ill this afternoon, so ill that she had to be put to bed. I came to do her work in the tribunal chambers, but thought you should be told of your sister's illness, so asked the sentry to let me speak to you."

In her trepidation, she hardly knew what words came to her lips.

There was silence ; then after Privat had gotten the information into his head, and had digested it, he said slowly : —

"Tell Jeanne Privat that I shall come to see her — let me see — day after to-morrow — no — the day after that, Thursday, my first free time."

Edmé looked up into his face. He was very tall and of a ruddy complexion, fully fifteen years younger than his sister.

"Is that all your message ?" she inquired, in order to gain time for thought.

"At four o'clock in the afternoon, if you like, but she knows the time well enough — from four to six."

Then without showing any further interest in the subject, the imperturbable Privat took up his bunch of keys and began to polish one of them upon his coatsleeve.

There was a pause.

Edmé summoned all her courage and spoke with as much composure as she could assume, although she felt that her voice trembled : —

"Citizen Privat, I have an urgent request to make you."

Privat blinked at her out of his stupid eyes.

"But I am prepared to pay for it."

A sign of animation seemed to come into the turnkey's face, but he did not move nor seek to question her.

"What I am about to ask may be very difficult for you to do, and that is why I am prepared to pay you *well*." She dwelt upon the last words, seeming to guess that she had struck the right note.

"How much are you prepared to pay?" he asked in his slow way.

Edmé drew a purse from the folds of her gown, and opening it disclosed a number of shining gold pieces. Privat's eyes were animated now.

"All that!" he exclaimed. "What do you want me to do for it? It must be something dangerous. I — I am not a brave man."

"It is merely," continued Edmé, holding the open purse in her hand, "to procure me speech with a prisoner."

"What prisoner?"

"Colonel Robert Tournay."

"But it is impossible; he is in secret confinement."

"I know he is, but what I ask is not impossible. There are five hundred francs here ; five hundred

francs, all for you, if you will but bring me to the
cell of Robert Tournay."

"I cannot do that; I have not the key."

"You know who has the key. Surely some of
this gold will enable you to get it. I leave the
means with you."

Privat's mind seemed to be going through the
process which served him for thought.

"At the further end of the south corridor," he
finally said, motioning with a key, "in half an hour,
the prisoner Tournay will be allowed to walk for
exercise. The south corridor is separated from
this one by a grated door. I will see that you get
through that door. That is all I can do."

Edmé pressed the purse into his huge palm,
which closed upon it greedily.

"Shall I come with you now?" she asked, her
pulse beating high between expectation, hope, and
fear.

"No, wait here in the shadow until I come to
fetch you to him. I shall also come to tell you
when you must leave the south corridor. You
will have to do so quickly and go back the same
way you came. If you are discovered here, I
shall get into trouble. You understand?"

"I understand," she answered.

CHAPTER XXIII

TOURNAY'S VISITOR

FOR three days Tournay and St. Hilaire worked away persistently at the bars of their window. They only dared work between the hours of one and four in the morning. Not only secrecy but great ingenuity was called for, as it was necessary that the bars should preserve in the daytime their usual appearance of solidity.

To do this, all the filings were kept, and at the termination of each night's work, this dust, moistened by saliva into a paste, was smeared into the fissure they had made. Their intention was to cut each bar nearly through, leaving it standing, but so weakened that it could be torn out by a sudden wrench.

On the morning which terminated their third night's labor, just as the first gray streak in the east announced the early coming of the long, hot summer day, the third bar had been cut halfway through. The two prisoners looked into each other's eyes. Both realized that they must work rapidly in order to complete their task in time.

" At all hazards we must begin earlier to-night," whispered St. Hilaire significantly. Tournay nodded. " There is still a good deal of work to be done, although a thin man might squeeze through," he said.

"Not a man of your breadth, colonel," replied St. Hilaire, carefully rubbing the dampened filings into the crevice. "We shall have to cut through all of them, and even then it will be a narrow passageway for your shoulders."

"Now for a little rest," he continued, descending from the table as quietly as a cat, and putting it in another part of the cell.

Tired out by their work and the attendant excitement, the two men threw themselves, fully dressed, upon their beds and slept until late in the morning. Their slumber might have continued until past noon had they not been rather unceremoniously awakened by the appearance of the turnkey and a couple of gendarmes by their bedside.

"What is wanted?" exclaimed Tournay sleepily.

"You are to be transferred to the conciergerie, citizen colonel, that is all," was the reply, although the tone implied a deeper meaning.

Tournay sprang from the bed, wide enough awake now, and with a sickening feeling at his heart. He looked at St. Hilaire, who was lying upon his own pallet outwardly indifferent to the announcement, but whose fingers silently stole under the mattress and closed upon the file that had been placed there the night before. St. Hilaire continued to lie there motionless, feigning sleep ; but his alert brain was busy with the problem as to where it would be possible for him to deftly

and successfully hide the useful little tool in case
the guards had also come to search their cell.

" Are you ready, citizen colonel? "

Tournay gave a quick glance at their window.
St. Hilaire rose to a sitting posture.

" Citizen colonel," he said, " will you take my
hand at parting? "

Tournay stepped to his bedside.   Outwardly
calm, the two prisoners clasped hands.   Tournay
felt the hard substance of steel against his palm.

Giving no sign of his surprise, he shook his
head sadly.   " It is useless," he said.

" Good-by, citizen colonel," said St. Hilaire carelessly, as one might bid adieu to a chance acquaintance.   " I am thinner than you, and I may grow
still more so if they keep me here many days
longer."   He gave an imperceptible glance of the
eye in the direction of the window.

The colonel turned away while the file slid up
his coat sleeve.

" I am ready, citizen officers," he said.

The two gendarmes preceded him into the corridor.   As he stepped over the threshold, Gendarme Pierre caught him quickly by the wrist and
the next instant had the file in his own possession.

It was done so adroitly and quickly that Tournay could have offered no resistance even had he
been so inclined.   The other gendarme was not
even aware of what took place.

" I like a clever trick," said Pierre with a
chuckle.

"You are quite a magician," was Tournay's re-joinder.

The tall gendarme gave his grim chuckle. "I am called Pierre the prestidigitateur," he said, "though you are yourself fairly adept at palming. What have you been doing with this little play-thing?" he continued, as they walked down the corridor.

"You mean 'What did I intend to do with it?' do you not?"

The gendarme examined the file carefully.

"No, I mean what have you been using it on," he said.

Tournay was silent.

"Oh, you need not hesitate to speak; it will be found out."

Tournay shrugged his shoulders, and made no reply.

"Well, you are right," said the gendarme. "It is for us to find out." And he relapsed into a silence that was not broken until they reached the conciergerie.

"You will hardly escape from this place though you had a whole workshop of tools," he said grimly at parting.

Tournay realized the truth of this statement, for he was now in the most dreaded of all the prisons of Paris, and he knew well what his trans-fer foreshadowed.

Tournay had no certain means of knowing whether their attempt to cut their way out of the Luxembourg had been discovered; and he still cherished the slight hope that St. Hilaire might be able to escape from the Luxembourg with the assistance of Gaillard.

Had they both escaped, St. Hilaire and he had formed a daring plan to rescue the Republic from the hands of those who were destroying it. And now, even though it was frustrated, he could not help going over all the details in his mind, although the thought of their complete failure added to his misery.

The news of the arrest of General Hoche had reached Tournay's ears some time before, and although it had caused him great pain to learn of the misfortune that had befallen his chief, he felt that the event would embitter the army, and that they would the more readily give their support to any plan that would of necessity liberate Hoche.

This plan had been made for Tournay to reach the army and enlist the officers in his support; then return to Paris with a sufficient force at his back to destroy the tyrants and overawe that part of the Commune that still idolized them. That would give an opportunity for the cooler and more moderate heads in the convention to come to the front, restore order, and form a stable government based upon the constitution.

St. Hilaire, meanwhile, was to remain in hiding; but the first approach of the national troops and the first blast of the counter-revolution was to be the signal for him to appear in the faubourgs, supported by all the followers he could muster, armed with all the eloquence he could command, to move the people to action, and fan to white heat the flame of opposition to the Terrorists which was already smouldering on every side.

But now all the fabric of the carefully spun scheme had been blown roughly aside by one puff of adverse wind.

Once in the conciergerie, a prisoner was not kept in uncertainty for any length of time. The next day after his transfer Tournay was summoned for trial. At first he attempted to defend himself with all the eloquence which the justice of his case called forth. All the fire of his nature was aroused, and as he spoke the attention of the crowded court room was held as if by a spell. Murmurs of applause rose from the multitude, even among those who had come in the hope of seeing him judged guilty.

But upon his judges he made no visible effect. They refused to call his witnesses. They suppressed the applause, and cutting short his defense hastened to conclude his trial. Tournay saw the futility of his defense. He read the verdict in the eyes of the judges, and sat down.

After the verdict had been given he was taken back to the conciergerie, " sentenced to die within eight and forty hours."

" Oh, for a month of freedom ! " he cried inwardly, as he reëntered the prison. " For one short month of liberty ! After that time had passed I would submit to any death uncomplainingly."

Withdrawing to the further end of the corridor

where he was permitted to walk for a short time, he sat down by a rough table where some of the lighter-hearted prisoners had, in earlier days, beguiled the time at cards. Here he rested his head upon his arm and sat motionless.

Then his thoughts returned to Edmé, or rather continued to dwell upon her, for no matter what he did or spoke or thought, no matter how absorbing the occupation of the hour, she was always in his mind, the consciousness of her presence was ever in his heart.

" Oh, for one little month of liberty," he cried aloud, " to make one attempt to rescue France, and to see you, Edmé, once again ! " He rose from his seat with a gesture of despair, and turning, saw her standing there before him. He stood in silence, looking at her as if she were the creation of his fancy, stepped for a moment from the shadow of the gray walls to melt into nothingness, should he, by speaking, break the spell.

She came toward him, putting her finger to her lips as a sign of caution. " Speak low," she whispered, " lest they hear you ! "

" Mademoiselle de Rochefort," he replied in a low voice, " is this really you? In God's name tell me how you come to be here ? "

" I have come to you," she answered simply, putting her hands in his. " When I heard that you had been arrested and put in prison, I knew that I should come and find you. You see all France was not wide enough to keep me from you."

"Then you are not a prisoner?" he exclaimed joyfully.

"No, I came in of my own free will. No one suspects who I am."

"Merciful God, do you know the risk you run? Why have you done this?"

"Have you not risked your life more than once for my sake? Did you think that Edmé de Rochefort would do less for you?"

"Edmé!"

For a moment the prison walls vanished. His shattered plans were forgotten. The redemption of the Republic became as nothing; he only knew that Edmé de Rochefort had proved beyond all human doubt her love for him, and that it was her loyal, loving heart he could feel throbbing, as he pressed her to his breast.

Only for a moment, then the full realization of the terrible risk she ran smote him with redoubled force. He turned pale. She had never seen him so deadly white before, and it frightened her.

"Hush," he whispered before she could speak, and stepping cautiously to the grated door he peered out between the bars. As far as the elbow of the corridor, he could see no one. With a sigh of relief he came back to her. His fears for her safety restored the activity of his mind.

"It is dangerous for you to go about the city. The merest accident, the slightest inquiry in regard to you might lead to your detection."

"I will be very careful," she replied submissively.

"Ah, Edmé," he said, "who am I to deserve such a love as yours? The thought of the risk you incur almost drives me mad. The knowledge of your love will make my last hours the happiest of my life."

"Do not speak of dying, Robert," she said. "There must still be hope. They dare not condemn you."

The words, "You do not know," sprang to his lips, but the look upon her face told him that she was as yet in ignorance of his sentence. He lacked the courage to tell her.

"It must come, Edmé; we should not be blind to that. I would gladly live, if only long enough to see France freed from the talons that rend it, and the true Republic rise from under the tyranny that is crushing it to death. I would gladly live for your love, a love I never dared to hope for either on earth or in heaven. Surely I ought to be the happiest of men to have tasted such bliss even for a moment; and to die with the firm belief that we shall meet beyond the grave."

She did not answer. The quick heaving of her bosom and the quiet sobbing she struggled to suppress went to his heart.

"Do not grieve for me so much," he whispered, drawing her to him; "after all, it will only be for a little while."

"For you who go the time may seem short," she answered mournfully; "but each year that I live without you will seem an eternity. I cannot bear it."

"Courage, dear one, I beseech you; do not grieve for me. Why, I might have met death any day within the past years. I have come to regard it with indifference. Not that I despise life," he added quickly. "Life with you would be more than heaven, but the very nature of a soldier's life makes him look upon his own sudden death as almost a probability. It is but a pang, and all is over."

"I will not grieve for you, Robert," she replied with firmness, "not while there is something to be done. Something that I can do. They shall not murder you."

"What are you going to do?" he asked quickly, fearing that some rash undertaking had suggested itself to her mind.

"This Robespierre rules through the fear he has inspired, but he is hated," replied Edmé. "The people accept his decrees like sheep, but they obey sullenly. They do not criticise him, but that bodes him the greater ill. It needs but one blast to make the whole nation turn against him. There must be men in the convention who are ready to rebel against him," she continued, talking rapidly. "I shall go to them."

"No, Edmé, you shall not. It would be" —

"Listen to what I have to say," she said, interrupting him with an imperative gesture. "I shall find them out; I shall go to their houses. It needs but a little fire; I will kindle it. I will plead with them. If they have any regard for their Republic they will listen to me. Your name,

Robert, shall not be mentioned, but it will be my
love for you that shall speak to them. In the
name of the Republic I shall plead with them, but
it will be only to save you. If they have any
courage or manhood left, they will accept now."

Robert Tournay looked at her with wonder and
admiration as, with a flush of excitement on her
cheek, she outlined clearly and rapidly a plan
strikingly similar to that evolved by St. Hilaire
and himself, — similar, but more daring, more
impossible; one that could not fail to be disas-
trous to her, whatever the ultimate result.

For a moment he feared to speak, knowing the
inflexibility of her will. "I pray you, Edmé,
abandon your design. It will only drag you into
the net and will not avail me."

"Robert, my mind is fixed; my action may
result in saving you, but if not, your fate shall
be mine also."

"Edmé! Do not speak thus. The thought of
you standing on that scaffold, the terrible knife
menacing your beautiful neck, will drive me mad.
Oh, the horror of it!" and he put his hand before
his eyes and trembled.

"Promise me that you will not do this," he continued pleadingly. "Robespierre's power will
come to an end, but the time is not yet ripe. Do
not try to save my life. Do not even try to see
me again." He took her head between his hands.
"Let this be our last adieu," he pleaded. "Listen! the turnkey is advancing down the passageway. I touch your lips; the memory of it shall
dwell in my soul forever."

She threw her arms about his neck for a moment, then before the heavy turnkey entered the inclosure she had passed quickly along the dark corridor through the wicket gate into the Tribunal Hall.

The chamber was dimly lighted by two smoky oil lamps, one on each side of the room; but they gave out enough light to enable her to see the way between the desks and chairs toward the door through which she had first entered from the street.

Edmé turned the handle of the door but could not open it. It had been locked on the outside. She ran to one of the front windows. By the faint light in the Rue Barillerie, she could discern an occasional passer-by. With an effort she raised the heavy sash and leaned out. It was between eight and nine o'clock, and the small street was very quiet. The few pedestrians were already out of hearing, and had they been nearer she would have feared to call out to them. She looked down at the pavement. The height was twenty feet; she closed the window with a shudder. Looking about the room she saw, what had before escaped her notice, a ray of light coming through the crack of a door into an adjoining room.

A number of voices in conversation was audible. She resolved to play again the part of Citizeness Privat. Whoever might be there, when he learned that she had been accidentally locked in while at work, would show her the way out.

The door opened wider, and a man came forth. Edmé, who had hastily taken up the same broom she had before used, pretended to be at work, while she summoned her self-possession. The man gave her no more than a casual glance as he went to a table, took out from a drawer a bundle of papers, and proceeded to look them over.

Edmé looked at him closely, sweeping all the while. Her first apprehension was quieted when she saw he was a very young man with rosy cheeks and a pen behind his ear. He was evidently one of the government clerks, staying late at the office to finish some piece of work.

She breathed more freely every moment notwithstanding the amount of dust she raised. The clerk put the bundle of papers under his arm with a gesture of annoyance, and went back to the other room.

Edmé waited a few minutes, put the broom under her arm, and approached the door which the clerk had left ajar. She could not help starting as she read the large letters on the panel of the door. The room which contained the apple-faced and harmless looking little scribe was designated " Chamber of Death Warrants."

" Here 's a pretty state of affairs, Clément," she heard a voice exclaim in a tone of annoyance. " The list of warrants for ' La Force ' to-morrow consists of thirty-seven names while I have only thirty-six documents."

" Count them again, Hanneton ; you know at school you were always slow at figures."

" I have compared the warrants with the list of names twice most carefully. I assure you one warrant is missing. See for yourself, ' *Bonnefoi*,

Charles de, ex-noble' is on the list, but there is not
a single Bonnefoi among to-morrow's pile of warrants."

"Have you looked through those of day after
to-morrow?"

"I have, both of the day after to-morrow and
the day following that. In fact, I have gone over
all the warrants for all the prisoners, but still no
Bonnefoi, Charles de, ex-noble."

"Lucky for Bonnefoi!"

"But unlucky for me. I shall be discharged
if I let these go out this way."

"I tell you what to do," said Clément, "take
one from the day after to-morrow. They are in
too great a hurry in the office these days to compare the lists; they just see if the number tallies,
and send off the warrants to the keepers of the
various prisons."

"But if I do that I shall still be one short, day
after to-morrow."

"No you will not," replied the facile Clément;
"you just take one from the day following that,
and so on and so forth. You merely keep the
thing going. Your lists and warrants will agree
as to number every day. No question arises,
and the only result is that some fellow gets shoved
along under the national razor just twenty-four
hours earlier than he would have, had not some
one, — I won't say named Hanneton, — but some
one who shall be nameless, made a little blunder."

"I rather dislike to do such a thing, Clément."

"Oh, Hanneton, my boy, I always said you were

slow. What's twenty-four hours to a man who
has got to die anyway? and then think of Bonnefoi; he 'll be overlooked for a long time. Some of
those fellows among the aristocracy have been in
prison two or three years already. They get to
like it and lead quite a jolly life there. I am told
they have fine times in some of the prisons. Bonnefoi will be wondering why they don't come to
shave him, but he won't say anything. Bonnefoi
won't peep. You can count on his silence."

" But my friend Clément, it will be discovered
some day."

" Well, I can't look ahead so far as that. If
you are found out you can say you made a mistake.
They can't any more than discharge a man for
making a mistake."

" I 'll do it, Clément. Here goes — good luck
to Bonnefoi."

" And good luck to the fellow you shove ahead
in his place; we 'll drink an extra glass to him
when we finish work to-night. Let's see what
may his name be."

" ' *Tournay, Robert, former Colonel!* ' Hello,
what 's that?" cried Clément, interrupting him.

" I did not hear ànything," replied Hanneton.

" The sound seemed to come from the next
room."

" Oh, it 's only that woman who is cleaning the
place. She has knocked over a table or a chair.
Come. Let's go out and get something to eat.
I 'm famished. We can return later, and finish
our work."

CHAPTER XXIV

TWO WOMEN

THE revelation that Tournay was condemned, the awful knowledge that he would be executed on the morrow, conveyed to her thus suddenly, made the room reel before Edmé's eyes. In her dizziness she fell against one of the tables and held to it for support.

In the quiet that followed the departure of the clerks she pressed her head and tried to think. At first her benumbed brain refused to work; then as the full significance of the clerk's action came back to her, when she realized just what he had done and what she in her turn might do, she stood erect, alert, and courageous.

The warrant for Robert's death; could she get possession of it? With a beating heart she glided into the chamber of death warrants.

A lamp was burning in the room, and there in plain view upon the table were three packets of black-covered papers. She bent over them hastily and at once took up the file marked : "Warrants of the eighth Thermidor." With nervous fingers she ran them through, looking at each name until she came to that of "Tournay, Robert, ex-colonel." At sight of the name she gave a half-suppressed cry, and took it quietly from the others. "They shall not send you to the guillotine to-morrow, Robert," she breathed. Her first thought was how to make way with the fatal paper. She looked round the room; it had one window and two doors. The window looked out upon the street. One doorway led back into the tribunal chamber. Through the other, a small one, the two clerks must have passed out. She hastened towards it, praying fervently that they had omitted to fasten it. Vain prayer, the clerks had not been remiss in their duty here. It was locked. Yet it was not a strong barrier. A few blows struck with some heavy object might break it through; or better still there was a pistol in the drawer of one of the desks; with that she could blow the lock to atoms. Either method would make a noise, but she must take the risk.

Just as these thoughts flashed through her mind, she saw to her consternation the door-handle turn, and heard the grating of a key on the outside.

"The employees returning," she thought, and had just presence of mind enough to pass her left hand, which still clutched the death warrant, behind her back, when the door opened, and she was face to face with a woman.

"Hello!" said the latter, "I expected to find Clément and Hanneton here. Who are you?"

"I — I am, — I came in the place of Madame — of Citizeness Privat."

"You seem a little put out, citizeness, at the sight of La Liberté. You have never seen me before? That's why, eh? Tell me, now, what are you doing here?"

"I am doing the work of Citizeness Privat, who is ill," replied Edmé, recovering her self-possession.

"Hum," said La Liberté with a slight sniff, as she closed the door and passed toward the centre of the room. Edmé slowly revolved on her heel, keeping her face toward La Liberté, and her left hand behind her back.

"What are you trying to hide there?" demanded La Liberté quickly, whose bright brown eyes took in every motion of Edmé.

"I have nothing to hide."

La Liberté's glance went from Edmé to the warrants on the table, and then back to Edmé's face again.

"You are hiding something behind your back," persisted La Liberté, trying to obtain a peep at it by making a circle around Edmé. Edmé continued to turn, always keeping her face toward La Liberté.

The latter stopped. "I will see what you have there," she declared with a toss of her head, her curiosity aroused to the burning point.

"You shall not. It does not concern you," was the firm reply.

For an instant each looked into the other's eyes in silence. Both breathed defiance; both were equally determined.

Then with a tigerlike spring La Liberté dashed forward, seized Edmé about the waist with one arm, while she endeavored to secure the parch-

ment with her other hand. Edmé quickly passed
the document into her right hand, bringing it forward high above her head. With the same cat-
like agility, La Liberté sprang for it on the other
side and managed to get hold of it by one corner.
There was a short struggle; a tearing of paper,
and each held a piece of the document in her hand.

" A warrant! " exclaimed La Liberté, darting
back a few paces and shaking out the piece of
paper in her hand. " You have been tampering
with these," she added quickly, putting one hand
upon the pile of documents on the table.

Edmé made no reply.

" Why did you take it? " inquired La Liberté,
taking her portion of paper near the light to examine it, while she kept one eye fixed upon her late
antagonist, in fear of a sudden attack.

The warrant had been divided nearly down the
centre; but the last name of the condemned man
was upon the piece held by La Liberté.

" Tournay! " she cried out in surprise. " Robert Tournay! What object have you in destroying this warrant? "

" I have not destroyed it," replied Edmé,
making the greatest effort to maintain an outward
calm. " It was you who tore it."

" Don't try any of those tricks with me,"
snapped La Liberté. " Come, what was your
object in taking this warrant? It is a dangerous
thing to tamper with those documents."

" I shall not answer any of your questions," was
Edmé's rejoinder.

For a space of ten seconds the two women stood again confronting each other, as if each waited for the other to move. La Liberté's eyes looked fixedly at Edmé, as if they would read her through and through.

"You are not what you pretend to be," she said finally; "you are no woman of the people." Then, suddenly flinging aside the torn paper, she rushed forward and seized Edmé's arm.

"I know who you are now!" she exclaimed excitedly. "You are an aristocrat! Don't deny it!" she continued passionately. "I came from La Thierry. I was a young girl when I left there, but my memory serves me well. Your name is Edmé de Rochefort. You are an aristocrat, and you love the republican colonel! You destroyed this warrant. You risked your life in the attempt to prolong his."

"Whoever I may be, whatever I attempted to do, you tore that paper. It was you who destroyed it," said Edmé as she wrenched herself free from the woman's grasp.

The only answer of La Liberté was a loud and scornful laugh. She approached Edmé again with a malignant glitter in her eyes; but Edmé held her ground and confronted her bravely.

"So you are Edmé de Rochefort," repeated La Liberté slowly. "I remember having seen you years ago when I was a girl of fifteen, at my father's mill near the village of La Thierry. You were a pale-faced girl then. You did n't wear coarse clothes then! You drove in your carriage, and did n't look at such as me; but I saw you, and hated you for being so proud. Then there was a certain marquis." A bright spot appeared on Edmé's cheek, but she did not speak.

" He came to pay his court to you, but he made love to me. He never even made a pretense of loving you. But he cared for me in his cold, selfish way. He took me to Paris, gave me everything money could buy, for a while. Then he left me, and went back to you. I hated you for that. You did not care for him. You did not marry him. That made no difference to me. Then there was another man. He was not for you. He was of my class, not yours. You had no right to his love. He never loved me, I know. I am too proud to say he loved me when it was not so. But he was kind to me. He was noble and generous, and I loved him. You had no right to him. I hate you for that more than all." Her passion wrought upon her so that her once pretty face was something fearful to behold. Edmé expected at each breath she would spring forward and tear her like a tiger cat.

" I care not for your hatred," Edmé retorted calmly. " I never willfully wronged you. Your hatred cannot harm me."

" No ? " demanded the frenzied La Liberté. " It can restore this paper. I can denounce you. I can send you with your lover to the guillotine."

" That does not terrify me," replied Edmé. " You can send the woman you hate and the man you profess to love into another world together.

That is all you can do. I am above your hatred."

La Liberté started to speak, then checked herself.

"You say you love him. Love," repeated Edmé in a tone of deep disdain. "You dare to call that love which would destroy its object? Such as you are not capable of love."

"If it were not that *you* loved him, I would let them cut me into pieces for his sake," retorted La Liberté fiercely.

"You say that you love him, and you are willing to send him to the guillotine," repeated Edmé.

"If it were not that it would be giving him to you, I would give my life a thousand times to save him," was the answer.

Edmé caught La Liberté by the arm.

"You have it in your power to cause my arrest. If you will not use that power, if you will give me only twenty-four hours, I may be able to save Robert Tournay's life. At the expiration of that time, whether I succeed or fail, I will surrender myself. I will denounce myself before the Committee of Public Safety."

La Liberté looked into Edmé's face searchingly but made no reply.

"You understand what I propose," Edmé continued in a cool, firm voice. "If you agree to it you can accomplish what you desire; the rescue of Robert Tournay and my death."

"Bah," said La Liberté with a shrug; "you are very heroic, but, Robert Tournay once out of danger, you would not give yourself up to the committee. In your place, I should not do it, and I will not trust you."

"I give you my promise to appear before Robespierre himself."

"Your promise," repeated La Liberté, "you ask me to accept your simple word?"

"The word of a de Rochefort," said Edmé with quiet dignity.

"The word of an aristocrat," continued La Liberté slowly. "You aristocrats vaunt your devotion to honor."

"And will you not trust it when Colonel Tournay's life is at stake?" asked Edmé.

"Yes, I will," La Liberté burst forth in fierce energy. "I *will* trust your word, and test your honor."

"Then for twenty-four hours you will let me go free? You will not have me watched nor interfered with in any way?"

"I give you *my* word," said La Liberté, drawing herself up, "and my word is as good as that of the proudest aristocrat."

Then changing her manner she asked quickly: "How do you propose to save Robert Tournay? What can you do?"

Edmé had no intention of imparting her plan to La Liberté, yet she did not wish to antagonize her by refusing to confide in her.

"There is not time to go into the details of it now. First help me to get away from here. Those clerks may return."

"I will prevent that," said La Liberté quickly. "I know where they sup. I will go there and delay their return. They are convivial youngsters and never refuse a glass or two. In the meantime you must see to it that those three files of warrants do not retain the slightest appearance of having been handled. Be sure that every object in the room is just as you found it."

By this time La Liberté was outside the door. Looking back into the room, she said: "When you have done that, go down this staircase, cross the street, and wait for me in the shadow of the building opposite. I will then conduct you to my house," and La Liberté's feet sprang nimbly down the stairs.

Quickly Edmé picked up the pieces of torn warrant, intending to take them away and burn them. Then she turned her attention to the documents on the table, and in a few minutes had them arranged just as she found them. She placed the chairs in a natural position before the table, and stepped back for a final survey to assure herself that she had not left a trace which might arouse the suspicion of the clerks.

No, there was nothing that Hanneton or even Clément would be likely to notice. She had been none too rapid in the arrangement of these details. The door of the adjoining chamber was unlocked and some one entered.

Edmé could tell by the footfalls that the person was traversing the room with measured tread. Then came the sound of a chair being drawn up to a desk. Then a dry cough echoed through the deserted hall as a man cleared his throat.

Edmé gave a glance toward the door that led down the staircase taken by La Liberté. It stood invitingly open, but to gain it she would have to pass the door that communicated with the tribunal. This also was open. She started on tiptoe across the floor.

The words " Bring me a light here, will you ? " fell upon her ears in a harsh tone of authority. She started at this sudden command. She had made no noise, yet the mysterious personage seemed to be aware of her presence.

" In the next room there, whoever you are, bring in more light ; this lamp burns villainously ! "

Edmé hesitated no longer but caught up the lamp from the table and entered the tribunal chamber. As she obediently placed the light upon the desk the man who was writing there looked up with impatient gesture. Although she had never seen him before, she had heard him described many times, and she knew that he was Robespierre.

" Well ! " he exclaimed, " who are you ? "

" I — I am here in place of the Citizeness Privat."

" The Citizeness Privat ? "

" Yes, she cleans up the rooms, and being ill " —

" Cleans ! " repeated Robespierre with a laugh, blowing the dust from the top of the table. " Is that what you call it ? ͵ This Privat is like all the rest, willing to take the nation's pay and give nothing in return. And you are also like the rest, eh?"

"I do not know what you mean. I am doing her work as well as I can. With your permission I will hasten to complete my task," replied Edmé.

In spite of her abhorrence of him she could not help looking at him intently, her eyes expressing the horror which she felt. To her, he was the embodiment of all that was evil, the very spirit of the Revolution. As her glance rested upon the white waistcoat, fitting close to his meagre figure, and as she thought of the cruel heart that beat beneath it, the vision of Charlotte Corday and the vile Marat flashed before her eyes with startling vividness.

What if heaven had decreed that she should be the means of ridding the world of this monster? What if the opportunity was about to present itself? She pushed the thought away from her, with the inward supplication, "God keep me from doing it."

Robespierre noticed the look of horror on her face, and attributed it to the fear his presence inspired. His small eyes blinked complacently.

"Stay," he said; "you have nothing to fear if you are a good patriotic citizeness. And you may be pardoned if you neglect your work for a few minutes to converse with Robespierre."

There was an insinuating softness in his tone as he spoke that made her nerves creep and increased her loathing for him. He sat leaning back negligently in his chair, and she stood looking down upon him like some superb creature from another world.

"By the power of beauty," he exclaimed suddenly, "you are a glorious woman! I have always said that only among women of the people is true beauty to be found."

She neither moved nor spoke, but stood still as a statue.

He leaned forward in his chair. "You shall lay aside your broom and dust-rags. I would see more of you. I have it. You shall be the Goddess of Beauty at our next great fête. In that rôle Robespierre himself will render you homage." Rising, he took one of her hands in his.

She shuddered. It was as if a snake had coiled itself about her fingers. The contact with her soft hand sent just a drop of blood to his sallow cheek.

"What sayst thou, O glorious creature? Wilt thou be a goddess of beauty and sit enthroned upon the Champ de Mars, dressed in radiant clothing, instead of these poor garments?" He spoke in low tones meant to be tender.

Again the vision of Charlotte Corday flashed before her.

"No, no!" she cried out, more in answer to the thought that terrified her than to his question.

"Fear nothing, fair one," he said soothingly. "Robespierre is only terrible to the guilty; to the good he is always magnanimous and kind. Some say that I abuse my power, but that is false. True, I condemn many, but 'tis done with justice; and I also pardon many. Should I receive no credit for my clemency?" he continued, as if he were arguing with some unseen personage.

He released her hand and leaned his elbow on the desk. Her hand fell cold and numb to her side, but the spell in which he had held her was broken. A sudden daring resolve entered her head.

"I have been told that you were a cruel monster, who condemned for the pleasure of condemning; who did not know the meaning of clemency," she said, "and therefore I am afraid of you."

"They have maligned me," he answered.

"Will you prove it by granting me a pardon, one that I can use as I may wish?"

Robespierre became alert on the instant.

"You would set some man at liberty?"

"Yes."

"Your lover, is it not?"

"I pray you, do not ask me."

"Do not ask you!" repeated Robespierre. "And yet you ask me to pardon him. Why should I do it?"

"To prove that you know what clemency is."

"I would rather show it in some other way. I should be a fool to set your lover at liberty, so that you both might laugh at me."

"I have not said that it was my lover."

"No, but I say so."

"You said a moment ago that you knew what mercy was, yet you cannot understand my feeling at the thought that he must die."

Robespierre took up a pen from the table and poised it over a sheet of paper. The pleading look in the beautiful eyes gave him great enjoyment, and he took a keen relish in prolonging it.

"A few words from my pen," he said tantalizingly, "would set the man at liberty. How would you reward me if I wrote them for you?"

"Oh, I pray you to do so," she cried out, throwing herself at his feet. "I pray you to write them. If you have the power, use it for mercy."

Robespierre gazed deep into the eyes which looked up at him imploringly.

"Who are you?" he demanded with the energy of sudden passion. "You are no woman of the common people. Who are you?"

"One who would have you do a noble action," she answered. "One who is pleading with you for your own soul's sake."

"Whoever you may be, you have bewitched me. Promise you will come hence with me, and I will write the release."

"Write it," she whispered faintly.

Robespierre dashed off a few hurried lines.

"What is the fellow's name?" he asked.

"Sign the paper," she murmured, dropping her eyes. "I implore you, do not ask me his name. Let me fill that in."

"I will free no man from prison unless I know his name," replied Robespierre.

"I will never tell you that," she replied, rising to her feet and going to the other side of the desk, "never."

"What foolish nonsense," he complained, sign-
ing his name. "Now," he continued, shaking the
sand box over the wet ink, "tell me his name,
and I will send this pardon to the conciergerie at
once. See, I have written 'immediate release'
upon it. You have only to tell me his name. Do
you still hesitate?"

There was a sudden rattle in the drawer on
Edmé's side of the desk. Leaning forward, she
brought one hand down upon the paper, while
with the other she pointed a pistol at Robespierre's
head.

He turned deadly white and drew back in his
chair.

"Would you murder me?" he gasped out.

"If you make one movement," she replied,
"Marat's fate will be yours." He cringed further
away from the muzzle of the weapon that stared
him in the face. With one hand she folded up
the document and put it in the bosom of her dress,
all the while keeping the pistol aimed steadily at
him.

"Now," she continued coolly, "you have the key
of the door. Make no movement," she added
quickly, bringing the pistol still nearer him, "but
tell me where to find it."

"It is in the door now," he snarled.

She came cautiously around the corner of the
desk, still keeping the weapon leveled at his
head.

He rose to his feet and sprang toward her.
The pistol snapped. He caught her by the wrist

"WOULD YOU MURDER ME?"

Then pinning both her arms to her side with his arms about her waist he breathed in her ear : —

" You cannot fire a pistol that is not loaded, though you *did* startle me. Now give me that paper."

Edmé did not speak, but struggled desperately to break from his grasp. She determined that he might kill her before she would give back the paper. So fiercely did she struggle that he had to exert all his strength to hold her.

" I 'll have that paper again if I have to strangle you to get it ! " he muttered through his teeth. He succeeded in holding down both arms with one of his, leaving his left arm free.

Before he could make use of it, he felt himself seized from behind. His nerves, strained by his previous fright, gave way completely at this unexpected attack. Uttering a cry, he released his hold completely.

" Save yourself; I will not hold you to your promise ! " cried a voice. Edmé waited to hear nothing more, but darted swiftly from the room, leaving the baffled Robespierre confronted by La Liberté.

For a moment he stood still, his surprise rendering him incapable of speech or action. La Liberté walked jauntily to the door through which Edmé had just vanished, locked it, and stuck the key in her belt beside the knife she always wore there.

" Do you know what you are doing, you mad creature ? " cried Robespierre, running to the door and putting his hand upon the latch. " Unlock this door at once."

"Wait a moment; I have something to say to you," was La Liberté's rejoinder.

"Give me that key instantly, do you hear?" he yelled, stamping his foot upon the floor. "You do not know what you are doing."

"I know," said La Liberté, nodding her head. "I have seen and heard everything; I have been watching you from the door of the back staircase."

"The back staircase!" exclaimed Robespierre, starting toward it.

"You need not trouble to go to it. I locked that door when I came in."

Robespierre came toward her, furious with passion. "I will have none of your escapades," he said fiercely; "give me that key or I will" —

"Keep off! keep off!" cried out La Liberté, bounding lightly out of his reach with a little mocking laugh. "Don't catch me about the waist; I carry my sting there."

"You wasp! I will crush you!" he cried out, foaming with rage.

"Better take care how you handle wasps," was her rejoinder as she perched herself upon the edge of a desk and shook her brown curls defiantly at him.

"Come, Liberté," he said, trying a coaxing tone, although his anger almost choked him; "I know you will open the door at once when I tell you that woman has obtained from me by a skillful ruse a pardon in blank. I don't know whose name will be filled in. Perhaps some great enemy of the

Republic will be set at liberty, unless I can send word at once to the conciergerie and forestall it."

"I know who will be liberated," sang La Liberté, swinging her feet.

"You do!" vociferated Robespierre in genuine astonishment. "Is this a plot? Are you concerned in it?" And he came toward her, his small eyes winking rapidly.

"You don't get it yet," laughed La Liberté, sliding over to the other side of the desk. "I am concerned in enough of a plot to keep you from sending to the scaffold a man to whom I've taken a fancy. I do not very often take a particular interest in any one person, but when I do, it is lasting." And she regarded him airily from her point of vantage.

"I'll send you to the guillotine," hissed Robespierre between his teeth, striking his clenched fist upon the desk in front of him. "I'll have you arrested to-night. I'll bear with you no longer. I have permitted you to swagger around in public, to come into the Jacobin Club and flourish your pistols, because it amused the populace, and I laughed with them at your antics; but now you have overstepped the line. This meddling with national affairs will cost you your life."

For a moment La Liberté confronted him from behind her barricade, her eyes darting fire.

"How dare you threaten me!" she cried shrilly.

"You have conspired against the Republic; you shall pay for it," he repeated, his fingers working convulsively as if he would like to lay hands upon her.

"My name is La Liberté," she said proudly, drawing herself up. "I am a child of the Revolution. I have drunk of her blood. Do you think, Robespierre, to terrify me with your shining toy, the guillotine? Bah! I snap my fingers at it;" and speaking thus, she advanced toward him, one hand resting on the dagger at her hip. He fell back before her, step by step, until they reached the door. Voices were heard outside and some one tried to enter.

"Break the door down, whoever you are!" cried Robespierre. "Kick the panel in; throw your whole weight against it."

"We are Hanneton and Clément, clerks; we found the rear doorway locked "—

"Break in, I say!" called out Robespierre impatiently.

The hall reverberated with the noise of an attack made by Hanneton's heavy shoes and Clément's shoulder.

La Liberté inserted the key in the lock. "I might as well open it now," she said, throwing back the door.

The two clerks stood on the threshold in open-mouthed surprise.

La Liberté passed them like a fawn and sped swiftly down the staircase.

"We were merely returning to finish up a little work," stammered Clément, who was the first to recover the use of his tongue; "but if we intrude "—

"Come in," interrupted Robespierre quickly.

" I have an errand of importance for you." Seating himself at a table, he dashed off two short notes. The clerks exchanged glances from time to time.

" Here ! " said Robespierre looking at Clément, and sealing the letters as he spoke. " You look the less stupid. Take this at once to the keeper of the conciergerie, then report to me in person at my house. You other fellow, take this to Commandant Henriot. You will find him either at the Hôtel de Ville or at the Jacobin Club. Tell him to report to me in person. Now go, both of you."

The two clerks did not wait to be twice bidden, and Robespierre followed them from the room.

An hour later the commandant stood before the president of the committee in his own house.

" Well," asked Robespierre, " have you executed the warrant ? "

" The Citizeness Liberté has been incarcerated in the Luxembourg prison," was the reply.

Robespierre's eyes blinked rapidly. " She is a child of the Revolution," he repeated softly, " and does not fear my toy."

Upon Henriot's heels entered Clément. Robespierre turned to him eagerly.

" Fifteen minutes before I reached the conciergerie, a prisoner, named Robert Tournay, was liberated on a release signed by you, citizen president. It was delivered by a woman," was the brief report.

An oath sprang to Robespierre's lips. " Tour-

nay!" he cried out. "So it was Tournay whom
that woman has freed. The man is dangerous,"
he continued, speaking to himself. "He should
have perished long ago had I not wished to get at
Hoche through him. But he shall not escape me;
nor shall the woman."

"Henriot," he exclaimed in his next breath,
"order every route leading out of the city guarded.
Lodge information at every section for the arrest
of Robert Tournay, and of one other, a woman."

"Yes, citizen president, and who" —

"Wait, I will write her description for you,"
cried Robespierre. "There it is. Now be prompt,
my patriot. We can still recapture our prisoner,
and then" — He did not complete the sentence,
but his teeth came together with a snap, and he
drew his thin lips over them tightly.

CHAPTER XXV

NO. 7 RUE D'ARCIS

THE order signed by Robespierre for the immediate release of a prisoner had not been questioned by the keeper of the conciergerie, and within a few minutes from the time when Edmé presented the document with a heart fluctuating between the wildest hope and the greatest fear, Colonel Tournay walked out of the prison a free man.

The sudden manner of his release, the fact that it had been effected by Edmé's own daring and sagacity, and that he owed his life to her whom he loved, made his brain reel. Then the recognition of the danger that still menaced him, and above all the woman who was by his side, brought him back to himself, and he was again cool, alert, and determined as she had always known him. Drawing her arm through his and walking rapidly in the shadows of Rue Barillerie, he said quickly: —

"The pursuit will be instant. Robespierre will ransack all Paris to find us. But I know a hiding-place. Come quickly."

She looked up at him. "I feel perfectly safe now," she said, and together they hurried onward.

Suddenly she stopped. "But how about Agatha!" she exclaimed, as the thought of her faithful companion came to her mind for the time.

"Agatha! Where is she?" asked Tournay almost impatiently, chafing at a moment's delay.

"At the Citizeness Privat's in the Rue Vaugirard. They will surely find and arrest her. Robert, we must not let them."

"The delay may mean the difference between life and death," replied Tournay, turning in the direction of the Rue Vaugirard; "but we must not let Agatha fall into Robespierre's clutches."

In a few minutes they passed up the Rue Vaugirard. "Which is the house?" asked Tournay anxiously.

"There; the small one with the blinds drawn down. Agatha will be anxiously waiting for me, I know. There she is now in the doorway. She sees us! Agatha, quick! Never mind your hat or cloak. Ask no questions. Now Robert, take us where you will."

Passing Edmé's arm through his own, and with Agatha on the other side, Tournay conducted the two women rapidly down the street.

At the same moment gendarmes were running in all directions carrying Robespierre's orders.

Two of them hastened to the house of Citizeness Privat. They found her in bed. Awakened from her sleep, she could only give meagre information about her lodgers. There were two of them; one, she thought, was still in the room across the hall. A tall gendarme opened the door and walked in without ceremony. He found the room empty, although a few articles of feminine apparel indicated that it had been occupied recently.

" Hem ! " sniffed the tall gendarme, " women ! " Then he called in his companions, and they proceeded to examine everything in the hope of finding a clue.

At that moment Robert Tournay, Edmé, and Agatha were approaching the Rue d'Arcis.

" It is only a step from here," said Tournay encouragingly as they crossed the bridge St. Michel. " Once there we cannot be safer anywhere in Paris. I know of the place from a fellow prisoner in the Luxembourg."

They passed through a narrow passageway and underneath some houses, and emerged into the Rue d'Arcis. Crossing the street, and looking carefully in both directions to see if they were unobserved, Tournay struck seven quick low notes with the knocker on the door. They waited in silence for some time; then Tournay repeated the knocking a little louder than before. They waited again and listened intently. Edmé's teeth began to chatter with nervous excitement, and Tournay looked once more apprehensively up and down the street.

" Who knocks ? " was the question breathed gently through a small aperture in the door.

" From Raphael," whispered Tournay, " open quickly."

" Enter."

The door swung inward on its hinges, and the three fugitives hastened to accept the hospitality offered them.

It was an old man who answered their summons
and who closed the door carefully after them. He
now stood before them shading with his palm
a candle, which the draft, blowing through the
large empty corridors, threatened to extinguish
altogether. The dancing flame threw grotesque
shadows on the wall. As the light played upon
the features of the old man, first touching his white
beard and then shining upon his serene brow,
Edmé thought she looked upon a face familiar to
her in the past, but, no sign of recognition appearing in the eyes that met her gaze, she attributed it
to fancy.

"Your name is Beaurepaire?" inquired Tournay.

"That is my name," was the old man's answer.

In a few words Colonel Tournay told of his
acquaintance with St. Hilaire, and explained how,
had their plan of escape succeeded, they would
have come there together. Unfortunately he alone
had escaped, — and now came to ask that he and
his two companions might remain there in hiding
for a few days.

"You came from Raphael," replied Beaurepaire with the dignity of an earlier time. "The
length of your stay is to be determined by your
own desire."

He led the way along the corridor, down a short
flight of steps, through a covered passageway, into
what appeared to be an adjoining house; Tournay
asked no questions, but, with Edmé and Agatha,
followed blindly.

Their aged conductor ushered them into a large room, which had formerly been a handsome salon; but the few articles of furniture still remaining in it were decrepit and dusty. The once polished floor was sadly marred, and appeared to have remained unswept for years. The room was wainscoted in dark wood to the height of six feet, and upon the wall above it hung portraits of ladies and gentlemen of the house of St. Hilaire. Here they had hung for years before the Revolution, dusty and forgotten.

At the end and along one side of the room ran a gallery which was reached by a short straight flight of stairs, and around this gallery from floor to ceiling were shelves of books.

Beaurepaire mounted the stairs, and looking among the books as if searching for a certain volume, pushed back part of a bookcase and revealed a door. He motioned them to ascend.

"In here," he said, pointing to a small room with low-studded ceiling, "the two ladies can retire. It is the only room in the house suitable for their comfort. You, sir," he continued, looking at Colonel Tournay, "will have to lie here upon the gallery floor. There is only a rug to soften the oak boards, but you are, I see, a soldier. To-morrow I will see what can be done to make the place more habitable."

Edmé and Agatha passed through the aperture in the wall, the venerable Beaurepaire bowing low before them.

"At daylight I will bring you some food; until

then I wish you good repose." He withdrew, and Colonel Tournay was left to stretch himself out upon the gallery floor to get what sleep he could.

It was daylight when he opened his eyes, and looking through the balustrade to the room below, saw a loaf of bread, some grapes, and a steaming pitcher of hot milk set on a large mahogany table which stood against the wall. He had evidently been awakened by the entrance of his host, for the figure of Beaurepaire was standing with his back to him, looking out of the window into the courtyard. The colonel kicked aside the rugs which had served him for a bed, and rising to his feet, started to descend.

The figure at the window turned at the sound of the tread upon the stairs, and Tournay stopped short with one hand on the rail. "He has shaved off his flowing beard overnight," was his astonished thought. Then the next instant he recognized that it was not Beaurepaire, but Father Ambrose, the old priest of La Thierry, who stood before him.

The latter approached with his usual dignity.

"Father Ambrose," exclaimed Tournay in surprise, "how can this be? Who, then, is this Beaurepaire?"

"He is my brother. I have lived here for more than six months. I saw you when you came last night, but waited until now before making myself known. Inform me, my good sir, how fares it with Mademoiselle de Rochefort?"

"You shall see her presently. She and Agatha

are in the chamber behind the secret panel. They are doubtless much fatigued from the excitement of yesterday, and we would better let them sleep as long as they can. In the meantime I will eat some of this food, for I am desperately hungry."

"Do so, my son," replied the priest. "I would eat with you, but for the fact that I never break my fast before noon."

Tournay helped himself to a generous slice of bread and a bunch of grapes.

"Tell me," he asked, as he began on the luscious fruit, "how do you obtain the necessities of life? Do you dare venture out to buy them?"

"I have not set my foot outside the door since I first entered. All the communication with the outside world has been held by my brother, who has managed to keep free from suspicion, and who goes and comes in his quiet way as the occasion arises."

A knock upon the door brought Tournay to his feet. He stopped with the pitcher of milk in one hand and looked at Father Ambrose.

"There is no cause for alarm," said the priest; "it is my brother's knock;" and going to the door he drew back the bolt.

Tournay set down the milk jug untasted, with an exclamation of surprise, as he saw Gaillard burst into the room, followed by the old man Beaurepaire. The actor, no longer dressed in the disguise of an old man, was greatly excited.

"Great news, my colonel!" he exclaimed without stopping to explain how he had found his way there. "Robespierre has been arrested by the convention."

Tournay sprang forward and grasped his friend by both shoulders. "At last they have done it!" he cried excitedly. "Gaillard, tell me about it. How was it brought about?"

"Embrace me again, my colonel," exclaimed Gaillard, throwing his arms about Tournay and talking all the time. "It was this way: I heard the cry in the streets that the convention had risen almost to a man and arrested Robespierre and a few of his nearest satellites. At once I ran to the conciergerie to try and see you. Everything was in confusion. The news of Robespierre's arrest had just reached there. 'Can I see Colonel Tournay?' I demanded of the jailer.

"'He is not here,' he answered, turning from me to a dozen other excited questioners.

"'He has not been sent to the guillotine?' I cried, with my heart in my mouth.

"'No; liberated by Robespierre's order last night.'

"'What!' I shouted, thinking the man mad.

"'The order was countermanded fifteen minutes after the citizen colonel had left the prison,' cried the warden in reply. 'Don't ask me any more questions. My head is in a whirl; I cannot think.'

"I, myself, was so excited I could not think; but when I collected my few senses I recollected that St. Hilaire had told you of a place of refuge in case of emergency. 'My little colonel is there,' I said to myself, and flew here on the wind. Everywhere along the way people were congratulating one another. The greatest excitement prevailed. No notice was taken of an old man of eighty running like a lad of sixteen. When I reached your door I took off my wig and beard and put them in my pocket. Ah, my colonel, we shall wear our own faces; we shall speak our own minds, now that the tyrant himself is in the toils."

" Will they be able to keep him there ?" asked Father Ambrose; "he will not yield without a struggle. The Jacobins may try to arouse the masses to rescue him."

" The populace is seething with excitement," said Gaillard. " Some quarters of the town are for the fallen tyrant; others are against him. In the Faubourg St. Antoine, the stronghold of the Jacobins, Robespierre is openly denounced by some, yet his adherents are still strong there and are arming themselves. The convention stands firm as a rock. ' Down with the tyrant ! ' is the cry."

"There is work for us," exclaimed Tournay. " Father Ambrose," he continued, turning to the priest, " I must go out at once. I leave you to tell the news to Mademoiselle de Rochefort. Tell her to remain here in the strictest seclusion until I return and assure her that we can leave here in safety. I leave her in your keeping, Father Ambrose. Now, Gaillard, let us go."

In the streets, Tournay found that his friend had not exaggerated the popular excitement. As

they walked along both he and Gaillard kept their
ears alert to hear everything that was said.

Suddenly a noise caused them to stop and look
into each other's faces with consternation.

"The tumbrils!" exclaimed Gaillard, in answer
to Tournay's look.

"That looks bad for our party," said Tournay.
"One would expect the executions to cease, or at
least be suspended, on the day of Robespierre's
arrest."

"There is no one to give a coherent order,"
replied Gaillard. "Some of the prison governors
do not know which way to turn, or whom to obey.
The same with the police. They need a leader."

As he spoke they turned into the Rue Vaugirard
and saw coming toward them down the street two
death carts, escorted by a dozen gendarmes. The
street was choked with a howling mass of people,
and from their shouts it was manifest that some
were demanding that the carts be sent back, while
others were equally vociferous in urging them on.
Meanwhile, the gendarmes stolidly made their
way through the crowd as best they could.

Many of the occupants of the tumbrils leaned
supplicatingly over the sides of the carts and implored the people to save them.

The crowd finally became so large as to impede
the further progress of the carts.

"My God!" cried Tournay, grasping Gaillard
by the arm. "There is St. Hilaire."

In the second cart stood the Citizen St. Hilaire.
He held himself erect and stood motionless, his

arms, like those of the rest of the prisoners, tightly pinioned behind him. But it could be seen that he was addressing the populace and exciting their sympathy. By his side was Madame d'Arlincourt, her large blue eyes fixed intently upon St. Hilaire; she seemed unmindful of the scene around her, and to be already in another world.

In the rear of the cart, dressed in white, was La Liberté. Her face was flushed and animated, and she was talking loudly and rapidly to the crowd which followed the tumbril.

Tournay sprang to the head of the procession. He still wore his uniform, and the crowd made way for him.

" Why did you take these tumbrils out to-day?" he demanded of the gendarmes. "Do you not know that Robespierre is in prison and the executions are to be stopped?"

" I have my orders from the keeper of the Luxembourg. I am to take these tumbrils to the Place de la Révolution," replied the officer; then addressing the crowd, he cried, " Make way there, citizens, make way there and let us proceed!"

"No, no!" cried a great number of voices, while others cried out, "Yes, make way!" But all still blocked the passage of the carts.

" The keeper of the Luxembourg had no authority to order the execution of these prisoners to-day. Take them at once back to the prison," ordered Tournay.

" Where is your authority? Show it to me and I will obey you," replied the police officer.

"This is not a day on which we present written authority," answered Tournay. "I tell you I have the right to order you back to the prison. It is the will of the convention."

"I take my orders from the Commune," replied the gendarme stubbornly. "I must go forward."

Gaillard had meantime worked his way to Tournay's shoulder, and the latter said a few words in his ear. Gaillard plunged into the crowd and was off like a shot in the direction of the convention.

"Citizens, let us pass!" cried the gendarmes impatiently.

"Citizens," Tournay cried out in a loud voice, "it is the will of the convention that no executions take place to-day. These carts must not go. I call upon you to help me." As he spoke he ran to the horses' heads. The crowd swept the gendarmes to one side, and in a moment's time the tumbrils were turned about.

Then a clatter of hoofs was heard, accompanied by angry shouts, and the crowd broke and scattered in all directions, as Commandant Henriot, followed by a troop of mounted police, rode through them.

"What is the meaning of this?" he roared out.

"Where shall we go, back to the Luxembourg or forward to the Place de la Révolution?" cried out the bewildered gendarmes who guarded the tumbrils.

"To the guillotine, of course, always the guillotine," answered Henriot. "About, face! Citizens, disperse!"

The crowd had closed up and were muttering

their disapproval, many even going so far as to flourish weapons.

"Citizens," cried Tournay fearlessly, "this man Henriot has been indicted by the convention. He should now be a prisoner with Robespierre."

"Charge the crowd!" yelled Henriot to his lieutenant. "I will deal with this fellow; I know him. His name is Tournay." And he rode his horse at the colonel.

The latter sprang to one side, and seizing a sword from a gendarme, parried the trust of Henriot's weapon. Catching the horse by the bridle, he struck an upward blow at the commandant. The animal plunged forward and Tournay was thrown to the pavement, while the crowd fled before the charge of the mounted troops.

Before Henriot could wheel his charger, Tournay was on his feet, and realizing the impossibility of rallying any forces to contend with Henriot's, he took the first corner and made the best of his way up a narrow and deserted street.

He was somewhat shaken and bruised from his encounter, and stopping to recover breath for the first time, he noticed that the blood was flowing freely from a cut over the forehead which he had received during the short mêlée.

As he stanched the wound with his handkerchief, he heard footsteps behind him, and turning, saw a man dressed in the uniform of his own regiment running toward him. Wiping the blood from his eyes, he recognized Captain Dessarts who had served with him for the past year.

"You are wounded, colonel!" exclaimed Dessarts, taking the hand which Tournay stretched out to him. "Can I assist you?"

"It is only a scalp wound, but it bleeds villainously. You can tie this handkerchief about my head if you will."

"I tried to help you rally the crowd, my colonel, but it was hopeless. Yet with a few good soldiers behind his back, one could easily have cleared the streets of those hulking gendarmes. Do I hurt you?" he continued as he tied the knot.

"No," answered Tournay. "Tie it quickly and then come with me."

"I must go to the barracks, Colonel Tournay," replied Dessarts. "Your old regiment has been disbanded. I am here with my company, ordered to join another regiment and proceed to the Vendée."

"Where are your men quartered?" asked Tournay excitedly.

"Two streets above here."

"Will they obey you absolutely?"

"To the last man, my colonel."

"Will you follow me without a question?"

"To the death, my colonel."

"Come then, and bring me to your men at once. Every instant is worth a life. Let us run."

CHAPTER XXVI

THE END OF THE TERROR

SURROUNDED by Henriot's mounted guards, the tumbrils lumbered slowly to the Place de la Révolution. There a large crowd had assembled to witness the daily tribute to the guillotine.

"You shall not be disappointed, my patriots!" cried Henriot.

They answered him with a cheer. The crowd here was in sympathy with him, and he felt grimly cheerful.

"My friends, you will cheer again when you learn that one hour ago Robespierre was set free by me. The convention is trembling. The Commune triumphs."

Again the crowd cheered.

Henriot rode up to the guillotine.

"Sanson," he cried out to the executioner, "here is your daily allowance. We have kept you waiting, but you can now use dispatch."

The occupants in the tumbrils had seen their last hope of deliverance vanish in the Rue Vaugirard. They were fully prepared for death. One after another they mounted the fatal scaffold and were led to the guillotine.

Some went bravely forward to meet their fate.

way out of the difficulty?" and he turned from one to the other with a shrug.

"Bah, no! They are the very ones to blame, I tell you," repeated d'Arlincourt.

"My dear count," cried Madame d'Arlincourt, "I cannot permit you to speak slightingly of our philosophers. They are all the fashion now. The door of every salon in Paris is open to them. The other night, at a great reception given by the Duchess de Montmorenci, half the invited guests were philosophers, poets, encyclopædists. They say that even some of the nobility were overlooked in order to make room for the men of letters."

The Marquis de St. Hilaire threw a small cake to the spaniel that sat on its haunches begging for it.

"We cannot very well overlook this new order of nobility of the ink-and-paper that has exerted such an influence during the last generation," he said carelessly.

"I should not overlook them if I had my way," cried the Count d'Arlincourt. "I should lock them safely up in the Bastille."

"Oh!" cried the ladies in one breath; "barbarian!"

"These men are doubtless responsible for the inflamed state of the public mind," said St. Hilaire, again taking up the conversation.

"Of course they are," agreed the count.

"And so are Calonne and Brienne," continued the marquis. "They mismanaged affairs during their terms of office."

Others almost fainted and were nearly dead from fear by the time they reached the hands of Sanson.

La Liberté came forward with a firm step. As she did so, the crowd set up a deafening shout. It was a shout of genuine astonishment at the sight of this well-known figure, though mingled with it were cries of satisfaction from those who had been jealous of her popularity. Some thought it was a new escapade on her part, and they applauded it all the louder because of its daring nature.

Even the red-handed Sanson opened his huge bull's-mouth with surprise as she appeared before him.

"Bon jour, Sanson," said she airily; "you did not look for me to-day, I imagine. Do not touch me," she exclaimed as he stretched out his large hand towards her. " I have sent too many along this road, not to know the way myself, alone." Then walking down until she stood under the very shadow of the knife she looked out over the sea of faces.

The mighty yell was repeated.

The pallor of approaching death was on her face, but unflinchingly she met the gaze of thousands, while with a toss of her chestnut curls she surveyed them proudly, taking the shouts as a tribute to herself.

Suddenly her face became animated and the color rushed back to her cheeks.

"Well done, my compatriot!" she exclaimed aloud; she no longer saw the crowd at her feet,

but stood transfixed, her gaze on the further corner of the square.

There Robert Tournay, at the head of some of
his own men, charged upon Henriot's troops. Steel
clashed upon steel, and Tournay's men pressed on.

"Bravely struck, my compatriot. Well parried,
my compatriot. That was worthy of my brave
colonel. One little moment, Sanson," she pleaded
as the burly executioner caught her by the arm.

"You have had twice the allotted time already,"
he objected; "you are keeping the others waiting."

"One more look, Sanson, just one! Ah, well
done, my brave."

"En avant," said the ruthless Sanson.

"Good-by, compatriot," murmured La Liberté,
a tear glistening in her eye. The knife descended,
and La Liberté was no more.

"Another!" said the insatiable executioner,
extending his huge hands towards the cart.

St. Hilaire looked into Madame d'Arlincourt's
face. Their eyes met full.

"Madame," he said, "in such a case as this you
will pardon me if I precede you," and stepping in
front of her he walked quietly up the scaffold.

Meantime Colonel Tournay, with Captain Dessarts at his shoulder and a company of his own
troops behind him, had dashed out of a side street
into the Place de la Révolution.

Tournay, with the ends of the blood-stained ker-
chief flapping on his forehead, and the sword
wrested from the gendarme waving in his hand,
urged his men forward.

Commandant Henriot, his forces augmented by a company of civic guards, charged upon them. The commandant's men outnumbered those led by the colonel, two to one, but in the shock that followed the tried veterans held together like a granite wall, and broke through Henriot's troops, hurling them in disorder to the right and left of the square.

Tournay saw the white-clad figure of La Liberté disappear under the glittering knife. He saw St. Hilaire standing on the scaffold with head turned toward Madame d'Arlincourt.

· "Soldiers, on to the guillotine!" cried the colonel, dashing forward at full speed.

The populace, who, between the blood of the executions and the battle going on in the square, were mad with excitement, pressed forward, and circled about the scaffold, angrily menacing the approaching troops, who seemed about to put an end to their entertainment.

"Sweep them away!" cried Tournay ruthlessly, his eye still upon the scaffold where St. Hilaire stood. "Use the bayonet!"

Meanwhile Henriot, by desperate efforts, had rallied his own troopers at the other side of the square, while his civic guards, having no further stomach for the fray, had fled incontinently.

"Colonel, they are about to attack us in the rear," said Dessarts warningly.

Tournay wheeled his men about as the enemy rode at them for a second time. Henriot, with his brandy-swollen face purple with excitement, was reeling drunk in his saddle, yet he plunged forward with the desperate courage of a baited bull.

"Down with the traitor!" he yelled. "The Commune must triumph; Robespierre is free, and the Republic lives."

With the answering cry of "Long live the Republic!" Tournay's men braced themselves firmly together.

"Fire!" commanded the colonel. A deadly volley poured into the commandant's forces.

"Charge!"

Henriot's troops were dashed back, scattered in all directions, and their drunken commander, putting spurs to his horse, fled cursing from the scene.

The populace, now thoroughly dismayed and frightened, parted on all sides before the soldiers. Tournay ran to the guillotine. He leaped up the steps of the scaffold.

"In the name of the convention, halt!" he cried.

"I know nothing about the convention," protested Sanson, laying his hand upon St. Hilaire's shoulder. "This man is sent to me to be guillotined — and " —

Tournay threw the executioner from the platform to the ground below, and cutting the cords that bound St. Hilaire set his arms at liberty.

Captain Dessarts formed his men around the scaffold to prevent interference on the part of the crowd. St. Hilaire took Tournay by the hand.

"You have come in time, colonel, to do me

a great service," he said. " Now give me a weapon,
and let me take part in any further fight."

Tournay gave him a pistol. St. Hilaire went
to the side of Madame d'Arlincourt. The crowd
began again to surge around the soldiers threateningly.

" Let the guillotine go on ! " " Let the executioner finish his work ! " were the cries from all
sides.

" Citizens," yelled Sanson, who had risen to his
feet and was now rubbing his bruised sides, " you
are a thousand. They are only a few soldiers.
Take back the prisoners and I will execute them."

" Make ready — aim," was Colonel Tournay's
quick command. The muskets clicked ; the crowd
fell back. " Fix bayonets, forward march." And
through the press Colonel Tournay bore those
whom he had saved from the guillotine.

No organized attempt was made to attack them,
and the party proceeded to the Rue d'Arcis unmo-
lested. Here Tournay turned to his captain.

" Dessarts, leave a file of men here and take the
others back to their barracks for repose, but hold
them subject to immediate orders."

" Very good, my colonel," and the soldiers were
marched away.

Madame d'Arlincourt showed signs of succumb-
ing to the effects of the terrible strain to which
she had been subjected, and St. Hilaire, supporting her gently, hastened to the door of his former
servant.

In another instant they were all inside.

They passed through the corridor and entered the wainscoted salon. As they did so the bookcase above moved gently. Edmé entered through the secret door and stood for an instant surrounded by a frame of dusty books, looking down upon them.

In her plain gown of homespun, with her skin browned by exposure to the air, and cheeks which had the glow of health in them despite the hardship she had undergone, Edmé de Rochefort was a different picture from that of the girl of five years before. Yet it was not the present Edmé that suffered by comparison.

With a cry of joy she hastened down the stairs. "I have been told the glorious news," she cried. "Have you returned to tell me it is all true? But you are wounded!" she exclaimed in the same breath, with a cry of alarm.

"'T is nothing," Tournay replied, folding her in his arms. "I do not even feel it."

"Is all the danger over?" she asked anxiously, looking up in his face.

"Not all over," he answered caressingly. "The result hangs in the balance, but we shall win, we shall surely win. At present we have need of a little food and repose. St. Hilaire and myself must go out again shortly. Has Gaillard come with a message? I expected him from the convention," he continued, addressing Beaurepaire.

"He has not returned," was the answer.

Edmé turned to assist Agatha in caring for Madame d'Arlincourt, while old Beaurepaire busied himself in setting forth some food upon the table.

At this moment Gaillard burst into the room, followed by Father Ambrose.

"I bring glorious news!" cried the actor excitedly. "Robespierre, at one time released by the aid of Henriot, has been rearrested. He has attempted suicide. Henriot, St. Just, Couthon, are also arrested. They will all be sent to the guillotine. The convention triumphs. The Commune is defeated. The Reign of Terror is at an end."

The news was received with a great shout of joy. "Listen," called out Gaillard, "and you will learn what the people think."

The booming of guns and the ringing of bells throughout the city verified his statement.

"We have won!" said Colonel Tournay.

"Let us celebrate the victory by this feast that Beaurepaire has provided!" exclaimed St. Hilaire.

Tournay drew Edmé into the recess of one of the large windows. The sound of a whole city rejoicing at the abolition of the Reign of Terror filled the air. In the room at the back the voices of Gaillard and St. Hilaire were heard in joyful conversation.

For a moment they stood in silence. She looked into his eyes and read the question there.

"Yes," her eyes answered.

"In order to save your life," he said, "Father Ambrose once stated that you and I were man and wife. It was a subterfuge, and had no other

A MOMENT THEY STOOD IN SILENCE

meaning. We now stand before him once again ;
will you let him marry us now ? "

" Yes, Robert."

With a look of pride and happiness upon his
face Tournay faced about and addressed the company.

" There can be no more fitting time than this,"
he said, " to present to you my bride," and he
looked proudly down at Edmé who still had her
arm through his.

" Father Ambrose," Tournay went on, " will
you marry us now ? "

The priest, who had evidently had a premoni-
tion of the event, was all prepared ; and in the
wainscoted salon, with the portraits of the old
régime looking down upon them from the walls,
Robert Tournay, a colonel of the Republic, and
Edmé de Rochefort, of the ancient Régime of
France, were made man and wife.

" Let us drink a toast to them ! " cried St. Hilaire as the happy party gathered about the table
after the ceremony.   " Long life and happiness to
Colonel Robert Tournay and his bride ! "

Beaurepaire filled their glasses with some rare
old Burgundy, which he drew from some hidden
stores in the cellar, and the toast was drunk with
enthusiasm.

St. Hilaire's eyes met Madame d'Arlincourt's,
and the look that was interchanged foretold their
future.

Tournay stood in silence for a moment, and
when he did speak there was a note in his voice

Here the philosopher smiled an assent.

"But the blame rests more heavily upon other shoulders than those of scribbling writers or corrupt officials," and the marquis paused to look around the table.

"I am all attention," cried the Countess d'Arlincourt, prepared for something amusing. "Upon whom does it rest?"

"Upon the nobility themselves," answered St. Hilaire.

For a moment there was silence; then came a storm of protests from all sides, only the chevalier and the philosopher making no audible reply, although the latter said to himself: —

"You are right, monsieur le marquis."

"St. Hilaire is in one of his mad fits," de Lacheville exclaimed.

"If it were not for the nobility there would be no poetry, no wit," murmured the poet.

"The nobility is the mainstay of the throne, the vitality of the country," said d'Arlincourt.

"What have *we* done?" cried the ladies in concert. "We ask for nothing better than to have everybody contented and happy." And they shrugged their pretty white shoulders as if to throw off the burden that St. Hilaire had placed there.

"Look at me," exclaimed St. Hilaire, rising and speaking with an animation he had not shown before. He was a man of twenty-five with a face so handsome that dissipation had not been able to mar its beauty. "I am a type of my class."

which showed how deep was his emotion. " I will give you a toast. Let us drink to the new France ; for after all," he continued, looking from one to the other, " we are all Frenchmen. The fate of France must be our fate. With her we must stand or fall. A new France has now risen from the ashes of the old. To her we turn with new hope."

" Long live the Republic ! " cried Gaillard.

Tournay, St. Hilaire, and Gaillard touched glasses and looked into one another's eyes. They understood one another as brave men do.

" Nations may rise or they may crumble into dust," said Colonel Tournay, " but Justice and Liberty are eternal. They will live always in the hearts of men."

" And Love also," whispered Edmé in his ear.

" Yes, truly, and Love also, sweetheart."

www.ingramcontent.com/pod-product-compliance
Lightning Source LLC
Chambersburg PA
CBHW030353030726
47497CB00002B/324